AUTUMN TEXAS BRIDE
THE BRIDES OF BLISS TEXAS, BOOK 3

Copyright © 2018 by Katie Lane

All rights reserved. Except for use in any review, the reproduction or utilization of this work in whole or in part in any form by any electronic, mechanical or other means, now known or hereinafter invented, including xerography, photocopying and recording, or in any information storage or retrieval system, is forbidden without the written permission of the publisher.

This book is a work of fiction. Names, characters, places, and incidents are a product of the writer's imagination. All rights reserved. Scanning, uploading, and electronic sharing of this book without the permission of the author is unlawful piracy and theft. To obtain permission to excerpt portions of the text, please contact the author at katie@katielanebooks.com Thank you for respecting this author's hard work and livelihood.

Printed in the USA.

Cover Design and Interior Format
© THE KILLION GROUP INC.

Autumn Texas Bride

 The Brides of Bliss Texas—Book 3

KATIE LANE

To my daddy, I miss you

CHAPTER ONE

"YOU FROM AROUND HERE? YOU look familiar."

Maverick Murdoch had hoped that sunglasses, a cowboy hat, and a week's growth of beard would be enough of a disguise. Obviously not. He tried not to show any reaction as he looked back at the old guy who sat behind the counter of the gas station.

"Nope. Just passing through." He handed the man three twenties.

The old guy put the money in the drawer of the cash register and pulled out change. "Well, if you have time for lunch, you should stop by Lucy's Place Diner. Carly's pot roast is the best in Texas." He turned and handed him the change. "And the Tender Heart Museum is sure worth taking a look at. Did you ever read the Tender Heart western series? The author, Lucy Arrington, lived right here in Bliss, Texas. Her family still does. Her great-nieces and nephews own some of the biggest ranches in the county, her great-grandson is soon to be elected our new mayor, and one of her great-granddaughters married our sheriff and the other is about to open up a bakery on Main Street."

Maverick wasn't interested in bakeries, old book series, or dusty museums. He was in Bliss for one reason and one reason only.

Intense, mind-blowing, tension-relieving sex.

He slid the change in the front pocket of his jeans. "Actually, I'm looking for a friend of mine. Do you know Summer Hadley?"

The old guy smiled, showing off a chipped front tooth. "I sure do. She's the great-granddaughter who's opening the bakery."

Maverick was more than a little surprised. Summer had never mentioned being a relative of a famous writer. Nor had she ever mentioned liking to bake. Of course, in college all they'd talked about was sports, and recently ... they hadn't talked about much of anything. It was hard to talk when your lips were busy doing other things.

"How do you know Summer?" the old guy asked.

"We're college friends." Friends with benefits. Really good benefits that Maverick couldn't seem to get out of his mind.

The old guy grinned. "I bet those Hadley triplets were as hard to tell apart in school as they are now. If not for their haircuts, I wouldn't have a clue."

"I haven't seen Autumn and Spring in a while, but in college the sisters were identical. I could only tell them apart by their personalities." Summer was direct, driven, and outspoken. Spring was bright, vivacious, and personable. And Autumn was ... weird. Or at least, that's how she'd acted around him. Whenever he'd stopped by their dorm room to see Summer, all Autumn had done was stare at him. It made him feel creepy. Unlike Summer, who made him feel hot.

"Where is this bakery?" he asked.

"Just head south on Main Street and you'll see it on your right." The old guy's eyes narrowed. "Are you sure we haven't met before? What do you do for a living?"

"I'm a . . . football coach." It was a little too close to the truth to be a good lie. Although the old guy seemed to like it. A big smile lit his face, and he walked around the counter to heartily thump Maverick on the back.

"Well, why the hell didn't you say so in the first place?" He held out a hand. "Emmett Daily. Folks will be happy as pigs in mud to hear that we've got us a candidate for the coaching job. Most of the town wanted to tar and feather Coach Wilson for taking that coaching job in Mississippi and leaving us high and dry right at the start of high school football season."

"Sorry, but I'm not here for a coaching position. I just stopped by to say hi to Summer."

Emmett's face fell. "Well, that's too bad. We sure could use a coach. Raff Arrington and Waylon Kendall have been trying to fill in at practice, but Raff has a baby on the way and ranch and house renovations to deal with, and Waylon is our sheriff and just got married. We need us a full-time coach."

Maverick understood the town's problem. Having grown up in Texas, he knew how important high school football was to the state. Everyone looked forward to Friday Night Lights and watching their gridiron heroes. He had been one of those heroes. One of the brightest stars in Texas . . . until he'd fallen. Now he was just a man looking to redeem himself.

And get laid.

He tipped his cowboy hat. "Thanks for the gas and the information, but I better get going if I want to catch Summer before the bakery closes."

"It isn't open. Blissful Bakery won't open until Labor Day weekend. Of course, Summer will probably be there. That little gal has been working day and night to get things ready."

Maverick had no problem finding the bakery. He could've thrown a football the length of Main Street. He parked next to the curb in front of the old brick building with the cloud-shaped sign that read Blissful Bakery. The large window was covered with brown paper, as was the door. It wasn't locked, and when he stepped inside, the scent of something sweet and sugary was thick in the air. He didn't eat refined sugar or flour. Both were the enemies of an athlete's body. But damn did they smell good. He'd only had a protein shake for breakfast, and his stomach grumbled with hunger.

The walls of the bakery were painted sky blue with fluffy clouds in the shape of cookies, donuts, muffins, and cupcakes. Little round tables with spindly-looking chairs filled the space in front of the window and display cases and a counter stood in front of a partition that separated the customer area from the kitchen. A rainbow neon sign hung on one wall. Summer's Blissful Bakery. But Summer didn't look to be around.

"Hello?" he called.

A white-haired lady stepped out from the back. She wore a floral dress and a sky blue apron that had "Blissful Bakery" printed across the bib. She was small and fragile looking, but there was a steeliness in her piercing blue eyes.

"I'm sorry, but we're not open for business yet." She held out a plate of donuts. "But you're welcome to a free sample."

The yeasty, glazed donuts looked as good as they smelled, but he shook his head. "Thank you, but I'm on a strict diet."

She placed the plate on the counter. "Me too. No sugar for me, I'm afraid. I'm a diabetic."

"And you work in a bakery?"

She laughed. "That does seem strange, doesn't it? But I love baking so much I couldn't give it up just because my doctor thinks it would be easier on me."

He understood that better than most. He had more than a few people telling him to take the easy way out and give up football. He refused to listen. Football was his life. He didn't want to live without it. But occasionally he needed a break from it. He glanced at the doorway that led to the back. "Is Summer here?"

"She just went to the post office to pick up some flyers she ordered for the grand opening, but she should be back any second." She held out a hand. "I'm Maybelline Marble. Retired school teacher and town baker. Although Summer is taking over as town baker."

He took her hand and gave her his middle name. "I'm Matthew. Nice to meet you, Ms. Marble."

Her eyebrows went up. "Matthew? I thought

you went by Maverick."

He was struck speechless. The football-loving guy at the gas station hadn't recognized him, but this little old grandmother had. She must've read his alarm because she reached up and patted his shoulder.

"No need to worry. I'm not the gossiping kind. And I understand perfectly why you don't want anyone to recognize you. I'm sure you're tired of people talking." She glanced at his cowboy hat, and then gave him a stern look. "But that's no excuse for bad manners."

He quickly took off his hat, followed by his sunglasses. "Sorry, ma'am. I guess I've spent so much time with football jocks in the last couple months that I've forgotten my manners."

"Then you were picked up by another team?" The woman did know football. Or maybe she just followed his career. Everyone seemed to follow his career. Probably because it was such a disaster. But he was going to fix that.

"Not yet," he said. "But I will be."

She studied him with her piercing eyes. His meanest coaches hadn't had stares as intense as Ms. Marble's. "You remind me of Summer. She has the same kind of drive and stubbornness."

Which was why he and Summer got along so well. They let very few things get in the way of their success. He glanced around. Although a small bakery in a Podunk town didn't seem very successful to him. Especially when she'd owned a clothing store in Houston. Of course, she no longer owned the store. When he'd stopped by to see her there, it had been locked up tight with a "For Lease" sign in the window. Maybe that was why she was here. Like him, she was regrouping after life had sacked her.

He started to ask Ms. Marble about why Summer had closed the store when he heard the back door open.

"Sorry I took so long," Summer said in a loud voice that carried all the way into the bakery. "I ran into Mrs. Crawley and the nosy woman wouldn't let me get away. Ms. Marble?"

"I'm in the front, dear," Ms. Marble called. "Visiting with your friend."

"My friend? Did Carly stop by? She said she was going to stop by and sample the—" Summer stepped out from the back and froze. "Maverick?"

She looked different from the last time he'd seen her. She looked more like the girl he'd known in college. Her dark black hair was pulled back in a messy ponytail, and besides the smudge of flour on her cheek, her face was tanned like when she'd played softball. He didn't like it as much as he'd liked the porcelain skin his lips had tasted every inch of. But tanned or not, he was happy to see her.

He smiled. "Surprise."

While Summer stared at him, Ms. Marble picked up a straw hat and white gloves from the counter. "I think I'll head on home and leave you two to visit. I glazed the donuts and they're right there on the counter, Summer. And don't forget the cookies in the oven. I think your new recipe for Cowboy Cookies is going to be a hit with the Tender Heart tourists."

Summer pulled her gaze away from Maverick to give Ms. Marble a hug. "Thanks for helping me. I don't know what I'd do without you. Autumn hasn't exactly turned out to be the best baking assistant. I sent her to the Walmart in Fredericksburg to get more flour and sugar, even though I ordered plenty from my supplier—anything to keep her out of the kitchen. She can't seem to follow a recipe to save her soul, and she either forgets to preheat the oven or turns it up too high. I'm starting to wonder if she'll ever get the knack of baking. Which is weird since she's good at everything else."

"No one can be good at everything." Ms. Marble smiled at Maverick. "It was nice meeting you, Maverick." She gave him a hug as if she'd known him all her life before she spoke to Summer. "Do you want me to lock the front door after I leave?"

"No. I'll get it." Summer picked up a set of keys from the counter, then shot a sassy look at Maverick. "There's no telling what kind of riffraff will walk right in if we don't."

When Ms. Marble was gone and the door locked, Summer walked back over to the counter where he was standing. She wore athletic wear and running shoes. He preferred the sexy dress and heels she'd worn the last time she'd come to his hotel room. A sexy dress with no panties underneath. The spandex sports tank and pants would be much harder to get off. But he would manage.

"So what brings you to Bliss, Mav?" she asked.

"Guess." He tossed his cowboy hat onto a nearby table before he stepped closer. "You want to play cheerleader and football player like last time? Or how about donut maker and sugar addict?" He pulled her into his arms and kissed her. But before he could get more than a taste of her lips, she kneed him right in the family jewels.

He released her with a groan and bent over, shielding his manhood from any more abuse. "What the hell, Summer?"

"What the hell is right!" she yelled. "What the hell do you think you're doing waltzing in here and acting like some sex fiend?"

He struggled to catch his breath. "I thought that's what you wanted. You seemed to like it the other times."

"Other times? What other times? Did you lose it after you screwed up in the NFL? That would certainly explain you drunk dialing me that one time and showing up here acting crazy?"

He stared at her in confusion for a moment before the truth dawned. "Oh, I get it. This is one of your new sex games. Well, I've got to be honest, I'm not liking it much. I was willing to play naughty pony and horse trainer. But innocent amnesia patient and town drunk isn't my cup of tea." He reached for his hat and pulled it on. "I think our friends with benefits is at an end."

"Friends with benefits?"

Maverick turned to find a man standing in the doorway that led to the back. A man who didn't look very happy. In fact, he looked flat-out pissed. Maverick got a bad feeling. A really bad feeling.

"Who are you?" the man asked.

Summer jumped in. "This is Maverick Murdoch, Ryker. I told you that I was friends with him in college."

Ryker's eyes narrowed on Maverick. "You didn't mention 'with benefits.'"

"Because there were no benefits. I haven't seen

him for years and was completely shocked when he walked in here out of the blue and tried to kiss me."

Maverick knew what was coming and braced himself before Ryker's fist connected with his jaw. It still snapped his head back and knocked off his hat.

Ryker shoved a finger in his face. "Don't you ever touch my wife again, do you hear me?"

Wife? Shit. He just kept making one mistake after another.

He held up his hands. "I'm sorry. I didn't realize Summer was married." He scooped his hat up from the floor. "I'll just let y'all get back to your . . . donuts." He turned and headed for the door, not remembering it was locked until it wouldn't open. Fortunately, before he had to turn back around and ask for the key, the lock turned and the door opened.

He recognized the inky black hair immediately. It was one of Summer's sisters. She was using her butt to push open the door so he couldn't see her face. Not that seeing her features would've told him which sister it was.

He held the door and moved out of the way as she stepped inside with her arms loaded down with grocery totes. One tote slipped, and Maverick grabbed the handles before it could hit the floor and gave it back to her.

"Thank—" Her face lifted to his, and she abruptly cut off as her eyes widened.

The hard punch of recognition made Maverick realize that he'd been wrong. The Hadley triplets weren't identical. There was only one triplet who had alabaster skin that tasted like vanilla ice cream. One triplet with dark curls that framed her face. One triplet with a tiny heart-shaped birthmark at the corner of her right eye.

And one triplet who liked to play games.

CHAPTER TWO

LOOKING AT MAVERICK MURDOCH HAD always been a favorite pastime of Autumn Layne Hadley's. He was like a piece of art—an exquisite masterpiece that you could stand and stare at for hours. His hair wasn't just blond. It was a blend of dark honey, golden wheat, and pure sunshine. His eyes weren't just blue. They were a mosaic of steely gray and soft cornflower with splashes of sparkling sapphire thrown in. He had thick eyebrows that lowered when he didn't like something or lifted when he was surprised. His nose was straight and prominent without being too broad or long. And his jaw was angular and manly—especially with a covering of golden scruff.

His lips were the only imperfect things about him. The curves of his top lip were uneven—one soft hill slightly higher than the other. But even that imperfection didn't take away from his hypnotic beauty.

Of course, she wasn't hypnotized now. She was stunned. What was he doing here in Bliss? He belonged on a football field. Or in a private hotel room in Houston. Or locked in the fantasies in her head. He did not belong in a public bakery. Her sister's bakery.

He studied her for only a second before he spoke in his whiskey-soaked Texas drawl. "Autumn, I presume."

Everything inside her tensed.

He knew.

She tried to say something. Anything. But she had never been able to talk to Maverick. At least not as herself. So she just stood there with her arms aching from the heavy grocery totes as a blush burned her cheeks. But that seemed to be enough to answer his question. His eyebrows lowered and his eyes turned as cold and hard as Artic ice. Without another word, he pulled on his cowboy hat and walked out the door.

When he was gone, Autumn's knees trembled so badly she worried she was going to slip to the floor amid all the bags of flour and sugar. But her sister's voice kept her from it.

"That man is as nutty as a pecan pie."

She whirled to find Summer standing there with Ryker, and her bad day grew worse. Did they know too? Had Maverick filled them in on her dirty little secret? If a person could die of embarrassment and guilt, Autumn was about to. She had spent most of her life being the perfect triplet. The one who never cussed, cheated, or lied. The one who followed all the rules, got the best grades in school, and kept her wilder sisters in check. And now that perfect bubble she'd been living in was about to burst big time.

She waited for Summer's disbelief and anger. But

her sister didn't even glance at her as she turned to her husband. "I hope you didn't believe a word he said, Ryker."

"I didn't." Ryker leaned in and kissed her. "The man is obviously unhinged."

Autumn released the breath she'd been holding. Maverick hadn't thrown her under the bus. He'd kept her secret. At least for now. But just in case he came back, she tried to do some damage control. "I couldn't agree more. Maverick has always seemed a little unhinged to me." She paused. "Umm, exactly what did he do?"

Summer waved a hand. "He strutted in like some Johnny Casanova and tried to kiss me. I had to knee him in the teabags to get him to stop."

"You kneed him in the balls?" Ryker smiled. "That's my girl. Although I wish you had mentioned that sooner. If I'd known you'd already abused him, I wouldn't have punched him so hard." He shook his hand. "The guy has a jaw of steel."

Autumn winced. Kneed and punched. No wonder Maverick looked so mad. "So did he say anything?" she asked.

"Too much," Summer said. "I guess ol' Mav is into some pretty kinky role playing. He wanted me to play pretty pony and horse trainer with him."

Autumn swallowed. "Roleplaying isn't all that kinky." When Summer sent her a confused look, she quickly added. "I mean, I'm sure there are other sexual activities that are much kinkier."

"How would you know? You're not exactly a sex expert. Have you been reading those erotic romances again?"

Ryker held up a hand. "Before this conversation gets any more uncomfortable, I'm leaving. I promised Cord I'd stop by and talk with him about some marketing strategies for his boot company."

Cord Evans was Ryker's father and a retired rodeo champion who now sold cowboy boots. Until just recently, he and Ryker had been estranged, but Cord had worked hard to mend his relationship with his son. It was nice to know that there were fathers out there who learned from their mistakes and tried to make things right—something that Autumn's father would never do. Holt didn't see himself as a deadbeat dad who had deserted his wife and four kids. He saw himself as a rolling stone that gathered no moss.

But he was still her father, and she felt a responsibility to check in on him occasionally. On her way to Houston, she'd stopped by the county jail where Holt was awaiting his trial for running a gambling racket. She thought he would've been humbled by his incarceration. He wasn't. He acted like he was at a five-star hotel as he joked with his guards and fellow inmates. He hadn't asked once how she and her siblings were doing. He just wanted to know if she'd brought him money for cigarettes and his defense attorney.

"Be honest, Ryker," Summer cut into her thoughts. "You're enjoying helping Cord market his new boot company. It's kept you from being bored silly after you sold Headhunters."

Ryker had sold his online job search company right before he and Summer had gotten married. He'd decided that he'd rather spend his days in a small town with the love of his life than in a big city with a billion-dollar company. Which made

Autumn love her new brother-in-law all the more.

"I wouldn't be bored if my wife spent more time with me," Ryker said. "I never should've given you the bakery as a wedding present."

Summer looped her arms around his neck. "We spend all night together. We can't spend all day together too. Besides, I think that working for your daddy is a perfect way to stay busy." She glanced down at the cowboy boots Ryker was wearing. "You can't deny that you love his boots. You also love showing off your business savvy to him."

Ryker pulled her closer and grinned. "You know me too well. Now walk me out so I won't embarrass your sister when I kiss you senseless."

Once they were gone, Autumn slumped back in the chair with relief. Her secret was safe. Or not really safe. Maverick now knew about the game she'd been playing with him. Although she couldn't see him spreading the news that he'd been duped by his college girlfriend's sister. Still, she didn't want him hanging around Bliss and accidentally letting the cat out of the bag. Or the triplet out of her perfect persona.

She got up from the chair and moved to the window. She peeled back just enough brown paper to see out into the street. Two women were browsing in the window of the Home Sweet Home antique shop, and Emmett Daily was talking to Old Man Sims outside the diner. She didn't see Maverick anywhere. She could only hope that he'd left town and would never come back.

A face popped into her line of vision, and Autumn almost jumped out of her sensible shoes. Thankfully, it didn't belong to Maverick. It belonged to her sister, Spring. Spring sent her a what-the-heck-are-you-doing look before she disappeared from sight. A second later, the door opened and her sister breezed in, looking like a bright daffodil in her yellow dress.

"Hey, Audie. Did you realize that your eyes peeking out the tear in the paper look creepy as heck to people walking by? This is a bakery shop, not a shop of horrors."

"It was a shop of horrors today." Summer walked in from the back. "And Autumn wasn't the creep. Maverick Murdoch was."

Spring put her purse on one of the hooks by the door. "I heard a football coach was looking for you. The phone at the sheriff's office has been ringing non-stop with the gossip." Spring worked for the sheriff, who also happened to be her husband. "I'm going to assume that this coach was Maverick. Is he coaching now? And why is he a creep? I've always liked him, and I thought you did too. You rooted for him when he was playing football for Chicago."

"That was before I knew he had turned into a sex fiend." Summer picked up the plate of donuts on the counter and brought them over to a table, then sat down. "And I don't think a professional football player would be vying for a small town coaching position."

Spring took a seat at the table. "I don't care about the coaching position. I want to hear more about Maverick being a sex fiend."

"He walked in and tried to kiss me. I had to knee him where it counts to get him to stop."

Spring laughed. "Well, that should teach him to

think he could start something back up with his old college flame. He probably raced out of town like his tail was on fire."

Autumn certainly hoped so. She didn't need any reminders of her walk on the wild side. Because despite the game she'd played with Maverick, Autumn wasn't wild. She was calm, subdued, and predictable. And she wanted her life to be the same way.

Her childhood had been turbulent enough to last her a lifetime, with her father leaving and her mother dying of cancer when she and her siblings were still in grade school. Autumn had lived through insecurity and chaos. Now, she just wanted to live a secure, peaceful life. Bliss was the perfect place for that. She planned to work in her sister's bakery during the day and read books at night. One day, she'd meet a nice, stable man who didn't have dreams of becoming anything more than a loyal husband and father. A man nothing like her daddy . . . or a bad-boy pro football player who wasn't ready to grow up.

"So everything is set for Waylon's surprise birthday party tonight." Spring picked up a donut and took a big bite. "All that's left to do is for you to bring the cake and cupcakes to the Watering Hole, Summer. And, Audie, you need to bring the presents."

"Presents?" Summer heaved a sigh. "Crap. I've been so busy baking Waylon's cake, I forgot to get him a present."

Autumn joined her sisters at the table. "No worries. I knew you wouldn't have time so I got a gift for you. I wrapped it, but you'll need to sign the card."

"You are a lifesaver, Audie. What did you get him?" Summer held up a hand. "Never mind. Whatever it is, I'm sure it will be perfect. You always get the perfect gifts. I just wish you were as gifted at baking."

Autumn hated to disappoint her sister. She hated to disappoint anyone in her family. But try as she might, she couldn't seem to get the knack of baking. She'd been reading cookbooks and watching Food Network's baking championships, but she still made stupid mistakes.

"At least I didn't burn the last batch of cookies," she said.

Summer rolled her eyes. "No, you just forgot the sugar."

"What? But I'm sure I double checked every ingredient in the recipe before I put them in the oven."

Spring patted her hand. "You'll get better. You just need a little more practice. I've never seen you fail at anything."

"Spring is right," Summer said. "But until you get better, I think I'll hire another person to help."

"Can you afford that?" Autumn asked.

"Of course I can. I married a filthy rich man, and Lucy Arrington's final book comes out in January and the royalty money should start rolling in."

Autumn was looking forward to her great-grandmother's book coming out too. She had read the entire Tender Heart series and was a true fan. She was also looking forward to the increase in her bank account the royalties would give her. She had always been a saver, but she'd used most of her savings to keep their clothing store, Seasons, from going bankrupt. Now she barely had enough for living expenses. Which was why she was hoping to rent the room above Ms. Marble's garage. The monthly rent on a tiny studio couldn't be very high and it was time she moved out of Waylon and Spring's guest room.

Spring tipped her nose up and sniffed. "Speaking of burning cookies."

Summer's eyes widened. "My Cowboy Cookies!" She jumped up and disappeared into the back.

Spring looked at Autumn and laughed. "I guess you aren't the only Hadley who burns things in the kitchen."

Autumn left Waylon and Spring's house early under the pretense of babysitting for her brother and his wife. Instead, she met up with Dirk and Gracie in the parking lot of the Watering Hole. Dirk came over immediately and opened her car door.

"Did Waylon act like he knew something was up?"

"No," she said as she got out. "But he might when he sees how full this parking lot is."

Gracie shook her head. "It's always full on Twofer Tuesdays. Waylon's not going to think anything is amiss. What excuse did Spring give him for wanting to stop by here before they head to dinner in Austin?"

She opened the trunk of her Audi and got out Waylon's presents. "She's going to tell him that she needs to drop some earrings by to Summer that she borrowed."

Dirk took the presents from Autumn and flashed a smile at her and Gracie. "You ladies are looking mighty beautiful tonight. I'll be the most envied man at the party. Although I'm pretty much the most envied man in town already. I have a beautiful wife. Three beautiful sisters. And three beautiful baby girls. A man can't get more blessed than that." He glanced at Gracie and winked. "Although a son might be nice."

Gracie pointed a finger at him. "Don't you even think about it until the triplets are potty-trained. I refuse to have four babies in diapers. Besides, you're going to be awfully busy after Election Day, Mr. Mayor."

Dirk smiled. "I'll always have time for my family. Now come on, pretty ladies, we have a party to get ready for."

The bar was as packed as the parking lot. Dirk ushered them through the crowd to the back where Spring had reserved some tables for the family. On the way, Emmett Daily stopped Dirk to talk about the need for a new football coach. His wife Joanna rolled her eyes at Gracie and Autumn.

"I swear it's all the man has thought about since Coach Wilson left. We can't even have a decent dinner conversation without him bringing it up."

"I think that's all every man in town has been thinking about," Gracie said. "And I do feel sad for the boys if we can't find a coach. They've worked so hard this summer."

"I'm sure a coach will show up. Right now I'm more concerned about getting the library built before the release day of Lucy's final Tender Heart book."

"How is that going?" Gracie asked.

"Much faster now that Dirk has called in a few favors from politicians he knows. And it's only right that we get a library. This is the hometown of Lucy Arrington, one of the greatest literary geniuses of all-time. Bliss should have a library with her name on it."

"Especially when she willed most of her book royalties to the Texas Library system," Autumn said.

Joanna glanced over and seemed surprised to see her. "Oh, Autumn, I didn't see you there." It wasn't unusual. Autumn was the Hadley sister who always blended into the woodwork. "I'm hoping to break ground on the new library in a few weeks," Joanna continued. "That will give us close to four months before January when the final book is released. Of course, we don't just have to worry about the building. We'll have to worry about ordering books to fill it."

"I could help you," Autumn said. "I used to order books for the bookstore I worked at in Waco."

"That would be wonderful. If you give me your number, I'll call you so we can talk."

Autumn had just finished giving Joanna her number when Summer called her name. She turned to see Summer and Ryker standing by the door. They were both loaded down with cake boxes. She hurried over to help.

"Get the one off the top, Audie," Summer said. "The rest are cupcakes, but that's the birthday cake and it needs to be taken to the refrigerator in the kitchen so the cream cheese frosting doesn't melt in this heat before Waylon gets here."

Autumn took the box and weaved her way through the crowd to the kitchen. Once she'd placed the box in the refrigerator, she headed back out into the bar to rejoin her family. Unfortunately, on her way past the bar, a man reached out and pulled her between a pair of long, muscled thighs that she remembered all too well.

When she looked into Maverick's eyes, her breath caught, and her heart thumped like a bass drum in a marching band. His eyes hadn't warmed up one degree. And when he spoke, his voice was even icier.

"Why, if it isn't the little imposter."

CHAPTER THREE

MAVERICK THOUGHT THAT THE BEERS he'd drunk while sitting in the hick bar would've cooled his anger. But as he stared into Autumn's eyes, he only got madder. They were the exact color of the flowers that grew along the edge of the creek that ran behind his childhood home in Bedford, Texas. The deep blue flowers were beautiful, but their ground-covering vines could hide all kinds of poisonous vipers.

"Why did you do it?" he asked. "Why would you pretend to be your sister?"

She pressed her lips together, drawing his attention to her mouth. A mouth he remembered all too well. When she'd come to his room, she'd always worn dark red lipstick that left lip prints on the hotel sheets . . . and on his skin. But now she didn't have on any lipstick.

She glanced around and spoke under her breath. "Could you please lower your voice?"

He was about to say he didn't give a shit if people overheard, but then he realized that he did give a shit. No one besides Autumn's family and Ms.

Marble had recognized him. And he wanted to keep it that way.

He slid off the barstool and took Autumn's hand, leading her toward the exit sign at the back of the bar. The exit looked like it was emergency only, but he opened the door anyway and pulled Autumn out with him. He led her around to the back of the building by a trash bin that reeked of booze and beer.

It was still light outside, the setting sun hot and bright. He took his sunglasses out of the neck of his shirt and slid them on. "So talk."

She didn't seem to be in any hurry. She just stood there, looking nothing like the hot, sultry woman who had filled his fantasies for the last few months. This woman looked frigid and uptight. While most women in the bar had been dressed in tight jeans or flirty skirts, Autumn wore a black dress that hit her just above the knee. It was fashionable and contoured to her tall, lithe body, but it was much too proper for a bar. It looked like something a middle-aged woman would wear to a funeral.

"What happened to the sexy red dress and heels?" he asked snidely. "Or do you save those for your unsuspecting victims?"

Her cheeks flushed a bright pink. He thought it was from embarrassment, but when she spoke he realized it was from anger. Her voice was as cool as her eyes. "I wouldn't call you a victim. You seemed to enjoy our time together quite well."

His temper snapped. "Because I thought you were Summer! I didn't think you were the weird, creepy sister." He wanted the words back as soon as they were out. Her eyes filled with hurt. But before he could apologize, she cut him off.

"If you'll excuse me, I have a birthday party to attend." She started to walk past him, but he took her arm and stopped her.

"I'm sorry. I didn't mean to hurt your feelings. I'm just a little ticked off about being made a fool of. And I don't get it. I just don't get why you would pretend to be someone you're not. That day in Houston, you were the one who stopped me on the street. The one who didn't correct me when I called you Summer. You came back to my hotel room, for Christ's sake. Why would you do that? And why would you go along with the entire friends with benefits thing? We're not friends, Autumn. We've never been friends. You barely said two words to me in college."

She hesitated for a long moment. When he'd almost given up on getting an answer, she spoke. "Because I had a crush on you."

He stared at her. "Excuse me?"

"I had a crush on you in college. That's why I acted like a mute idiot whenever you were around. And don't look so surprised, Maverick. Lots of girls had crushes on you. You were the star quarterback. The hero of the university—if not most of Texas."

It was true. He *had* been a hero. He'd help take the Longhorns to the playoffs three years in a row and brought home the trophy once. Wherever he'd gone, he'd been slapped on the back and hailed the conqueror—all because he could throw a fifty-yard pass straight into the arms of a receiver. He had rarely missed. Which was why the Chicago Bears had drafted him in the first round. They'd wanted a superhero. Unfortunately, what they got was a screwed-up loser.

He studied the woman in front of him and tried to make sense of everything. "So you had a crush on me in college, and when you ran into me in Houston you decided to fulfill your quarterback fantasies. Is that it?"

She took a deep breath and released it. "Something like that."

He didn't know why the truth pissed him off. Over the years, he'd run into a lot of women who had star athlete fantasies. Some he had even taken up on their offers. But with those women, he had always kept his guard up—being careful what he said and did just in case it ended up on social media. With Summer, he thought he could relax and let down his guard. She was a trusted friend who wouldn't post pictures of him naked or tweet about everything he said.

Except she hadn't been Summer. She'd been Autumn. He knew nothing about Autumn except that she liked to role play and pretend she was someone she wasn't. And if word got out about any of their sexual exploits, his image would be even more tarnished than it already was.

He pointed a finger at her. "If anything we did gets out to the press, I'm suing the hell out of you. Do you understand me?"

Before she could answer, someone called her name. "Audie! Are you out here?"

"I have to get back," she said. "My sisters will be worried." She hesitated. "But I promise you that I'm not going to say a word about anything we did. And I hope you'll do the same. In fact, I think it would be a good idea if you left town as soon as possible."

"Don't worry. I have no desire to stay in this Podunk town for any longer than I have to."

Her shoulders relaxed. "Good." She started to leave, but then stopped and turned to him. "How many beers did you have? Are you okay to drive?"

He was a little taken back. No woman had ever asked him that before, not even his mother. Of course, his mother hadn't cared enough to ask. She'd been too busy fighting with his father.

"I'm fine," he said.

She nodded. "Well, goodbye, Maverick. I hope everything goes well for you."

A breeze blew through the alleyway, fluttering a lock of dark hair over her face. Without much thought, he lifted a hand and brushed it out of her eyes, his fingertips sliding over the soft skin of her cheek. Desire flooded through him, but he wasn't going to be sucked into her game again. His body might remember her body, but he didn't know this woman. He didn't know her at all.

"Goodbye . . . Autumn."

She studied him for a moment longer, then turned and disappeared around the corner of the building. Once she was gone, Maverick stood there for a moment feeling desire, anger, and even a touch of sadness. Sadness that the friend he'd thought he had hadn't been a friend at all. Autumn had just been someone else who used him.

He turned and headed to his truck. It wasn't anything like the big blue half-ton pick up he'd bought right after signing with the Chicago Bears. He had sold that truck to one of his teammates after the Bears dumped him. He'd had numerous trucks after that. Each time he signed with a team, he'd gone out and bought a new truck in the team's colors. And each time he got dropped from the roster, he'd sold it. This truck wasn't big or shiny or new. This truck was a good twenty years old with rusted paint and more dents than a demolition derby car. But it fit him. He wasn't the new shiny quarterback who everyone wanted anymore. He'd been driven hard and beat to hell and back. But he'd keep running. He'd damn well keep running.

He reached in his front pocket for the keys. When he couldn't find them, he remembered leaving them on the bar. He started to head back in to get them when his cellphone rang.

He pulled it from his pocket and glanced at the caller ID. He didn't recognize the number, but he'd gotten a lot of important calls in the last few months from unknown numbers. He answered immediately.

"Maverick."

"Hi, Maverick, this is Neil Mackle from the San Diego Chargers."

His gut seized up and he clenched the phone a little tighter. "How are you, sir?"

"I'm fine, thank you." There was a long hesitation. Maverick knew that hesitation. He'd lived through it many times before and it had always resulted in bad news. And one time, life-changing news. His gut tightened even more as Neil finally spoke. "The coaches and I have reviewed your tryout and decided to pass."

It was hard not to scream out his frustration. He had worked his butt off preparing for the tryout with San Diego, and he had called in every favor to get it. And he'd done well. Better than well. He'd done great. "But why? I thought y'all were happy with my tryout."

"It was an impressive tryout, but there are other things to consider besides your athletic ability, Maverick. You know that. Football isn't just a physical game. It's a mental game. Players need to be in the right frame of mind before they can perform to their full capabilities—especially quarterbacks."

"Is this about what happened in Tampa? Because I just lost my temper is all. I can promise you that it won't happen again."

"It's not about Tampa. Although your temper and all the fights you seem to get into don't make you a coach's dream player." Neil paused again, and Maverick couldn't take it anymore.

"Just say it," he said. "Just say that you think I can't handle the pressure of being a pro quarterback."

Neil sighed. "We don't think you can handle the pressure. And your pro record has proven that. Three NFL teams have given you a chance as their back-up quarterback. And all three have regretted it."

Damn. Maybe he didn't want the truth. He bent over at the waist and tried to ease the cramp in his stomach as Neil Mackle continued.

"You always perform great in practice, but every time you're put in the game, you choke. You throw more interceptions than completions, you fumble the ball, stay too long in the pocket, and can't seem to focus. It's puzzling. Everyone in the league is trying to figure it out. You are the perfect quarterback. You're tall. You're strong. You're fast. You're smart. And you have the best, most accurate arm I've seen in a long time. It's just too bad that your mind keeps screwing things up."

There was no way to argue the point. His mind had been screwing things up for a long time. "It's just nerves," he said.

"If it was just nerves, we could work with that. But the team therapist doesn't think that's it. He thinks it's something more."

During the entire conversation, Maverick had been holding it together. He couldn't hold it together anymore. "It was the shrink? That skinny bald guy with the glasses who probably doesn't know one end of a football from the other? That's the person keeping me from being placed on the roster? You've got to be fuckin' kidding me."

"He's one of the best sports psychiatrists in the business, Maverick. And if he thinks you have a problem, maybe you need to seek professional help."

"The only thing I need to seek is a team who doesn't listen to bullshit from people who don't know crap about football." Maverick hung up. He turned on a boot heel and started for his truck. Then he remembered he didn't have his keys. He whirled around and headed for the door of the bar.

Once inside, he slipped off his sunglasses. The Watering Hole had gotten even more crowded. He had to weave his way around groups of chatting people to make it to the bar. His keys weren't there.

He tapped the guy on the shoulder who was sitting on the same barstool he'd been sitting at. "Have you see some keys?"

The guy swiveled around, and then swayed, almost falling off the stool. Maverick steadied him. "Thanks, man." He grinned drunkenly. "And I saw those keys. I gave them to the bartend—do I know you? You look awful f-f-familiar."

"I don't think so." Maverick went to motion for the bartender, but the guy grabbed his arm.

"Nope. I know you. I never forget a face." The guy studied him for a second before he pointed a finger. "You're Maverick Murdoch." Before Maverick could ask him to keep that under his hat, he turned and yelled down the bar. "Hey Timmy! It's your old friend, Maverick Murdoch."

A big ol' boy at the end of the bar turned. Maverick recognized him immediately. Although he hadn't gone by Timmy in college; everyone had called him Tank. He'd been an offensive linebacker for UT Maverick's freshman year. And they had never gotten along. Not only had the guy sucked at holding the defensive line, he was also a jackass. Something Maverick had once told him. Which meant this wasn't going to be good. Not good at all. Because Tank was still pretty much built like a tank.

Tank got off his barstool and parted the crowd with his huge hulking body as he made his way over to Maverick. When he reached him, a wide smile spread across his face.

"Why I do believe you are right, Pete. It *is* the great Maverick Murdoch—the pride of the Longhorns. Of course, as it turned out he isn't anything to be proud of. He's just a piece of shit choker who couldn't handle the pressure of the NFL." His smile got bigger. "Isn't that right, Mav?"

If it had been another day, Maverick would've ignored him, gotten his keys, and left without saying a word. But it wasn't another day. It was a damned-assed bad day. A day where he'd discovered that his friend with benefits had been an imposter and lost his last hope of playing football this season. Or maybe forever. And he just couldn't take one more shot to his ego. He just couldn't do it.

He smiled. "Fuck you."

That was all it took for one hell of a bar fight to break out.

CHAPTER FOUR

AS SOON AS SPRING TEXTED that she and Waylon were on their way, Autumn volunteered to get the cake from the kitchen. She needed a moment to collect herself after her run-in with Maverick.

Why had she told him that she had a crush on him in college? Why hadn't she come up with some other excuse for playing the game she'd played? Not that there was any excuse for tricking your sister's old boyfriend into bed. And that's exactly what she'd done. She'd tricked Maverick into having sex with her. If he had known she was the weird Hadley triplet, he never would've asked her back to his hotel room. He never would've kissed her and made her want more. He never would've slipped off her clothes and turned her world upside down.

That's why she hadn't told him. After all those college fantasies, she had to know what it felt like to be held in Maverick Murdoch's arms. And now she knew. It felt amazing. But what she also knew was that he hadn't been holding her. He'd been holding Summer. That knowledge kept her from making more of their time together than there was. It had been a brief walk on the wild side. Something she could smile about when she was old and gray and sitting in her rocker, surrounded by her children and grandchildren who thought their mom and grandma was just a sweet little old lady with no exciting past.

That's where she wanted to put her affair with Maverick: In the past.

She smiled at the cook who was frying chicken wings in the kitchen as she pulled the cake box out of the refrigerator. Not wanting to have to deal with the box when she got to the table, she set it on the prep counter and took the cake out.

Summer had done an amazing job. The cake looked just like a sheriff's star. The cream cheese frosting was a shiny gold and Waylon's name and Happy Birthday looked like they were engraved into the icing. She carefully carried the cake to the swinging doors that led out into the bar.

She pushed one door open with her butt, then glanced both ways before she stepped out. But she'd only taken two steps when she heard someone yell "Hey, Timmy! It's your old friend Maverick Murdoch."

She froze in her tracks. Maverick was still there? She edged closer to the bar and peeked between two cowboys. Sure enough Maverick was talking with a giant of a man who had arms the size of tree trunks. Or not talking so much as listening. The giant seemed to be doing all the talking. When he was finished, Maverick finally spoke. And you didn't have to be a lip reader to know what he'd said.

Autumn watched in horror as the giant drew back his huge fist and swung it straight at Maverick's face. Fortunately, Maverick ducked in time. Unfortunately, the giant's fist hit the guy behind Maverick and caused him to sail onto the bar, sending beer bottles and glasses flying.

Then all hell seemed to break loose. Someone yelled "Fight!" and men just started swinging at anything. Even the two cowboys in front of her started shoving each other.

Autumn stepped back against the wall and tried to guard Waylon's cake as she watched the giant pick Maverick up in a bear hug and attempt to squeeze the life out of him. And from Maverick's red face it looked like he was doing a pretty good job.

She should've ignored the swell of concern that welled up inside her. It wasn't like Maverick hadn't asked for it by talking back to someone the size of a semi-truck. And once Maverick passed out, the big man would probably let him go. Wouldn't he? The thought of Maverick lying dead on the floor had Autumn lifting the cake over her head and weaving around the groups of fighting men. When she reached Maverick and the giant, she yelled above the din.

"Let him go!"

The giant didn't seem to hear, but Maverick did.

"What the hell are you doing?" he wheezed. "Get out of here before you get hurt."

She ignored him and yelled again. "Let him go now!"

The giant finally looked at her, and his arms

loosened but didn't completely release. "Not until he admits that he's the biggest pussy in football."

That seemed easy enough. Autumn looked at Maverick. "Say it."

Maverick blinked. "Hell no."

She rolled her eyes. What was it with men? Couldn't they ever let go of their egos? "Fine. I'll say it." She yelled at the top of her lungs. "Maverick Murdoch is the biggest wussy in football!" For some reason that got people's attention and the fights that had broken out stopped and everyone turned to her. She blushed with embarrassment before she looked back at the giant. "Now let him go."

The giant shook his head. "Nope. He has to say it. And I said pussy, not wussy."

Autumn lifted an eyebrow. "That word is extremely derogatory to women. It's wussy or nothing." She looked at Maverick, but she could tell by the stubborn set of his jaw that he wasn't going to call himself a wussy either. Not even when the giant squeezed harder and his pretty sapphire-splashed eyes bugged out. So she did the only thing she could do. She smashed Waylon's beautiful birthday star cake into the giant's face.

He released Maverick immediately, then stood there for a second like a red velvet abominable snowman. Finally, he wiped the cream cheese frosting from his eyes. Eyes that looked extremely angry.

"I'm sorry," she said. "But you should've listened when I asked you to let him go."

The giant glared back at her for a moment before he grabbed her wrist in a vise-like grip. "And you should keep your pretty little nose out of other people's business."

"Let her go, Tank." Maverick said in a threatening voice that Autumn had never heard before. Not even when they had played principal and naughty student.

Tank jerked her closer and put a beefy arm around her waist. His teeth flashed through the gold frosting. "Or what?"

The punch Maverick threw was so fast that Autumn didn't even see it connect with Tank's jaw. All she saw was the flash of fist and tanned muscled arm. Tank stood there for a second before he released Autumn and his eyes rolled back in his head. Then he crashed to the floor like a felled tree. A felled tree covered in Waylon's birthday cake. Summer was going to kill her. Not to mention what Spring would do when she found out her husband didn't have a cake.

Completely exasperated, Autumn turned to Maverick. "Wouldn't it have been easier to just say what he wanted you to?"

Maverick studied her as if she were a science project gone wrong. "You hit him in the face with a pie."

"Actually, it was a cake."

A smile broke across his face. Maverick had always had a breathtaking smile. It reminded Autumn of the sun peeking through the clouds of an overcast day—brilliant and blinding. "You smashed a badass offensive lineman in the face with a cake." He tipped back his head and laughed.

She didn't see the humor. "It's not funny. Summer spent hours making that cake. And it's completely ruined all because you were too cocky to give in."

He stopped laughing and looked at her. "If anyone should know how cocky I am, it's you." She knew by the sexual glint in his eye that he wasn't talking about his ego.

She blinked away the image of just how cocky he was. "I think it's best if we put the past behind us. And why haven't you left town?"

"I forgot something." He reached out and brushed a finger over her cheek. He studied the smudge of gold frosting for only a second before he placed his finger in his mouth and sucked it off. Just like that, Autumn was lost in a tidal wave of sexual desire. She didn't know what she would've done if the crowd hadn't suddenly parted to reveal Waylon standing there.

"What is going on here?"

Spring moved up next to him, looking as baffled as her husband. But unlike Autumn, her sister had always been good at recovering from shocks. After only a second, she turned to Waylon and pinned on a bright smile.

"Surprise!"

Once Waylon got over his surprise, he didn't waste any time trying to figure out what happened. There seemed to be conflicting versions on who started the fight. Tank's friends all claimed that it was Maverick who had thrown the first punch. And since Autumn hadn't witnessed the entire confrontation, Waylon arrested both Maverick and Tank. Tank put up a fight when he came to, and it took Waylon, Dirk, and Ryker to get him handcuffed. But Maverick didn't say a word as Waylon cuffed his hands behind his back and led him out the door.

Once they were gone, Hank, the owner of the Watering Hole, cleared everyone out of the bar so he could clean up the mess. Autumn, Spring, and Summer walked out together.

"Well, I wanted to give my husband a surprise on his birthday, and he sure got one." Spring glanced at Summer. "And it's all your old boyfriend's fault."

Autumn should've kept her mouth shut, but she couldn't. "Like I told Waylon, I don't think Maverick threw the first punch. If he had hit Tank before I got there, the man would've been laying on the floor. He only punched him after Tank grabbed me."

"And that big oaf only grabbed you because you smashed him in the face with my cake." Summer searched the parking lot of people getting into their vehicles, no doubt looking for Ryker. "Do you know how long it took me to get the shape of that star just right?"

"I'm sorry, but he wouldn't stop squeezing Maverick."

"It sounds like Maverick asked for it." Dirk walked up with Gracie. "Even if he didn't throw the first punch, you don't tell a man that size to f-off and not expect to start a fight."

"Like I said before, something's not right with Maverick," Summer said. "He's not the same person he was in college."

Autumn couldn't argue the point. Even though they hadn't done much talking when they were together, she'd recognized the change in Maverick too. At UT, he'd worked hard at his grades and football, but his intensity to succeed had been tempered by a playful charm. He'd smiled more, laughed more, and had constantly teased Summer about being too driven and intense. Now he was the one who was too intense. Although that intensity had made for some steamy memories.

Ryker appeared and slipped an arm around Summer. "It seems that Maverick is going through a tough time. I read that the Chargers were considering him after their backup quarterback got injured. But I just saw a tweet that said they went with someone else."

"Maybe another team will give him a chance," Autumn said, hopefully.

"Doubtful," Dirk said. "Maverick has had his three strikes. I'd say he's out of the NFL for good."

If it was true, then Maverick must be devastated. Football was his life. And maybe that's why he'd agreed to be friends with benefits. He was hoping that sex would help him forget about his problems. Now it looked like he only had more. And Autumn couldn't help feeling responsible. If he hadn't come to Bliss looking for her, he'd never have gotten into the fight.

"What will he do if he can't play football?" she asked.

"He's hardly the first football player who hasn't made it in the pros," Ryker said. "I'm sure he'll find something to do. Sportscaster. Coach."

"You're right, Rye. He does have other options." Dirk squinted his eyes like Granny Bon did whenever she was mulling something over. Only a second later, he looked at Gracie. "We better get home, honey. There are a few calls I need to make before we turn in."

"Come on, husband of mine," Summer said to Ryker. "I want to go home and see if anyone's answered my ad for another baker."

When her siblings and their spouses were gone, Spring hooked her arm through Autumn's. "It looks like it's just you and me, Audie."

As they walked to the car, Autumn couldn't help asking, "Do you think Waylon will keep them in jail for long?"

"I guess it depends on how much damage they've done and how sorry they are. He might just let them cool off in jail for the night and release them in the morning after they pay for damages." Spring glanced over. "But be honest. You're not really worried about Tank as much as you're worried about Maverick."

Autumn stumbled over a crack in the parking lot. "What makes you say that?"

Spring laughed. "Come on, Audie. It was quite obvious in college that you had a major crush on the guy. You couldn't say more than two words to the man without blushing. And it was hard to miss the moon-eyed looks you gave him."

Autumn should've known that Spring would be the one to put two and two together. Her sister had always been observant. "Did Summer know?"

"Of course not. Summer was too wrapped up in softball and thinking up ways to make money to notice you crushing on Maverick. And even if she had noticed, she wouldn't have been upset about it. It's not like you were flirting with him and trying to get him into bed."

Autumn cringed. She hadn't tried to get Maverick into bed when her sister had been dating him, but she'd wasted no time when she ran into him after college.

She had been stunned when she'd seen him walking down the street in downtown Houston. So stunned that she'd called out his name without even thinking. He'd turned and flashed his megawatt smile. "Summer?" She should've corrected him. But she hadn't been able to form one word with his smoldering blue eyes pinned on her. He'd taken her silence as assent. And when he'd pulled her into his muscled arms for a hug, all her morals had flown right out the window. She hadn't thought about Summer or the golden rule of never dating a man your sister was dating—or had dated. All she'd thought about was fulfilling her deepest fantasies.

Which made her the worst sister in the world.

"You don't have to look so guilty, Audie," Spring said. "It was only a crush. You're too levelheaded to date a man like Maverick. I like Mav, but he's selfish. And our daddy proved that selfish men leave nothing in their wake but heartache."

Autumn *was* levelheaded enough to know that Maverick wasn't serious relationship material. His heart belonged to football, and she didn't want a man who couldn't give her his heart completely. Their brief time together had been sexual. Nothing more.

"Speaking of Daddy," Spring said once they were in the car. "He called me the other day."

"No doubt to ask for money for his defense."

"That's exactly why he called. But he didn't get any. After he stole my car and vintage trailer, I promised myself that I wasn't going to be fooled by

Daddy again. But I still worry about him. How was he when you visited him in jail?"

Autumn backed out of the parking space. "Like Daddy. Incarceration hasn't fazed him at all. He tells jokes to all the guards and has made friends with the other inmates. He also has a new girlfriend. I overheard her asking to see him as I was leaving."

"Let me guess," Spring said. "She was a bleached blond with no brains and fake boobs like his last two girlfriends. Of course, no one with brains would date Holt."

Autumn pulled out on Main Street. "I don't know about her intelligence, but she wasn't big boobed or bleached blond. She also looked a lot younger than Holt."

Spring snorted. "Obviously, Holt has bamboozled her into believing he has money. Poor woman doesn't realize she got a Lame Daddy instead of a Sugar Daddy." She glanced out the side window. "Looks like Waylon has gotten Tank and Maverick tucked in tight."

Autumn followed her gaze to the sheriff's office and the jailhouse that was attached to it. There were two lights on. One in one jail cell and one in the other. She couldn't help wondering which one held the giant and which one held her guilty secret.

Nor could she help wondering how long her secret would remain a secret.

CHAPTER FIVE

SHERIFF WAYLON KENDALL TURNED OUT to be a big football fan, which worked in Maverick's favor. Instead of booking him, Waylon seemed more interested in talking football. Once Tank was snoring loudly in his cell, Waylon sat in Maverick's cell and asked him questions about playing for the Longhorns and in the NFL until his deputy showed up for the night shift.

When Waylon was gone, Maverick tried to sleep. It was impossible with Tank's snoring and the hard cot that didn't quite fit his long frame. He ended up staring at the ceiling and thinking about his conversation with Neil Mackle. He was still upset about the phone call. If the San Diego Chargers' coaching staff thought he needed a shrink, then the rest of the NFL probably did too. No wonder no one wanted to take a chance on him. They all thought he was nuts. And maybe he had been after Robby died. He'd been volatile and out of control, drinking, partying, and getting into fights with even his teammates. And he'd been a disaster on the football field—fumbling, staying too long in the pocket, and throwing interceptions. But he'd worked thorough that. He was fine now. Completely fine.

All he needed was a chance to prove it. And he would get that chance. He wasn't giving up. He'd try out for every team in the league if he needed to. And if that didn't work, he'd move to Canada and try out for their league. Hell, he was even willing to move to Italy and work for pizza. He had lost everything else. He couldn't lose football too.

He rolled over on the cot to try and get some sleep and his arm brushed against something sticky on his shirt. He lifted his arm to examine it in the light from the hallway. It was a smudge of gold frosting.

The image of a prim and proper woman in a black funeral dress smashing a cake in Tank's face popped into his head, and he couldn't help but laugh. Autumn wasn't as prim and proper as she looked. Of course, he already knew that.

Thoughts of their sex play had him instantly aroused. In an attempt to get rid of his hard-on, he got up and did sets of squats, followed by crunches and pushups. He finally fell asleep in the wee hours of the morning. What felt like only a few minutes later, he opened his eyes to find Waylon unlocking his cell.

The sheriff glanced over at the cell where Tank was still snoring. "I think we'll leave sleeping beauty where he is for now, but you can come with me."

He followed Waylon down the hallway to a reception area where a short-haired Hadley sister was waiting with a cup of coffee. He now knew the difference between the triplets. This was the only season he hadn't kissed.

"Good mornin'." Spring flashed a bright smile and held out the cup. "I didn't know how you liked it so I just left it black." She glanced at the sheriff. "Which is how most ornery men seem to take it."

"Thank you," Maverick accepted the cup, even though he didn't drink anything with caffeine in it.

"You're most welcome. I don't know if you remember me, but I'm Spring. I'm the youngest triplet and the one who used to talk your ear off whenever you came to see Summer."

Maverick nodded. "I remember."

"You probably also remember my sister Autumn. She's the quiet, shy one."

Not as shy as you think.

Again he nodded. "Yes, I remember Autumn." In fact, he couldn't seem to forget her. And he wanted to. He wanted to forget every moment he'd been played by her. Unfortunately, despite what his mind wanted, his body seemed to enjoy the memories of the time they'd spent together. Even now, he got semi-erect at just the mention of her name.

"Well, I guess I better get back to work." Spring glanced at the sheriff and smiled impishly. "I have a real taskmaster as a boss."

Waylon shot her a stern look that wasn't all that stern. "Behave, or I might have to fire you."

She sashayed around the receptionist desk and sat down. "You tried that once and it didn't work, remember?"

"I remember very well, Miss Hadley."

Spring tipped up her chin. "Mrs. Kendall. And don't you forget it."

Waylon laughed before he held out a hand to the

open door on his right. "Come on into my office, Maverick."

Maverick followed him into the room. "Mrs. Kendall? Spring is your wife?"

Waylon closed the door. "Yes, and I thank my lucky stars every day." He walked over and sat down behind the desk. There was a computer sitting on it, and once Maverick sat down he could see the screensaver. It was three dancing pugs wearing pink tutus.

Waylon followed his gaze and smiled. "What can I say? I like pugs in tutus." His smile faded. "So I guess it's time to address what happened last night."

Maverick couldn't help feeling a little nervous. All he needed was a police record of a bar fight to add to the NFL's belief that he was mentally unstable. Hopefully, Waylon was such a football fan that he'd only give Maverick a slap on the wrist and a bill for the damages. Maverick might not have a job, but he had a good-sized bank account. He hadn't squandered the money he'd gotten from signing with the Chicago Bears.

Waylon sat back in his chair. "Timmy and his friends are still saying you threw the first punch. I don't believe it, especially after hearing Autumn's side of things. But since Tank *was* the only one to get injured, that leaves me in a sticky situation."

"I didn't throw the first punch, but I'm not sorry for hitting Tank. As far as I'm concerned, he deserved what he got."

Waylon nodded. "He's an asshole, all right. And I'm not real happy about the reports I got of him manhandling Autumn. I figure we'll get all of this settled when y'all go in front of the judge."

"Judge?" Maverick's neck muscles tightened. "I was hoping we could deal with this without bringing in a judge."

Waylon studied him for a long moment. "Since this is your first offense in Bliss, it might not be necessary to bring you up on charges. Of course, I can't just let you go scot-free either."

"Of course not. I'm more than willing to pay for any damages that occurred during the fight."

"Surprisingly enough, there wasn't that much damage done besides a few broken glasses . . . and my birthday cake." Waylon grinned. "That Autumn is more of a pistol than I thought she was."

The man had no idea.

"I'd be more than happy to pay for the glasses and buy you another cake," Maverick said.

Waylon shook his head. "As much as I would've liked to see the sheriff's badge cake that Summer made me, I don't really need the extra calories. Spring has brought home so many baked goods for me to sample recently that I'm starting to get a sheriff's gut."

Maverick doubted that. The man looked to be in perfect shape. "Then how about if I donate some money to the town? Or a local charity?"

"Actually, I was thinking more of your time than your money."

Maverick stared at him. "Are we talking community service?"

Waylon gave a brief nod. "That's exactly what I'm thinking."

Maverick wanted to decline. He didn't have time to pick weeds or help out in a library. He had to find another team that was willing to give him a chance. And if he wanted to make that team, he had to stay in shape. Which was a full-time job. This was the first entire day that he'd gone without weight training or running in years. But it wasn't like he had much choice.

"I'd be happy to do a few hours of community service."

"Actually, I wasn't thinking about a few hours. I was thinking more like a few months."

Maverick jerked to attention so quickly that he spilled the coffee he still held in his hand. He barely noticed the wet heat seeping through his jeans. "A couple months? Doing what?"

Waylon smiled. "Coaching our high school football team."

It only took him a second to get over his shock and realize that he had walked right into a trap. One he wasn't about to stay in. He shook his head. "I'm sorry. I get that you need a coach, but I can't do it. I don't coach. I play."

Waylon's eyebrows lifted. "For whom? I heard that the Chargers have decided to go with another backup quarterback."

Maverick hated how quickly news traveled. You could talk to someone one second, and the next second your conversation was being tweeted to the world. "San Diego isn't the only team in the NFL."

"True, but they were the only team looking for a quarterback this late in the season." Waylon sat up and cupped his hands on the desk. "I understand how much you want to play pro football, Maverick. In college, I wanted to play pro baseball in a bad way. But then I got injured and I had to accept the fact that it wasn't going to happen."

"It's going to happen for me," Maverick snapped.

"I don't doubt it. You seem pretty determined to succeed, and I've never seen a quarterback with your arm. I think any team would be lucky to have you." Waylon paused. "It just doesn't look like anyone is going to pick you up this season."

Waylon's words were like a hard punch to Maverick's stomach. He didn't want to accept them, but he knew they were true. He wasn't going to play this season. But that didn't mean he wasn't going to play next season.

"I have to train. I don't have time to coach a team properly."

"What better place to train than at a high school with its own gym and track? And if the boys train with a professional football player, they should be more than ready for the season."

Maverick knew when he'd been pushed into a corner, but he couldn't help making one last-ditch effort to get out. "And what happens if I decline your offer?"

Waylon shrugged. "Then I guess I'll have to charge you with disorderly conduct and let the judge set your penalty."

"You know if I fought this in front of a judge, I'd get off. Tank and his friends are lying."

"Of course you will." Waylon paused. "But not without a lot of media attention. And somehow I can't see you needing any more bad press. What you do need is some good press. And I'm thinking that volunteering to help out a small town high school football team is as good as it gets."

Maverick wanted to argue, but he'd run out of arguments. He had a choice: He could agree and spend three miserable months in Bliss or he could decline and put another black mark on his already marked-up football resume. Another black mark would no doubt convince the NFL that he *did* have some major problems and wasn't a good risk.

Although word of the fight was bound to get out.

"The media will find out about the fight anyway," Maverick said. "Everyone in town was there and saw it."

Waylon smiled. "You don't know very much about small towns, do you? We gossip among ourselves, but we're pretty close-lipped when it comes to spreading bad news about our town to folks who don't live here. Once everyone hears that you're coaching our boys, you'll be the town hero who can do no wrong. And I doubt Timmy will want to post about getting lights knocked out."

Before Maverick could come up with another argument, Spring breezed into the room. "I hate to interrupt, but Timmy just woke up and is breathing fire. I figure some of Ms. Marble's cinnamon-swirl muffins will help calm him down so I'm heading over to the bakery. Did y'all want anything?"

"No muffins for me," Waylon said, "but I'd love one of Carly's western omelets from the diner. And bring Maverick whatever he wants."

Spring looked at him with hopeful eyes. "So are you going to coach our boys?"

He accepted his fate. "It doesn't look like I have a choice."

Spring sent him a sympathetic look. "There's no need to look like you just lost your best friend, Mav. I was stuck in Bliss once myself and everything turned out just fine and dandy." She glanced at Waylon and smiled softly. "I found the love of my life and a town filled with friends."

Maverick wasn't looking for the love of his life. And he certainly wasn't looking for friends. He would do his time, but he had no intentions of getting attached to anyone in Bliss, Texas.

Especially a troublemaking triplet.

CHAPTER SIX

A UTUMN WOKE UP MUCH LATER than usual. She had spent most of the night worrying that Maverick would crack under Waylon's interrogation and spill the beans about what he was doing in Bliss and how Autumn had tricked him into bed.

And she *had* tricked him. Not that getting him into bed had been her plan at first. When she'd first seen him in Houston, she'd only planned on playing the triplet switch game until they said goodbye. But when he'd started to walk away, she'd blurted out a dinner invitation. And during the main course, she'd made up her mind to have Maverick for dessert.

She wanted to blame her uncharacteristic behavior on the two glasses of wine she'd had with dinner—she'd never been able to hold her liquor. But deep down, she knew it hadn't been the wine. It had been her infatuation with Maverick coupled with the headiness of being someone other than herself. All her life she'd been logical, responsible Autumn who thought everything through before she did it. She followed the rules. She never caused problems. But that night at dinner, she'd taken on her sister's persona. And not just Summer's, but her other siblings as well. She had been as sassy and controlling as Summer, as free-spirited and gregarious as Spring, and as devilish and naughty as Dirk when she'd accompanied Maverick back to his hotel room. Once in his room, she'd pushed him against the closed door and kissed him like there was no tomorrow, then slipped off her dress and offered her body to his talented fingers and scorching lips.

Thinking they'd only have the one night together, she'd taken everything she wanted from him. But before she left his hotel room, he'd asked to see her again. After three amazing orgasms, she couldn't say no. They met two more times before she closed the store, but she made sure both times were just about sex. No dinner. No drinks. No conversation. Just hot sex that she could never confuse with anything else. Once the store was closed, she brought an end to her Maverick games and resumed her calm, mundane life.

And then Maverick had showed up in Bliss.

Now she didn't feel calm. She felt petrified with anxiety that her family would find out what happened in Houston. Her sweet, religious grandmother would probably have a heart attack if she found out that her prim and proper granddaughter was really a sex-starved wanton. Not to mention how shocked Dirk and Spring would be. And Summer, poor Summer, would be completed blindsided that her own sister had betrayed her in such a way.

There was an unspoken rule between sisters: You didn't date each other's boyfriends—past or present. And you especially didn't trick them into bed by impersonating your sister. What if Maverick had told someone about their affair and it had gotten out to the media? Summer would've been the one who suffered. It might have even affected her relationship with Ryker. Autumn never would've forgiven herself if Ryker had broken it off with her sister because of her.

Thankfully, that hadn't happened. And if Autumn could just get Maverick out of town, no one in her family would ever be the wiser.

She quickly got out of bed and almost tripped over the hound dog and cat that were sleeping on the floor. Sherlock lifted one droopy eyelid for only a second before he went back to sleep. Watson, on the other hand, got up and followed Autumn to the bathroom where he sat on the toilet and groomed himself while Autumn showered.

She hoped to catch Waylon before he left for work so she could find out what had happened to Maverick. But by the time she was dressed and got downstairs, Waylon and Spring had already left. She tried calling Spring, but her sister didn't answer. She would just have to stop off at Waylon's office on her way to the bakery.

After making sure that Sherlock and Watson had food and water, she grabbed her purse and headed out the front door. She was on her way down the porch steps when she glanced next door and noticed Ms. Marble struggling with the grocery bags she was taking out of her trunk.

Autumn hurried over to help the older woman.

"Let me get those, Ms. Marble." She took the heavy bags.

"Thank you, dear," Ms. Marble said. "I thought you'd be at the bakery by now."

"I'm running a little late this morning." She glanced at all the bags in the trunk. It was a lot of groceries for just one person. "Are you baking today?"

"Actually, I just found out this morning that I'm going to have a new tenant in the apartment over my garage, and I wanted to stock it with a few snacks."

Autumn's heart sank. "You rented your little apartment?" She had been counting on renting the apartment from Ms. Marble. Now she would have to find another place to live. She couldn't continue to stay with Spring and Waylon.

"Yes, and I must admit that I'm surprised by how popular the studio over the garage has become." Ms. Marble picked up a bag and headed to the side door of her house. Autumn followed behind her, feeling more than a little depressed that she hadn't talked to Ms. Marble sooner about renting the apartment.

Ms. Marble opened the door that led into the kitchen. "I also bought extra groceries because I'm hoping your grandmother will have dinner with me one night while she's here for the grand opening of the bakery."

"Oh, I'm sorry no one told you, but Granny Bon won't be able to come for the grand opening after all. She's too busy at work." Her grandmother worked at a transitional home for foster children in Waco. While Granny Bon loved the job, Autumn worried about the long hours her grandmother kept. "I wish she would retire and move to Bliss." She followed Ms. Marble into the kitchen and set the groceries on the counter.

"There's no need to be in a hurry to retire." Ms. Marble set her bag down. "I didn't retire from teaching until I was almost seventy. But I agree that your grandmother needs to cut back a little—maybe find a good man to spend her spare time with."

Autumn laughed. "I don't think Granny is interested in dating."

"I don't know why not. She may not be a spring chicken, but she's still young enough to find a special someone."

Autumn had never thought about her grandmother dating. Granny Bon had always seemed quite content to remain single. But maybe Granny wasn't as content as she was letting on. Autumn acted like she was perfectly happy with her life when she was around her family, but since her siblings had gotten married, she had started to feel like the odd man out. Which was probably another reason why she'd continued the affair with Maverick. When she'd been with him, she hadn't felt like a single in a double world.

"Maybe you could find her a man here in Bliss so that Granny will be more willing to move here after she retires," Autumn said. It was no secret that Ms. Marble was good at matchmaking. She had been instrumental in getting all of Autumn's cousins and siblings to the little white chapel.

"That's my plan," Ms. Marble said. "Your grandmother, you, and your siblings have become like family to me. Call me selfish, but I want all of you to live here so I can enjoy your company."

Autumn gave Ms. Marble a tight hug. "You're like family to us too, Ms. Marble."

After a moment, Ms. Marble drew back. "We better get the rest of my groceries inside before my milk spoils in this heat. I'll be happy when fall arrives and we get cooler weather."

Once Autumn helped Ms. Marble get her groceries put away, she made her excuses. "I should get to the bakery. It's just two more days before the grand opening, and I need all the baking practice I can get." She also needed to talk to Waylon and make sure Maverick was gone.

"Baking isn't about practice," Ms. Marble said. "It's about love." Before Autumn could ask what she meant, she held out the two grocery sacks she had set aside for her new tenant. "Before you leave, would you mind taking these up to the apartment over the garage? My old knees can't take those stairs."

Once inside the apartment, Autumn was even more disappointed that Ms. Marble had rented the space to someone else. The little studio with the small kitchenette and bathroom would've been perfect for her. It was next door to Waylon and Spring's house and only a block from the cute Victorian Ryker had bought Summer. But there was no sense crying over something she couldn't change.

Autumn put the bags on the counter in the kitchenette. Worried that there might be something perishable, she put the groceries away. It was a pretty healthy selection. There were baby carrots and celery sticks, apples and pears, protein bars and drinks, a can of almonds, almond milk, and a jar of organic almond butter.

She was putting the groceries away in the cupboard when she heard Ms. Marble coming up the stairs. A second later the door opened, and she couldn't help teasing the older woman.

"You certainly like to keep your tenants healthy, Ms. Marble. There's not one cinnamon-swirl muffin in the bunch."

"Let me guess. You're here to welcome the new coach."

She froze at the deep, familiar voice. She slowly turned to see Maverick standing there looking like he'd gotten less sleep than she had. His eyes had dark circles under them. The scruff on his face was thicker. And his hair was mussed. Still, he looked as hot as ever. But his gorgeousness was eclipsed by the fact that he was there when he should be gone.

"Why are you still here?" she asked.

He smiled sardonically. "You're looking at the new head football coach of the Bliss High School . . . whatever they call themselves."

Panicked was too gentle a word to describe how she felt. When she spoke, her voice hit a high note that she hadn't hit since seventh grade choir. "What are you talking about? Why would you volunteer to coach the football team?"

"I didn't." He dropped the duffel bag he carried to the chair and tossed his cowboy hat onto the small table in front of the window. "I was bulldozed into it by your sister's husband. Who, no doubt, started hatching his plan last night when we were talking football. I either coach or get brought up on charges."

Autumn slowly shook her head. "But you can't stay here. You can't live in the same town as I do."

"Why? Afraid your dirty little secret will get out?"

She was, but that wasn't the only reason she wanted him gone. She couldn't be around Maverick and remain the calm, logical Hadley triplet. When he was around, she lost all her inhibitions and sanity. What had happened in Houston proved it—not to mention what had happened last night at the Watering Hole when she'd jumped into the middle of a bar fight. And this wasn't a big city where no one cared what you were doing. This was a small town where everyone cared what you were doing.

She started for the door. "I'll talk to Spring. I'm sure she can talk Waylon out of this crazy idea."

He stopped her in her tracks. "Spring already knows all about the crazy idea." When she turned to him, he waved a hand around. "She was the one who arranged for me to have this ... closet to live in while I'm here."

"But she wouldn't do that. Especially when she knows I had a—"

Maverick cut her off. "You told your sisters about our affair? What happened to keeping our mouths shut?"

"I would never tell either of my sisters what happened in Houston. Spring just knows that I had a crush on you in college. Obviously, she thinks I'm over it." She realized what she'd said when Maverick looked confused.

"You're not?"

She tried to backpedal. "Of course I am." She cleared her throat. "I'm going to fix this. I'll convince Waylon that you being the new coach is a bad idea."

"And just how are you going to do that?"

She thought for a moment. "I'll tell him that you have a drug problem and would be a horrible influence on young boys."

"Like hell you will. I don't want that getting out to the media." He toed off his cowboy boots. "Now if you'll excuse me, I need to get some shut-eye before I meet my team this afternoon." He punched the air three times. "Go. Fight. Win."

Not concerned at all that she was still there, he pulled off his t-shirt, revealing sculpted bronzed muscles that Autumn had touched and tasted every square inch of. But she didn't have time to walk down muscle memory lane. She had other things to worry about. Like living in the same town with her dirty little secret.

"You can*not* live here."

He neatly folded the shirt and hung it over the back of a chair. "Too late. I already am." He flicked open the button of his jeans, lowered the zipper, then pushed them down his lean thighs. She tried to look anywhere but at the bulge beneath the black cotton of his boxer briefs, but her eyes seemed to have a will of their own. He turned and his butt and leg muscles flexed and released in flawless balance as he walked to the bed and stretched out on the mattress like a jungle cat exhausted from toying with its prey.

That's exactly what Autumn was—Maverick's prey. She was trapped in the same town with an arrogant predator who could kill her off with the truth at any time. Or worse, kill her with desire for the gorgeous body stretched out before her.

Desire he easily read.

He tucked a pillow beneath his head and closed his eyes. "Sorry, honey. This horse has run its last race with an imposter as his jockey. Close the door when you leave."

Anger consumed her. Not just at Maverick for his arrogance, but also at herself for wanting to ride him like a jockey. But things had changed between them. As Summer, she had been the popular overachiever seducing the famous football player. As Autumn, she was the pathetic introvert crushing on the famous football player. And she didn't like it. She didn't like it one bit.

"Just for your information," she said, "I have no desire to ride a washed-up gelding that's been put out to pasture. I prefer strong, successful studs." She whirled and walked out the door, slamming it as hard as she could behind her.

She headed straight to Waylon's office. She could've taken her car, but she needed the walk to cool her anger. She wanted to be clear-headed when she talked to her brother-in-law.

But hopes of talking Waylon into rethinking his position died a quick death when she got to Main Street and ran into Emmett Daily. "Did you hear the great news?" he said with a bright smile. "We got us a professional football player for our high school coach." Before her mouth could finish dropping open, he headed down the street.

She stood there watching as he stopped to tell everyone he met the "great" news. There were loud whoops of celebration, and her last spark of hope flickered out. Waylon couldn't change his mind now. Not without the entire town revolting. They wanted a coach, and he'd given them one.

She just wished it hadn't been the man she'd played horse trainer and naughty pony with.

CHAPTER SEVEN

MAVERICK DIDN'T GET THE NAP he needed. After Autumn had called him a useless gelding, he was too ticked off to sleep. A part of him had wanted to jump up from the bed and prove that he was no gelding. It wouldn't have been difficult to do. He'd been semi-erect from the moment he'd walked into the room and seen Autumn. The dress she'd had on wasn't as ugly as the one she'd worn the night before. It was still too conservative for his tastes, but it had shown enough long legs and soft cleavage to make him want to tumble her into the sheets and prove his virility.

Of course, he didn't need to prove his virility to a manipulative liar. And as far as he was concerned, that's all Autumn was. A liar who had gotten him stuck in this town for three long months.

After she'd left, he got up and took a shower. He stood under the cool spray until his desire and temper cooled and his muscles relaxed. He wanted to be pissed at Autumn for getting him into this jam, but the truth was he had only himself to blame. He shouldn't have returned to Houston after the first time. He shouldn't have let a one-night stand turn into anything more than a happy memory.

But the sex had been too good.

Autumn might have manipulated him, but she was the best lover he'd ever been with. Most women wanted him to take control during sex and prove that he was the big stud quarterback. And never one to disappoint, he'd worked his ass off to make sure women left his bed happy. But Autumn hadn't let him take control. From the moment they'd stepped into his hotel room, she was the one who called all the plays. She'd told him what she wanted and how she wanted it.

For once, he didn't have to be the man in charge. She set up the game plan and all he had to do was follow her lead. She led him to a place filled with mind-blowing kisses and explosive orgasms. She led him to a place where he could find release from the demons that plagued him. And that's why he'd followed her to Bliss—the hope that she could help him find that same release.

Instead, he'd ended up in shackles.

After the shower, he stepped out of the bathroom to get his shaving kit from his duffel bag. Everything he owned was in the bag. For the last six months he'd been a nomad, traveling to any NFL team willing to give him a chance. It was a hard life, but one he'd gotten used to. He reached for the zipper on his duffel, but then froze when a woman spoke behind him.

"I now understand why you're so popular with the ladies."

He whirled around to see the little old woman he'd met at Summer's bakery standing in the kitchenette. He quickly wrapped the towel he carried around his waist and started to apologize. But then he realized that he wasn't the one who should be sorry. The assertive people of this town were started to tick him off.

He scowled. "I guess in Bliss I'll need to make sure my doors are locked."

Ms. Marble smiled. "I apologize for walking in unannounced. I didn't realize you had arrived. Autumn didn't say a word. Of course, she's a quiet little thing." She held up a bowl that was wrapped in what looked like miles of plastic wrap. "Chicken salad. Fat-free mayonnaise and plenty of walnuts and grapes. I figured a strapping young man would need more to eat than the carrots and celery I bought you."

Her generosity lessened his anger. "Thank you." He waited for her to leave, but she didn't seem to be in any hurry.

She pulled out some plates from the cupboard. "Go ahead and get dressed while I dish it up for you."

He wanted to decline the offer, but his grumbling stomach wouldn't let him. He'd already declined the breakfast Spring had offered him, and his body needed fuel. He grabbed his duffel and headed back to the bathroom. When he finished shaving and dressing, he stepped out to find Ms. Marble sitting in one of the chairs by the table. The late afternoon sun reflected off her white hair like a blinding halo, but he got the feeling that Ms. Marble was no angel.

"Much better," she said when she saw him. "I prefer a clean-shaven man to a scruffy one." She pointed to the plate of food and glass of milk. "Come eat. The boys will be getting out of school soon, and you'll want to be at practice to introduce yourself."

So that was why she'd brought food and filled his refrigerator with snacks. She wanted to make sure the coach of her beloved football team had enough energy to do a good job. He took the chair on the other side of the table. "Yeah, I wouldn't want to miss that."

Ms. Marble sent him a stern look. "Sarcasm is one of those things that's best used in moderation."

He really wanted to tell her exactly how he felt about being the new football coach. Instead, he nodded. "Yes, ma'am." He picked up his fork and started to eat. It was good. Really good. He didn't usually eat mayonnaise—fat-free or otherwise—and had forgotten how deliciously creamy it was.

Ms. Marble watched him eat with a satisfied smile on her thin lips. When he was almost finished, she spoke. "I realize you're upset about being stuck in Bliss. It can't be easy becoming a high school coach after being a professional quarterback."

"I'm not making a career change. I'm fulfilling a sentence."

She studied him with an unnerving gaze. "At one time or another, we all feel like we're serving sentences—like we were dealt a bad hand in the game of life. We have two choices: We can toss our cards on the table and fold, or we can take a good look at our hand and see if there's a way to come out a winner." She smiled. "I don't take you for a folder."

Before he could reply, she changed the subject.

"How did your reunion with Summer go?"

"She wasn't quite the girl I remembered," he said dryly.

"Summer has found love. That changes people."

He took a drink of the almond milk she'd poured him. "Usually not for the better."

"So you're a cynic."

"Just a realist."

"What seems real to people sometimes isn't real at all. It's just a misconception," Ms. Marble said. The woman was a fount of wisdom. Wisdom that he didn't want or need.

"There was no misconception with my parents. It was hate at first sight. Too bad they had kids before they realized it."

Her eyes filled with compassion. "I'm sorry. Divorce is a hard thing for a child to live through."

"Oh, they didn't divorce. My parents are still living in wedded misery." He wiped off his mouth with a napkin before he pushed back his chair. "Thank you for the chicken salad, Ms. Marble. But I better get to the high school. I wouldn't want the sheriff to think I'm not keeping my word and toss me back in jail." He got up, and when he noticed she was having a hard time getting to her feet, he walked over and helped her. She held onto his hand long after she was standing. She had a wrinkly, fragile-looking hand, but a surprisingly firm grip.

"You might not be able to see it now," she said, "but I think there's a reason you landed in Bliss, Texas, Maverick Murdoch. And I don't think it has anything to do with football."

Ms. Marble was intuitive. He'd give her that.

There was a reason he'd landed in Bliss, Texas. And it didn't have anything to do with football. It had to do with a deceitful woman who Maverick intended to stay away from.

Football was to Texas what basketball was to Indiana—except with more money thrown at it. High school stadiums were usually as big and elaborate as college stadiums. Weight rooms had all the newest training machines. And locker rooms were filled with all the best equipment that money could buy.

So Maverick was a little taken aback when he pulled up to the high school football stadium. Not that it could be called a stadium. There was no media box. No concession stand. No bathrooms. No scoreboard. And no locker rooms. There was just a field, two goalposts, and a single set of bleachers.

He got out of his truck and walked out on the field. Even the grass looked pathetic. But still there was something about stepping out on an expansive field of green, even a pathetic one, that made him feel at home. The house he'd grown up in had only been a block away from a high school stadium. And when his parents' fighting had gotten to be too much, he and his brother had walked to the stadium and climbed the chain-link fence to the field—or he had boosted Robby over and then climbed the fence.

He and his brother had always played the same way. Maverick was the star quarterback and Robby was the star receiver. But Robby had always struggled to catch the ball, even when Maverick had thrown it right into his hands.

The pain Maverick had been hiding from punched him hard in the chest. But instead of giving in to it, he started to run. He usually stretched before he ran, but this time he just accelerated into a hard sprint. When he reached the opposite goal line, he touched it, then turned and sprinted back the other way. He repeated it until his lungs and muscles were burning. He welcomed the physical pain. It was preferable to the mental pain.

He slowed down and stopped to catch his breath when he saw Waylon Kendall getting out of his sheriff's SUV.

"Hey, Murdoch!" Waylon yelled with a friendly wave. He was dressed in sweats and running shoes. Without his uniform, he looked much less intimidating. He even acted less intimidating. His smile was bright as he jogged toward Maverick. "You're here."

"Where did you expect me to be?"

Waylon stopped in front of him. "As far from Bliss as you could get."

"I wish. But I didn't want every lawman in Texas breathing down my neck." He glanced around. "So is this the practice stadium?"

"The practice stadium and the playing stadium." Waylon laughed. "By your shocked look, I'd say you were expecting something more elaborate."

"A peewee football field is more elaborate than this."

Waylon shrugged. "We're only a triple-A school. And we don't have any oil money paying our bills.

But this humble little field has worked for over fifty years and seen lots of boys turned into good men."

"Were you one of those boys?"

"I played a little. But baseball was my sport."

"Wimpy ball beater," Maverick said with a grin.

Waylon laughed. "Dumb pigskin flinger." They smiled at each other for a second before Waylon glanced over Maverick's shoulder. "Here come the boys."

Maverick turned, hoping that at least his team would be impressive. They weren't. A few of the kids crossing the field looked athletic, but most of them looked like they belonged anywhere but on a football field.

Waylon seemed to read his disappointment. "You know that new stadium you were thinking about? Well, the next county over just got finished building one. All of our most promising players from last year transferred there."

"Which probably explains why your coach bailed."

Waylon nodded. "But now we have a big NFL player to whip us into shape." He grinned. "Things work out if you let them." He lowered the bag he had slung over his shoulder and untied the drawstring.

The bag was filled with footballs, kicking tees, and drill cones. As Waylon was pulling the equipment out, Maverick's gaze returned to the boys who had almost reached them. One of the more athletic-looking kids reached out and tugged down the sweatpants of an overweight kid. The overweight kid stumbled over his pants and landed face first in the grass. The other boys laughed, and again Maverick's mind returned to Robby. His brother had been overweight as a kid. Which was why he couldn't run fast or climb fences. While Maverick had found solace from his parents' fighting in football, Robby had found it in food. Of course, no one had bullied his little brother. Maverick had been there to watch out for him . . . until he wasn't.

Waylon finally noticed the boys' laughter and glanced over his shoulder. "What's going on?" Not one of them answered. The overweight kid had pulled up his sweatpants and was struggling to get to his feet. "Stuart, what happened?" Waylon asked.

"Just me being clumsy, sheriff," he said. Smart kid. He knew that adults couldn't stop bullying. They usually just made it worse.

Waylon studied him for a moment as if he knew the kid was lying before he glanced at Maverick. "Did you see what happened?"

All eyes turned to Maverick. Some of the boys recognized him immediately. They punched each other and whispered under their breath. The others were just waiting for him to answer the sheriff.

He shook his head. "Nope. Didn't see a thing."

Waylon looked back at Stuart one more time before he let it go and introduced Maverick. "Boys, I'd like you to meet your new coach, Maverick Murdoch. For those of you who don't know him, he's been a quarterback for numerous NFL teams, including the Chicago Bears."

The kid who had pulled Stuart's pants down smirked. "Back-up quarterback, you mean. And according to what I've read, you're not even that now."

It took a real effort to keep a smile on his face. "It sounds like you know football. That's good. That's real good. I'm going to make a guess and say that you're the quarterback of the Bliss . . ." He pulled a name that started with a b out of a hat. "Bulldogs."

The boys laughed, and Waylon quickly corrected him. "Bobcats."

"Right. You're the quarterback of the Bliss Bobcats."

The kid's smirk got bigger. "Yes, sir." The way he drew out the sir made it anything but respectful. Great. Not only did Maverick have to deal with a misfit team, he also had to deal with a smartass, bully quarterback. His life for the next three months was going to be hell. And if his life was going to be hell, he might as well have some company there.

He looked at the kid. "What's your name?"

"Race. Race Dunkin."

"No kidding? Now that's a perfect football name. Of course, it would work better for a running back. But hey, who wants to be a running back when you can be the man in charge?" He winked as if sharing a secret. "Okay, Race, since you're the man, I'd like you to be my demonstrator for the warm-up drills we're going to do. You'll show the team how they're done properly, and then they'll follow your lead. Let's start with fifty-forties." When Race only stood there looking baffled, Maverick gave him a surprised look. "You know what those are, right? You start at the goal line and run as fast as you can to the forty-yard line and back."

"That's simple enough," Race said. He headed

to the goal line, then sprinted out to the forty and back. Maverick had to admit that he was fast. When the kid was finished, he jogged back to the group looking smug. "Did you time me?" He leaned over at the waist to catch his breath. "How fast was I?"

Maverick shook his head. "Sorry, I forgot to time you. I'll do it next time."

Race looked up. "Next time?"

"Yeah. You have twenty-four more times to do it. That's why they're called fifty-forties. You run forty yards fifty times. Twenty-five out and twenty-five back." Race looked appalled, and Maverick had to bite back a smile. "Is there a problem? I just thought an ace quarterback like yourself could handle a little running. If you can't, just say the word.

"I can handle it!" Race snapped. He headed back to the one-yard line while Maverick turned to the rest of the boys.

"Okay, while Race is demonstrating his athletic ability, why don't we do some stretches?"

A skinny boy with bright orange hair that resembled a rooster comb looked back at Race. "But shouldn't we be watching him so we'll know how to do it?"

Shit. This was going to be a tough three months. Maverick could only thank God that this motley crew didn't have a chance of going to the playoffs. Otherwise, three more weeks would be tacked on to his sentence. "I think you can figure it out when the time comes."

While Waylon had the boys do different stretches, Maverick walked around and got their names and positions. He put off talking to Stuart until the very last. Even then, he couldn't seem to look the kid in the eye.

"I'm going to assume you're a defensive lineman, Stuart."

"I don't have a position, sir."

Maverick glanced at Waylon who explained. "Stuart is new to Bliss High, and Raff and I couldn't decide the best place to put him." Which Maverick figured translated to "*Stuart sucks, but we didn't have the heart to kick him off the team because he's new to the school and fat. So we left that fun job for you.*"

He blew out his breath. "We'll figure that out later. For now, I want everyone to run a couple laps around the track to warm up your muscles, then come back here and we'll run a few plays to see where we stand."

The skinny redhead, whose name was Wesley or Wyatt or something with a *W*, spoke up. "But what about the fifty-forties?"

Maverick glanced back at Race, who had stopped running and was throwing up on the twenty-two yard line. "I think we'll leave those to our star quarterback." He clapped his hands. "Now hit it!"

The boys raced off. All except Stuart, who followed at a slow, shuffling jog. Maverick watch him for only a second before he turned to find Waylon studying him.

"What?" he asked.

Waylon shook his head. "Nothing. So what do you want me to do . . . Coach?"

The title annoyed Maverick. But whether he liked it or not, that's what he was.

CHAPTER EIGHT

THE GRAND OPENING WEEK OF the Blissful Bakery went off without a hitch. Everyone in town stopped by at one time or another to check out the new eatery. Summer had kicked Autumn out of the kitchen and had her working the register. Unlike the rest of her siblings, she had never been a people person. Thankfully, most everyone in Bliss was talkative, and she only had to say a few words to keep any conversation going.

The only one who hadn't shown up at the bakery was Maverick. Autumn thanked her lucky stars for that. She had spent the last week hiding from the man. When he'd walked into the diner while she was ordering lunch for her and Summer, she'd ducked into the kitchen and gone out the back door. When she pulled into the gas station and had seen him talking with Emmett, she'd pulled right back out again. And when she'd seen him running down Main Street, she'd quickly crossed the street.

Thankfully, Maverick was too into eating healthy to stop into the bakery. The entire town was gossiping about what the new coach ordered at the diner—egg white omelets and vegetables for breakfast and grilled chicken and fish for lunch and dinner. She couldn't see him ruining his perfect body with a donut or cupcake.

But everyone else in town stopped by for a sugary treat. After a week of non-stop customers, Autumn was thankful when Saturday afternoon rolled around. Summer still hadn't gotten any applications for bakers, and she'd decided to close the bakery on Sundays so she'd have at least one day off. Autumn was looking forward to a day off too. A day when she could curl up on the porch swing with a good book.

With it being so close to closing time, the customers had dwindled down to a group of teenage boys who seemed to be having trouble deciding what to order. Although they weren't looking at the menu so much as Autumn and Spring. Spring didn't work on Saturdays and had stopped by to help at the bakery. When the boys started whispering and punching each other, Autumn figured she knew what they were whispering about. All boys seemed to have sexual fantasies about identical sisters.

She glanced at Spring, and they both rolled their eyes.

"Should we have a little fun?" Spring said. Before Autumn could reply, her sister cupped her face in her hands and gave her a big kiss on the lips. "See you later at the slumber party, sweet sister. Remember, you don't need to bring any pajamas." She winked before she disappeared in the back.

When she was gone, Autumn glanced at the boys. Their mouths hung open like three largemouth bass. She bit back a smile. "Can I help you boys?"

After only a moment, the leader of the group recovered and smiled cockily. "Men. We're men, not boys." He winked at his friends. "And what do you have to offer?"

She lifted an eyebrow and pointed to the menu above her head.

He leaned on the counter. "Is that all?"

Before she could put the cocky teenager in his place, the bell over the door jingled. Another teenager stepped in. This one was chubby with soft brown eyes that widened when he saw the other boys. He started to back up, but the cocky kid at the counter stopped him.

"Well, if it isn't super-sized Stewie." He looked at his friends. "You better order up, guys. Once Stewie starts eating, there won't be a cookie crumb left." While his friends laughed, he turned back to Autumn. "I'll take a couple glazed donuts and two chocolate cupcakes with sprinkles, sweetheart."

Autumn was about to tell the obnoxious boy that he wasn't getting anything but a swift kick in the pants when the door opened again. This time, it wasn't a teenager. This time, it was a man. A man whose biceps bulged beneath the sleeves of his t-shirt as he pushed open the door. So much for her theory on healthy eaters staying away from bakeries.

Maverick smiled. "Well, good afternoon, boys."

The three teenagers exchanged looks before they mumbled a reply. "Hey, Coach."

The chubby teenager was a little slower with his response. "Hello, sir."

Maverick only nodded before his eyes zeroed in

on the kid standing at the counter. "And there's my star quarterback."

Autumn couldn't hold her tongue any longer. "He's not a star quarterback. He's a bully. He was harassing that poor boy and calling him names." The chubby teenager's face turned bright red, and he looked down at the floor. She hated to embarrass him, but something needed to be done. Unfortunately, it turned out that Maverick wasn't the one to do it.

His eyes widened in shock. "Race?" He slapped a hand on the bully's shoulder as if they were the best of friends. Although it was probably a little harder than he intended because the young man cringed. "You can't be talking about my boy, Race. Why he's the leader of my team. The main man. The hero of the town who's going to lead our team to victory. He would never bully anyone." He glanced at the chubby teenager. "Isn't that right, Stuart?"

Stuart kept his eyes on his run-over tennis shoes and nodded. "That's right, sir."

Maverick looked back at Autumn. "See. Obviously, you don't know the difference between bullying and playful teasing."

Autumn felt her anger rise. "I know the difference. And there is nothing playful about calling someone super-sized Stewie. That is just cruel and hurtful. And if you won't do anything about it, I will." She came around the counter and pointed a finger at the door. "Get out. We don't serve bullies here."

Race took a step back and looked at Maverick. Maverick merely shrugged. "What can I say, son. Women just don't get jock humor. But it's just as well. We quarterbacks can't be filling up on sugar. We need to eat clean and keep our perfect machines running at maximum capacity." He thumped the kid on the back. "And you have one perfect machine. You didn't falter once while running those bleachers this morning. Makes me think that my drills for my star player are just too easy."

Race's face lost all color, and Autumn wondered if he was about to pass out. Was Maverick punishing his team just because he was mad about having to be their coach? It certainly looked that way. All three boys seemed terrified of him. Race couldn't wait to get away.

He motioned at his friends. "Come on. Let's get out of here."

"Now, don't party too much the rest of the weekend," Maverick called after them. "I have some fun surprises for y'all on Monday." The boys glanced at each other before they hurried out the door. When they were gone, Maverick looked at Stuart. He didn't say a word. Not one word to the poor kid. He just stared at him until Stuart started to fidget.

"I-I-I'll see you on Monday, sir," he said as he edged to the door.

Since Maverick didn't seem to have a speck of kindness in his heart for the boy, Autumn quickly stepped in. "You don't have to leave, Stuart. I have some freshly made Cowboy Cookies in the back. After what you've been through, they're on the house."

Stuart glanced at Maverick and shook his head. "Thanks, but a football player shouldn't eat sweets." He hurried out the door.

When he was gone, Autumn turned to Maverick. He didn't even look like he thought he'd done anything wrong. He just stared back at her. For the first time since college, her hero-worshipping blinders fell off and she realized she didn't know Maverick at all. She had only seen him as the talented quarterback who had led their college football team to one championship after another. The charming boyfriend who had always teased Summer with some witty remark. And the hot lover who knew exactly how to make a woman burn. But she had never taken the time to know his beliefs, values, and morals. And now she was wondering if he even had any.

"How could you not see what was going on?" she said. "That poor boy is being bullied and all you could talk about was your star quarterback who happens to be the cocky jerk doing the bullying."

"I saw what was going on."

"And you did nothing about it." She rarely lost her temper. She had always been the calm and collected sister. But she was too angry to be calm and collected. "How could you do that? How could you let a sweet boy be humiliated like that?" When he didn't reply, she made the only assumption she could. Her eyes widened. "You don't care because you were a bully in high school too. Which is why you think Race's behavior is perfectly okay." She pointed a finger at him. "Well, it's not okay. And I plan to talk to the principal at the high school about what just happened first thing tomorrow. Hopefully, he'll be man enough to do something about it."

"Don't be stupid. That's the worst thing you can do."

Her eyes widened. "Stupid? I'm not stupid. You're stupid. You're a stupid, insensitive wussy!"

Annoyance flickered in his eyes, and he took a step closer. "A wussy? Listen, lady, I'm not a wussy. And the only stupid thing I've done in the last few months is let a conniving woman seduce me into bed."

She glanced back at the kitchen before she glared at him and spoke in a low voice. "I did not seduce you. You're the one who invited me back to your hotel room."

"Summer. I invited Summer back. And only after she—you—spent the entire dinner looking at me like I was a dessert you couldn't wait to gobble up."

She wanted to deny his words, but she couldn't. She had wanted to gobble him up. Ever since college, she had wanted to gobble him up like a triple layer chocolate cake. But not anymore. "That was before I knew what a bully you are. It's quite obvious that you are bullying your entire team because you're mad about having to be their coach. Now I wouldn't have sex with you on a bet."

His gaze swept over her from head to toe and then back again. The disgust in his eyes was easy to read. "You and me both."

"Good," she snapped.

"Great," he snapped back.

They stood there glaring at each other. Autumn refused to flinch first. She was through running from Maverick Murdoch. Unfortunately, while she was waiting for him to flinch, she couldn't help noticing the way a strand of golden hair curved over his forehead. Or the way the late-afternoon sunlight coming in through the window brought out the different shades of blue in his eyes. Or the way his golden-tipped lashes feathered over his cheeks as he lowered his gaze to her mouth.

Her insides started to melt, but she refused to give into the longing. "You need to leave." Her voice sounded breathless.

"I'm going," he said in an equally breathless voice. But he didn't go. He just stood there, heating her lips with his gaze. She didn't know what crazy thing she would've done if the bell over the door hadn't jingled and caused whatever it was that arced between them to break.

Maverick stepped back first. He glanced at the door and nodded. "Good afternoon, ma'am."

Autumn turned to the beautiful woman with long blond hair that hung well past her waist. Autumn recognized the woman immediately. She was the same woman who had been visiting Holt at the jail.

Up close, she looked much younger than Autumn had previously thought. In fact, she looked to be around Autumn's age. Which wasn't surprising. Holt had dated younger women before and took great pride in it. But what was surprising was seeing her here. Why would Holt's new girlfriend come to Bliss? There was only one answer: Holt had sent her. No doubt to see if she could get money for his defense attorney.

Autumn wasn't having it. Ever since she and her siblings were little, her father had shown up needing money. Each time he arrived, he disrupted their lives and caused havoc. Now he was trying to cause havoc by sending one of his loser girlfriends to do his dirty work. Autumn did not doubt for a second that the woman was a loser. No one but a loser would date Holt. Well, Autumn wasn't going to let her get away with it. Her sisters and brother had just found happiness. She wasn't about to let her father's girlfriend show up and cause problems.

Her voice was cool as she spoke. "Can I help you?"

The woman didn't introduce herself as Holt's girlfriend. She didn't introduce herself at all. She just stood there and stared at Autumn for a long moment before she nodded at the window. "I came about the baker's job."

Autumn's eyes narrowed. A job? What was the woman up to? The only thing that made sense was that she didn't know Autumn had seen her at the jail and was trying to pull a scam—either to get closer to the family before she asked for money or to help herself to the cash drawer when no one was looking. The latter seemed more likely. Holt was not above sending his girlfriend to steal for him. Spring had no doubt told him about Summer's new bakery and he felt like his daughter should share her wealth.

Autumn stared straight back at the woman. "I know who you are, and I'm not going to let you take advantage of my family. So if you thought you were going to get something from us, you're dead wrong. Go back and tell that to my daddy."

The woman's green eyes registered hurt and then anger. "I don't want anything from you." She turned and walked out. When she was gone, Autumn looked at Maverick. "And you need to leave too and never come back. What we had is over, and I have no desire to start it back up."

He studied her for a moment before he walked out. After the door closed behind him, she couldn't help feeling a little stunned. She wasn't the assertive sister who told people off. She was the calm, collected sister who kept her cool no matter what. But in the last few minutes, Autumn had told off a bully, Holt's girlfriend, and Maverick. Her actions had been completely out of character.

They'd also been something else.

Empowering.

CHAPTER NINE

MAVERICK WALKED OUT OF THE bakery thoroughly pissed off. He was pissed at Race for being a bully and at Autumn for butting her nose where it didn't belong. But mostly, he was mad at himself for walking into the bakery in the first place.

He'd always prided himself on avoiding temptation. And the bakery was temptation with a capital T. If the delicious smell of baked goods weren't enough to tempt him beyond his endurance, there was Autumn. Autumn, with hair glossier than the shiny glaze on the chocolate cupcakes. Autumn, with eyes bluer than the gooey filling of the blueberry tarts. Autumn, with lips more delectable than the glistening strawberries in the strawberry pies.

He'd almost taken a taste of those strawberry lips. If the woman looking for the job hadn't interrupted them, he would have. It would've been a huge mistake. The last thing he needed was to get involved with Autumn Hadley. Anyone who pretended to be someone else had a few screws loose. And Maverick wasn't about to get Waylon ticked at him for messing around with his sister-in-law.

Standing outside the bakery, he took a few deep breaths to clear his lungs of the sweet smell of baked goods and his mind of the sweet image of Autumn's lips. Then he stretched his calves for a few minutes before he returned to his run. He had only gone a block when he saw Stuart sitting on a park bench looking like he didn't have a friend in the world. Which it seemed like he didn't.

For a second, Maverick wanted to run back to the bakery and buy the kid a dozen donuts to make him feel better. Then he realized that he couldn't do that. Not only had Autumn banned him from the bakery, but also sympathy and sugar weren't going to fix Stuart's problems.

He had done some research on the kid and found out that he and his mother had moved here to live with his grandparents after his parents' divorce. His grandfather was the one who had pushed him to join the football team, no doubt hoping it would help him lose weight and make some friends. But it wouldn't do either unless Maverick could figure out a way to get the kid over his depression. No one wanted to hang out with a depressed teenager who wouldn't say more than two words at a time. And maybe that was the key. Maybe he just needed to get the kid talking.

He slowed his pace and yelled across the street. "Hey, Stuart!" When Stuart looked up, he motioned. "Get off your butt and come running with me."

If the look on the kid's face was any indication, the last thing he wanted to do was run with his hardass coach. He got up and slowly jogged across the street. Maverick had to almost run in place to keep from out distancing the kid. As they slowly moved down the street, he searched for a conversation starter.

"Beautiful day."

"Yes, sir."

"Like I've told you before, you don't have to call me sir, Stuart. Coach is fine. Or you can call me Maverick."

"Yes, sir."

Maverick rolled his eyes, but kept trying to engage the kid. "So what are you doing tonight? You have a hot date planned?"

"No, sir."

"Yeah," Maverick said. "Me either. I thought I'd grab dinner at the diner and head back to my apartment and watch some television. Do you have a favorite show?"

"No, sir." Sweat had started to trickle down Stuart's temples, but he didn't seem to be as out of breath and struggling as he'd been the first few days of practice when they'd run laps. At least that was some improvement.

"Favorite movies?"

"No, sir."

"What about a dog? Do you have a dog or a pet?"

"No, sir."

Maverick finally gave up, and they continued to slowly jog down the street without saying anything. He was about to release Stuart, and himself, from the torture when he noticed the extra slap of running shoes on cement. He glanced behind him to see a little blond-headed girl with messy braids running behind them.

She grinned a gapped-tooth grin. "I can run faster than you guys. Wanna see?" Before Maverick could answer, she took off past them. When she got to the corner, she turned around and raced back, wedging her way in between them. "See? You guys are slowpokes."

"We're not slowpokes," Stuart said. "We're training for our first big football game."

Maverick could've pointed out that a slow jog wasn't exactly training, but since it was the most words he'd heard out of Stuart, he kept his mouth shut and let the conversation continue.

The little girl cocked her head and looked at Stuart. "You're football players? But you're fat." She glanced at Maverick. "And he's old."

Stuart didn't defend himself, but he defended Maverick. "He's not old, dummy. And he's not playing football. He's our coach."

She looked back at Maverick. "Can I be on the team? I'm faster than him." She pointed at Stuart.

"You're not faster than me," Stuart said. "I could beat you if I wanted to."

"Prove it? On your mark, set, go!" The little girl raced off, and Stuart only hesitated for a second before he took off after her. Surprisingly, he caught her and passed her. Maverick had never seen the boy run so fast, and he was impressed. Maybe Stuart wouldn't make such a bad football player after all. He was definitely big enough. If Maverick could teach him how to hike the ball, he might make a pretty good center. He smiled at the thought of Race having to depend on Stuart for the ball and to block the defense from crushing his ass.

Yes, that might work out just fine.

Maverick stopped running and waited for them to race back. Stuart got there first, but it cost him. His face was red and he was chugging like a freight train. The little girl was only a stride behind him, and she wasn't panting as much as wheezing. He recognized the wheezing immediately. It was the same sound his friend in high school had made when he was having an asthma attack.

He crouched next to her and rubbed her back. "It's okay. Try to relax. Do you have an inhaler?" The little girl nodded. "Where is it?" he asked. "In your pocket?"

She shook her head. "M-My m-mom's purse. M-Motor Lodge."

They had just passed the Bliss Motor Lodge, so Maverick scooped her up in his arms and headed back the way they'd come.

"What's wrong with her?" Stuart asked as he followed.

"Asthma. If you have a phone with you, get it out. If we can't find her inhaler, we might have to call 911."

"Yes, sir." Stuart pulled his cellphone out of his sweatpants pocket.

When they reached the motor lodge, Maverick headed for the office, but switched directions when he saw a woman coming out of one of the rooms looking panicked. It was the same woman who had been at the bakery earlier.

"She's here!" Maverick yelled. When the woman turned to him, he added. "She needs her inhaler."

The woman turned and ran back into the room. She reappeared only a moment later and sprinted to him.

"It's okay, Carrie Anne," she said as she took the little girl from him. "I'm here, baby. Mama's right here." She sat down in the parking lot and cradled her daughter on her lap, then handed her the inhaler. Carrie Anne seemed to know exactly what to do. She shook it, placed it in her mouth, then pushed the button and inhaled. Only seconds later, her breathing evened out and the color returned to her cheeks.

She smiled at her mom. "I'm okay now, Mama."

Her mother's eyes filled with tears, and she pulled her daughter close and rocked back and forth. Maverick wasn't sure if she was trying to soothe Carrie Anne or herself. The woman looked pretty shook up. Of course, he couldn't blame her. He was pretty shook up himself. And Stuart didn't look much better. His face was pale, and he still clutched his phone as if ready to dial 911 at a second's notice.

It was amazing how much that reminded him of Robby. Robby had always been so willing to do whatever was needed of him. Especially if Maverick had asked. He'd adored his big brother and done anything to get his praise. And Maverick hadn't praised him enough. He hadn't praised him nearly enough.

He reached out and placed a hand on Stuart's shoulder. "You can put the phone away now." He squeezed his shoulder. "Good job."

Stuart placed the phone back in his pocket. "Is she okay? I shouldn't have raced her. That was just me being dumb. She's just a kid."

The mother looked up. "You let my daughter run a race?"

Before Maverick could explain, Carrie Anne jumped off her mother's lap. "I'm going to play football, Mama." She pointed at Maverick. "This is the coach, and he thinks I run fast enough to be on the team."

The woman stood and glared at Maverick. "What were you thinking having my daughter run?"

Maverick held up his hands. "I didn't have her do anything, ma'am. She just appeared out of nowhere and started running with us."

She turned to her daughter. "Carrie Anne Buchanan! You know better. You're not supposed to be running or playing hard. Nor were you supposed to leave the motor lodge. All I said you could do was swing on the hitching post out front."

Carrie Anne's bottom lip came out. "But there's nothing else to do in this dumb, boring town. When we left Wyoming, you said I was going to have my own room. And my own horse. And lots of friends and a grandpa. But all we've done is travel around all summer and stay in dumpy motel rooms and eat peanut butter and jelly sandwiches. I hate peanut butter and jelly sandwiches! And I hate having no friends!"

Her mother's face turned red. But it wasn't her embarrassment as much as the defeat in her eyes that caught Maverick's attention. He understood that look. He felt pretty defeated himself. But at least he had a job and plenty of money in the bank. It sounded like this woman didn't have either. And she certainly hadn't been welcomed to Bliss by Autumn Hadley. He wondered what had happened to cause such hostility. Autumn seemed like the kind of person who stuck up for the underdog.

She'd certainly stuck up for Stuart.

"That's enough, Carrie Anne," she said before she turned to Maverick and Stuart. "Thank you for helping her. I'm sorry if she interrupted your run."

Maverick held out a hand. "Maverick Murdoch, I'm the coach of the high school football team. And this is Stuart Simpson, one of my players."

The woman shook his hand, and then Stuart's. "Christie Buchanan. It's nice to meet you. Now if you'll excuse us . . ."

Before they could walk away, Maverick stopped them. "Would it be okay if Carrie Anne joined the team?"

Both of them turned around, Christie looked surprised and Carrie Anne looked like she'd just gotten the best Christmas present ever. "Please, Mama. Please can I play football?"

Maverick clarified. "I didn't say you'd be playing football. You're not old enough. But I could use someone to help me coach . . . and hand out towels and water during timeouts."

"I could do that!" Carrie jumped up and down. "I could so hand out water and towels."

"I'm sorry," Christie said. "But we're not staying in Bliss. I just wanted to . . ." She shook her head. "It doesn't matter. We're leaving first thing in the morning."

No doubt on gas fumes, Maverick thought. But before he could offer her some money, she pulled a disappointed-looking Carrie Anne away. She still had enough gumption to yell at Stuart, "I could've beat you if I'd had my inhaler!"

Stuart snorted. "What a brat."

"Nothing wrong with being a little feisty." Maverick should've started running again. He hadn't gotten anywhere close to his goal of ten miles. But he didn't feel much like running anymore. He turned and walked back to the diner where he'd parked. "She just wants a friend. It's not easy being the new kid in town." He shot a glance over at Stuart. "Some people become overly extroverted and other people become overly introverted."

Stuart looked at him. "You're talking about me, aren't you?"

"You have been acting like a major introvert. And if people don't know you, they can't like you."

Stuart released a sigh and went back to watching his running shoes hit the sidewalk. "I had lots of friends back in Indiana. They didn't care if I was fat or slow. They liked me for who I was. And there were no—" He stopped before he finished, but Maverick knew what he was going to say. Bullies.

It was hard not to confide in the kid. But if Stuart knew Maverick was aware of Race's bullying, he'd expect him to take care of it. And while Maverick was working on a plan, Stuart needed to stop being such a loner and make friends with the other kids.

"I'm sorry you had to move away from your friends, Stuart," he said. "But things happen in life that we might not like. We still have to make the best of them."

Stuart glanced at him. "Like you being here instead of playing pro football?"

Maverick hadn't been talking about himself, but now that the kid brought it up, he couldn't deny it. "Exactly."

They kept walking for a few minutes before Stuart spoke. "It doesn't look like you've made any friends."

The kid had a good point. Besides the time he spent coaching, he worked out by himself, ate by himself, and spent the rest of the time holed up in his tiny apartment watching ESPN . . . and thinking about Autumn. He'd declined dinner offers from Waylon and offers from Ms. Marble to sit on her front porch or come over for morning coffee. He wanted to do his time and leave without forming any kind of attachment. But he couldn't expect Stuart to make friends if he refused to.

"You're right. I've been doing the same thing you've been doing. I've been feeling a little sorry for myself and shutting everyone out." They reached his truck where it was parked by the curb. "But I tell you what. If you make the effort, I'll make the effort. We're both stuck in this grease spot on the highway so we both should try to make the best of it."

Stuart smiled for the first time since Maverick had met him. "It *is* a pretty small town."

"Hell yeah, it is. I mean, they don't even have a movie theater."

"Or a McDonald's."

"Or a gym."

"Or a Wendy's." Stuart thought for a moment. "Although the diner has great double cheeseburgers. And those cupcakes at the bakery looked good. Too bad we're in training."

Maverick laughed. "Too bad. Now get out of here and go make some friends."

"Yes, sir . . ." Stuart grinned. "Coach."

CHAPTER TEN

THE FOOTBALL SEASON WAS A big deal in Bliss. After Labor Day, every business had "Go Bobcats" signs in their windows. Lucy's Place Diner had a special Bobcat Burger. Emmett's Gas Station had a blowup Bobcat that greeted you on the way in to get gas. And the Blissful Bakery had cupcakes and donuts decorated with navy blue and gold sprinkles—the school's colors. But regardless of all the town's spirit, the Bobcats lost their first two games. Most people thought it had to do with losing so many players to the high school that had built the new stadium. They believed their new team just needed a little time and experience.

Autumn didn't agree. She was convinced it was their new coach. She had attended the games and spent most of the time watching Maverick. And while he stood on the sidelines and acted like a coach, he had no excitement or enthusiasm for his team. It was like he was just going through the paces and serving his time until he could leave.

She wanted to be angry, just like she'd been angry at him in the bakery for not standing up for the poor kid who was getting bullied. But her anger was eclipsed by disappointment. Disappointment that the hero she'd idolized for so long was just a man. And not even a good one. Which made her wonder if she had the same character flaw as her mother. Dotty Hadley had idolized Autumn's father. As far as she was concerned, Holt could do no wrong. Time and time again, she would take him back, and time and time again, he would prove himself unworthy of that love.

Not that Autumn loved Maverick.

Thankfully, her relationship with Maverick was purely physical. It would've been a disaster if she'd fallen in love with an egotistical man like her father who put his own needs before anyone else's. There was little doubt that Maverick was egotistical and selfish. His time here in Bliss had proven it. She couldn't help feeling stupid for wasting her time crushing on such a jerk . . . even if he was hot and amazing in bed.

The front screen door slammed, pulling Autumn from her woolgathering. She glanced up from the pumpkins and gourds she'd been decorating the porch with to see Spring standing there looking like a fresh peach in her white jeans and peach top.

"The porch looks great," Spring said. "I especially like the lanterns you mixed with the gourds and pumpkins. Where did you get them?"

"At the antique shop, Home Sweet Home. Savannah gave me the family discount." Savannah was married to the Hadleys' cousin, Raff Arrington.

"I love Savannah," Spring said. "She's so nice. And so is Raff, once you get to know him. Waylon and I are meeting them at Whispering Falls for a picnic this afternoon. Why don't you come with us?"

"No, thanks. This is my first day off this week and after I finish decorating the porch, I intend to spend it reading. Besides, I'm sure Waylon doesn't want me tagging along with you everywhere. It's bad enough that I live here. Although I think I figured out a solution to that problem."

"It's not a problem. Way and I love having you here." Spring glanced at the hound dog snoozing on the porch and the cat curled up next to him. "And so do Sherlock and Watson. We'd all be devastated if you moved away."

"I'm not moving away. I'm just moving to the land the Arringtons gave us. I thought I'd live in your little vintage trailer."

"You know I would let you if someone wasn't already living in it."

"Someone's living in your trailer? Who?"

"Christie Buchanan and her cute daughter, Carrie Anne. They're new to town. Waylon stopped to help them when they had car trouble, and the little girl pretty much informed him that they had to leave town because they didn't have any money to pay for another night at the motor lodge. Waylon offered to help them, but the woman stubbornly refused the money. So Waylon called me."

Autumn smiled. "Smart man." Everyone knew how good Spring was at fixing people's problems. "And my kindhearted sister talked her into moving into the trailer."

Spring shrugged. "I just told her that we needed a caretaker for our land so she'd be doing us a favor."

"That was sweet of you, Spring. But what exactly do we need taken care of? There's nothing out there but ground hogs and the occasional cow from Zane's ranch."

Spring's eyes glittered with devilry. "But you're forgetting about squatters. Folks who just show up and take up residence on any piece of land they want and you can never get them to leave."

"There's a problem with that in Bliss?"

Spring smiled. "Of course not, but Christie is from Wyoming and didn't have a clue."

Autumn shook her had. "You know the poor woman is going to stay up all night watching for squatters that will never show up, right?"

"I told her that if they see that someone's already living on the land, they won't squat." Spring's eyes grew thoughtful. "Now I just have to figure out how to get her a job. I offered her one at the bakery, but she must be as good in a kitchen as you are because she looked repulsed by the idea. Or maybe she's already met Summer."

Autumn laughed. "You are bad, Spring. I'll keep my ears open for anyone who needs a job. Do you think they have food?"

"I stocked the trailer before they moved in, and I've been spreading the word around town that we need to make them feel welcome. Which means plenty of casseroles and pies will be headed their way."

"I'll take over some cupcakes and cookies from the bakery. I bet the little girl will love that."

Waylon stepped out on the porch with a picnic basket and blanket. "Are you ready, honey?" Sherlock jumped up and loped over to him. Waylon laughed. "I wasn't talking to you, honey hound dog." He gave the dog a good ear scratch. "But I guess you can come too." He looked at Autumn. "Grab Watson, Audie, and let's load up before the day gets away from us."

It was nice to be included, but Autumn wasn't about to be the fifth wheel. "Thank you, Way, but I think Watson and I are going to spend the day right here in this porch swing."

"You sure?"

"Positive. But pick me some fall wildflowers if you find any. I want to do a table centerpiece with them."

Waylon grinned. "Deal." He took Spring's hand. "It looks like it's just going to be you, me, and Sherlock. Raff called and said that Savannah's feet were swelling so he wanted her to stay home and put them up. That man is the worst mother hen I've ever seen."

"He's just being protective because she's carrying his first child," Spring said. "I bet you will feel the same way when I'm pregnant."

Waylon studied her. "Are you?"

"No, but maybe that's something we can work on while picnicking." Spring winked at Autumn before she tugged Waylon down the porch steps.

Once they were gone, Autumn finished decorating the porch. She had just put the pillar candles in the lanterns when the sound of a motor starting pulled her attention over to Ms. Marble's house. She almost choked on her own spit.

Maverick was leaf blowing Ms. Marble's lawn . . . without a shirt. She had seen his perfectly honed body naked before. She'd even touched and tasted it, but that had been in the artificial lighting of a hotel room. She had never seen the sculpted muscles and tanned skin beneath a bright September sun. She became totally fascinated by the way each ridge of his back flexed as he wielded the handheld leaf blower.

He turned in her direction, and she quickly ducked down behind a group of pumpkins. Although it was doubtful he would notice her. The old straw cowboy hat he wore was tugged low on his forehead and he seemed focused on his job. Still, she crawled on her hands and knees to the corner of the porch and peeked over the hedge that grew above the railing.

The temperature had finally dropped from the hot summer temps, but it was still hot enough for Maverick to work up a sweat. She hadn't realized how sexy sweat was until she saw his muscles glistening with it. She watched with bated breath as it trickled over hard pectoral and rippled abdominal muscles before it was absorbed in the waistband of his faded jeans.

By the time he stopped to take off his hat and wipe his forehead, she was feeling more than a little hot herself. She was having trouble breathing and her clothes felt damp. Or maybe it was just her panties that were damp. She leaned closer to get a better view when someone cleared their throat behind her.

She turned so quickly in her crouched position that she fell on her butt. She glanced up to see Ryker's father standing there. Autumn wanted to crawl in a hole and hide.

Cord Evans had been her teen idol in junior high and high school. All the girls had thought the six-time rodeo champion was the hottest man alive.

And he was still hot with his rugged features, dark hair with a touch of silver at the temples, and pretty brown eyes. Eyes that looked thoroughly confused about what she was doing crouched on the porch. She was pretty confused herself. Why had she been lusting after Maverick Murdoch when she had just been thinking about what a jerk he was? Obviously, her body hadn't gotten the memo.

She cleared her throat. "Hi. I was just . . . checking the hedge for bugs."

He glanced at the hedge she'd been hiding behind, then his gaze lifted to Ms. Marble's house. A smile tugged at one corner of his mouth, and she knew he'd figured out what she'd been up to.

"Yep," he said. "You sure don't want your hedges getting bugs." He took off his hat and held out a hand. Her face burned with embarrassment as she took his callused hand and let him help her to her feet. Once she was standing, she was too humiliated to think of something to say. Thankfully, Cord took over the conversation. "I stopped by to talk with your sister Spring. Is she home?"

"She and Waylon went on a picnic. Is there something I can help you with?"

"I heard Spring was asking around for a job for a woman who was down on her luck, and I might have something."

"That's wonderful. Does she need to have any certain skills?"

"Just be willing to help an old cowboy who doesn't have a clue how to deal with all that Facebooking and tweaking."

She smiled, feeling a lot less embarrassed. Cord was a nice man who wasn't the type to spread gossip about how the weird Hadley triplet was spying on the new coach. "I think you mean tweeting," she said.

He released a sigh. "See what I mean? I don't know the first thing about social media. But my son has gotten it into his head that I need to figure it out if I want my boots to sell better. He thinks that since my name is on the brand, I'm the one who people want to follow and chat with. And I don't mind chatting to folks. I just prefer to do my talking face to face, instead of on a face book."

"I understand. But once you figure out social media, it's not really as bad as you think. It took me a while to get used to it too."

"I don't think I'll ever get used to posting something and waiting around for people to like it or comment on it. That's why I need to hire some young person who gets it."

"I'm sure Christie will be able to help you." If Christie didn't know about social networking, Autumn would teach her. It sounded like the woman desperately needed a job, and Cord would be a nice man to work for. "Can I get you something to drink, Cord?" she asked. "I have some sweet tea made." She started for the door, but tripped over the leg of a wicker chair. She would've gone down to a knee if Cord hadn't caught her.

"Easy there. You okay?"

"I'm fine." She winced. "I just stubbed my toe."

He grinned. "That's the problem with going barefoot. If you had on the pair of Cord Evans cowboy boots I gave you that wouldn't have happened."

She laughed. "You're absolutely—"

She cut off when she saw Maverick standing at the bottom of the porch steps, looking sweaty, delicious . . . and a little mad. His cowboy hat was pushed back on his head and his eyes were narrowed on Cord.

"Who are you?" he asked rudely.

Cord released her and turned. "I'm Cord Evans." He held out a hand. "And I don't need an introduction to you, Maverick. My son Ryker told me you are coaching our high school team. The entire town is pretty thrilled about getting a pro football player."

Maverick visibly relaxed and shook Cord's hand. "Nice to meet you, Mr. Evans. You were one of my idols growing up—right behind Troy Aikman."

Cord laughed. "That's a good man to be behind." He glanced back at Autumn. "I'm assuming you know Miss Hadley."

Maverick's smirk was infuriating. "Autumn and I go way back."

"Ahh." Cord put on his hat. "Well, I guess I better be going."

"But what about your sweet tea?" Autumn asked.

Cord shook his head. "Thank you, but I need to get back to the ranch. I have builders working on my new house and barn and I like to keep an eye on things." He tipped his hat. "I'll be seeing you, Autumn." He nodded at Maverick. "Nice meeting you."

Autumn waited until Cord had driven away in his truck before she turned to Maverick. She tried to keep her gaze off his naked chest and pinned on his face. It wasn't easy. "Is there a reason you came over?"

Maverick shrugged. "I thought you were being manhandled by some cowboy."

She was surprised. "And you came over to rescue me?"

"Gut reaction. I forgot you're the type of woman who doesn't mind a little manhandling."

Before Maverick had shown up, she'd been so good at controlling her anger. Now, she didn't even try to control it. She marched down the porch steps and stood in front of him. "You don't know me at all, you arrogant ass."

His eyebrows lifted. "Are you saying you didn't ask for my man hands to be all over you?"

She couldn't say that. There was a time when she had begged him to touch her. But not any more. "That was a big mistake. One I don't intend to make again. I want nothing from you."

He studied her for a moment before a smile spread over his face. "I think you're lying, Autumn Layne Hadley. I think there's a lot you want from me." He lifted a hand and brushed a strand of hair from her face, his fingers tips gliding over her cheek. She couldn't stop the heat that flashed through her body. "Which is why you played your sister. And why you went back to my hotel room. And why you continued the entire 'friends with benefits' thing."

He paused, and his smile got even bigger and cockier. "And why you hide behind shrubs and watch me." His gaze lowered to her mouth, and his voice grew low and sexy. "And it's only a matter of time before you'll give in to that desire and come knocking at my door." His gaze lifted. In his eyes, she saw the same hot desire that swirled around

inside of her. "And I might just answer."
He turned and walked out the gate.

CHAPTER ELEVEN

MAVERICK FELT A LITTLE CONFUSED after leaving Waylon and Spring's. He wasn't sure what had happened. One second, he'd been helping Ms. Marble clean up her leaves, and the next second, he was shutting off the leaf blower and vaulting the low shrubs that separated the front yards with every intention of decking the guy who held Autumn in his arms. And he would've if the guy had been some dude trying to cop a feel instead of Ryker's dad. Still, seeing her in the arms of another man had not sat well with him. Which was crazy. What they'd had was over. Hell, what they'd had was all a farce.

Except it didn't feel like a farce. The memories of their steamy summer affair still plagued him. He stayed up nights trying to fit together the hot, passionate woman who'd rocked his world with the cool, distant woman who couldn't seem to stand the sight of him. Of course, today had proven that she could stand the sight of him. She'd been spying on him as he worked in the yard. And it had turned him on to no end. She might say she didn't want him anymore. But she was lying. She wanted him. And he wanted her too. He wanted to see exactly what it would take to turn cool autumn into sizzling summer.

"You look like you could use a break."

He glanced at the porch to see Ms. Marble sitting in her favorite hickory rocker. She was wearing one of the big hats she always wore when she stepped outside and white gloves that came up to her wrinkled wrists. She picked up a glass of iced tea from a tray on the table next to her. "Come sit down and have a cold drink. It's unsweetened and decaffeinated."

"Let me just finish up and I'll be right there." He started up the blower and quickly finished blowing the leaves into a pile. As he worked, he couldn't help glancing at the house next door.

Autumn was no longer arranging pumpkins on the front steps. She seemed to have a knack for decorating. He had to admit that the porch looked nice. Suddenly, he remembered another time she'd been decorating. It was in college when he'd caught her and Summer decorating his car before a big game. Although now that he thought about it, it hadn't been Summer doing the decorating. She'd been sitting on the hood of his car texting while Autumn had been writing *Good Luck, Mav!* in white shoe polish on the back window. With a heart for the dot of the exclamation point.

The car decorating brought up other memories: The time when he'd left his history homework in the triplets' dorm room. By the time he went back to get it, the theme paper he'd been working on had been edited, neatly typed out, and placed in a folder. He'd just assumed Summer had done it. And like the dumb jock he was, he'd traveled to California for an away-game and completely forgot to thank her when he got back. But it hadn't been Summer. Summer hated doing her own homework. There was no way she would've done his.

He glanced at the house next door. Autumn had told him that she'd had a crush on him, but until this moment, he hadn't realized what that meant. She'd liked him. And not just in a sexual way. She'd really liked him. He didn't know why that made him feel happy. But it did. He couldn't keep from smiling when he joined Ms. Marble on the porch.

"You certainly seem to enjoy yard work," she said as she handed him a tall glass of iced tea. "I appreciate your help. I had a lawn boy, but he went off to college. Something they all seem to do." She glanced up at the huge oak tree in her front yard that still had plenty of leaves on it. "And I'm afraid that there are a lot more where those came from."

"I don't mind doing it while I'm here. And when I leave in a couple months, I'll see if one of my players would like to take over the job."

"I would appreciate it." She watched him guzzle down half of his tea, then poured him some more from a pitcher on the table. "A couple months? So I assume you don't think our boys will make it to the playoffs."

He could've lied like he did to everyone else in town when they asked him about the team. He could've said that they were just young and needed some time. But he couldn't bring himself to lie to Ms. Marble. Especially when she'd given him a place to live and had made him sugar-free, gluten-free cookies. The cookies had been horrible, but still a kindness he couldn't repay with a lie.

"No," he said. "I don't think the boys will make it to the playoffs. We'll be lucky to win a game." It couldn't have worked out better if he'd planned it. The sooner the season was over, the sooner he could leave Bliss forever. Autumn was screwing with his mind too much. He needed to stay focused if he wanted to get back in the NFL.

He wasn't surprised the wily old woman could read his mind. "I would imagine you're not too upset about that," she said.

"No, but I'm not trying to make them lose. I'm working them hard at practice and teaching them everything I know. If they don't win it's their fault, not mine."

Ms. Marble rocked and stared out at her lawn for a long moment before she spoke. "Did you know that my father was the foreman of the Arrington Ranch before it was divided into three ranches? He spent a lot of time training wild horses and cattle dogs. He once told me that the best way to train any animal was to love it first. If you love an animal, they'll love you back and do just about anything to please you."

"Look," he set down his glass. "I appreciate the advice, but I'm only here for a few months. That's all. I'm not going to ignore the kids and my coaching responsibilities, but I'm not going to become their best friend or most beloved coach either. It's better that way. If they don't get attached to me and I don't get attached to them, then when I leave, no one gets hurt."

She glanced over at him. She had the most penetrating eyes. They seemed to stare right through him. "Well, I can't argue with that. It does hurt when people you love leave, doesn't it? I've lost two husbands, my best friend, Lucy Arrington, and countless other friends who have moved away or died. And every time you lose someone, it feels like your world is ending."

Maverick understood the feeling. His world had ended when Robby died. Now he was just going through the motions in an empty void. Football was the only thing that mattered to him. If he lost it, he would lose everything.

"I'm sorry to hear about your losses," he said.

"It was hard, but I never regretted loving them." Ms. Marble smiled. "The love and joy they gave me in return was well worth the hurt I experienced when they were gone."

She was wrong. Nothing was worth the hurt he felt after Robby's death. Nothing.

He got up from the rocker. "Thanks for the tea, but I need to do some training." Before he could leave, she reached out and took his hand in her white-gloved one.

"Those boys deserve a coach who cares about them. They don't deserve someone just doing his time. And I'm not telling you this because I want you to win games. Being a good coach isn't about winning games. It's about coaching young men and women into winners."

She was right. Good coaches weren't about winning games as much as building character in their teams. But Maverick didn't want to be a good coach. He wanted to be a great football player. So he only nodded, then turned and headed back to his apartment.

It was too bad that Ms. Marble's words stuck with him like a toothache, making him feel like the worst human being ever. He was still struggling with his guilt when he arrived at the high school gymnasium thirty minutes later. He intended to work off that guilt by punishing his body in the weight room. Unfortunately, before he could unlock the side door of the gym, he heard yelling coming from the stadium next door.

It was probably just some teenagers letting off steam. Still, he couldn't help glancing over. He saw Stuart crouched beneath the bleachers, obviously spying on whoever was yelling. Maverick tried to ignore the kid, but damned if he could. He crammed the keys back into the pocket of his athletic shorts and headed over to the bleachers. When he ducked underneath and tapped Stuart on the shoulder, the kid almost jumped out of his Nikes.

"Shit!" He whirled around with his arm held up like someone was going to punch him.

"Calm down," Maverick said. "What are you doing?"

"I was going to run laps."

"Under the bleachers?"

"No, around the track. But when I got here, I saw Race working out with his father and I . . ." Stuart's face turned red.

Maverick sighed. "You hid. Damn, Stuart, you gotta stop running from Race and stand your ground. You're bigger than—" Loud yelling cut him off, and he looked out from beneath the bleachers to see Race high-stepping through the tire obstacle while a man with a buzz cut verbally abused him.

"If you can't go faster than that, you're nothing but a wimp! Now get those knees up! Not like that, you idiot. Go back and try it again."

Stuart moved up beside Maverick. "I guess we know now where Race gets his bullying. His dad's been yelling at him like that ever since I got here."

Maverick shouldn't get involved. This was none of his business. But damned if he could stand there and let Race's dad verbally abuse his son. "Stay here, Stuart." He ducked out from beneath the bleachers and walked around to the field. As soon as Race saw him, he stumbled on one of the tires and went down.

"Get up!" his father yelled. "I swear you are the clumsiest kid I've ever seen. No wonder you can't win a game."

Before there could be any more verbal abuse, Maverick walked up and held out a hand to the asshole. "You must be Race's daddy. I'm Coach Murdoch."

The man studied Maverick for a moment before he shook his hand. "Dan Dunkin." Some of Maverick's anger must've been telegraphed in his handshake, because pain flickered in Dan's eyes before he pulled his hand away. "My ex-wife told me that Race had a real professional football player as a coach. Of course, I didn't believe her. Women don't know shit about football."

Maverick understood why Race's mom had divorced the jerk. He glanced at Race. "So you're doing a little extra work?"

His dad answered for him. "When I heard he'd

lost his first two games, I figured I better get my butt down here and light a fire under him. I can't have my son being a loser."

No, one loser in the family was enough. "You don't live here?"

"No. I live in Amarillo with my new wife and her kids. Now her son is an athlete. He's only fifteen and already plays varsity." He glanced at Race. "Of course, his mama don't baby him like your mama does you." He shook his head. "No wonder you suck."

Race's face turned bright red, and he clenched his fists. As much as his father needed a good pop in the mouth, Maverick couldn't let that happen. He stepped between them. "I'm going to have to disagree with you on that. Race is one of the most talented quarterbacks I've ever seen."

His father snorted. "Then why aren't you winning games?"

It was a good question. One Maverick knew the answer to. "Because quarterbacks don't win games. Teams do. And there's only one person to blame if a team can't win: the coach. So if you want to yell at someone for sucking and being a loser, yell at me. I certainly haven't done my job the last few weeks."

The man stared at Maverick as if he didn't quite know what to say to that. After a moment, he cleared his throat and motioned at Race. "Let's get you home before your mother calls the cops on me for kidnapping."

"Actually, I'll be happy to take Race home," Maverick said. "There are a few plays I wanted to go over with him."

His father nodded. "Don't go light on him. He needs a firm hand."

The only person that needed a firm hand was Dan Dunkin. Right in the face. "I think I've figured out what Race needs," he said.

The man shrugged before he turned to Race and pointed a finger. "Stop being a wimp and win some games." He turned and walked off the field. When he was gone, Race wilted down to the grass like all the energy had been sucked out of him. And damned if Maverick didn't want to give the kid a hug. Of course, all Race had to do was talk to cause that urge to dissolve.

"I don't need you to protect me from my dad. I can handle him just fine without you butting your nose into my business." Race ripped up a handful of grass and flung it. "I hate him. I hate him so much. I wish I could divorce his ass like Mom did."

Maverick sat down on the ground and rested his arms on his bent knees. "I wanted to divorce both of my parents, but, unfortunately, that's not how it works."

Race glanced at him. "Did they yell at you and make you feel like shit?"

"No, they yelled at each other and made me and my brother feel like shit."

Stuart walked up. "My parents fought all the time too. It was kind of a relief when they got a divorce."

Maverick expected Race to have some smartass remark. He didn't. He just nodded. "Tell me about it. I cheered when my dear old dad walked out the door. I hate that me and my sister have to see him twice a month. Of course, he isn't as hard on her as he is on me."

Stuart sat down. "At least he wants to see you. My dad hasn't even called."

"Count your blessings. All my old man can talk about is football and what a great quarterback he was in high school." Race grabbed another handful of grass and threw it. "I'm tired of trying to live up to his expectations." He glanced at Maverick. "And I'm tired of living up to yours. I'm tired of running bleachers and fifty-forties and all the other drills you think up for me to do." He looked at Stuart. "And I'm tired of getting sacked twenty times a game because my center can't keep the lineman off my ass."

Stuart hesitated. "I can keep the lineman off your ass."

Race's eyes widened. "You've been letting me get sacked on purpose?"

Stuart's jaw tightened. "You deserved it for all the bullying." Maverick had to bite back a smile. So Stuart had gotten back at Race after all.

"Why you little shit!" Race dove on Stuart and knocked him to the ground. Maverick might have intervened if Stuart hadn't easily pinned Race. When Race's face turned red from lack of oxygen, Maverick spoke up.

"That's enough, Stuart."

Stuart released him, and Race sat up and glared at him. "You are such a tub of lard."

"And you're as big of a bully as your dad," Stuart snapped back.

Race's face lost all color, and Maverick figured Stuart's words had hit home. He let them sink in for a moment longer before he got to his feet.

"Come on, let's run a couple plays."

Race stood. "Didn't you hear me? I don't want to be your star quarterback anymore."

"I heard you." Maverick tossed him the ball. "And that's good. I don't need a prima donna star quarterback. What I need is a talented young man who wants to be part of a team." He paused and accepted his fate. "My team."

CHAPTER TWELVE

THE THIRD FOOTBALL GAME OF the season was an away game in a town only a thirty-five minute drive from Bliss. All the townsfolk caravanned in a long line of vehicles with shoe polished back windows showing their support for the Bobcats. Autumn had painted "Go Bobcats!" on the back window of her Audi and a picture of a bobcat that looked more like a pointy-eared dog with whiskers. Spring and Ms. Marble went with her to the game because Waylon had gone on the bus with the team.

Their opposition had a brand-new stadium much nicer than the one at Bliss High. It had a concession stand, locker rooms, and actual bathrooms instead of porta potties. Dirk and Gracie were already there when they arrived. Dirk had saved them seats high in the bleachers right behind their Arrington cousins.

While the rest of her family had taken to the Arringtons like ducks to water, Autumn was still a little shy around her new cousins. As they climbed the steps to their row, Spring and Ms. Marble stopped to chat while she followed along, feeling awkward.

Ms. Marble talked to Gracie's brother Cole about a new colt that he had high expectations of, while Spring talked to his wife Emery about their daughter Lucy, who was around the same age as Dirk's triplets and was home with a babysitter. Cole's cousin Zane wasn't interested in talking as he was busy offering up bites of cheesy nachos to his wife Carly, who owned Lucy's Place Diner and was pregnant with their first child. Zane's sister Becky and her husband Mason Granger sat next to Zane and Carly. Becky ran their small cattle ranch and Mason was the only lawyer in town. Above them, Raff and his wife Savannah sat. Savannah held a giant pickle in one hand and a Butterfinger candy bar in the other. She was close to nine months pregnant and ready to deliver at any time.

When she saw Autumn, she winked. "Cravings."

Once they reached their row, Autumn sat down between Dirk and Gracie. They had brought the triplets. Lucinda and Luana sat on Dirk's lap while Luella sat on Gracie's. Autumn immediately relieved her brother of Lucinda. The little girl was the spitfire of the bunch ... and the talker.

"Aww-dee," she said with a big toothy grin.

Autumn laughed. "You betcha, I'm your Aunt Audie." The baby gave her a wet slobbery kiss right on the mouth. Of course, once Ryker and Summer showed up, Autumn lost her place in Lucinda's affections.

"Wy-ka!" she screamed.

Ryker grinned and moved into the row behind Autumn. "How's my girl?"

Lucinda almost jumped out of Autumn's arms to get to Ryker, and Autumn laughed. "You might as well take her. She won't be happy until she's with you."

"Come here, Sassy," Ryker took the baby and lifted her above his head as she chortled with glee.

Summer smiled as she moved in next to him. "Who would've thought that a computer geek would be so good with kids?"

Ryker lowered Lucinda and smiled at his wife. "I'm thinking we need to get a couple of these."

"I'm thinking you might be right," Summer replied.

Spring, who was spreading out a blanket on the bench next to them latched onto that like a dog to a bone. "You're trying to get pregnant?"

Ryker shrugged. "What can I say? I keep forgetting to go to the pharmacy."

Summer laughed as they took their seats. Within minutes, she was doing what she did best—taking charge.

"That poor mascot needs a new costume. He looks like a drowned cat rather than a ferocious bobcat." Summer did have a point. The mascot's costume was pretty bedraggled. "And the cheerleaders should be cheering," her sister continued. "It doesn't matter if the game hasn't started yet, they need to be getting the crowd's spirit up instead of standing there gossiping. When I was cheer captain, I made sure my girls cheered from the time the first person arrived to the time the last person left."

"Yes, we know, Miss Overachiever," Spring said. "And every cheerleader hated you for it."

When Summer looked hurt, Ryker leaned over and gave her a kiss on the cheek. "Maybe they didn't love you, but I do." He bounced Lucinda on his knee and looked around. "Has anyone seen Cord?" Ryker still referred to his father by his first name. And since they had been estranged until recently, Autumn could understand why. "He said he was coming tonight and was going to try and talk his new assistant into coming with him."

Autumn turned around to look at him. "So he gave Christie a job?"

Ryker nodded. "And all I can say is thank God. Cord might know how to wrangle a horse and ride a bull, but he doesn't have a clue what to do on social media. He keeps posting pictures of his breakfast. I'm hoping Christie Buchanan will know more."

"Well, if she doesn't, Autumn can teach her," Spring said. "She did all the social media for the store, and she was amazing at it."

Ryker looked at Autumn a little skeptically, and she laughed. "Just because I'm shy around people doesn't mean I'm shy on social media. It much easier to talk to people when they aren't actually in the same room with you."

Ms. Marble suddenly stood up, the blue and gold ribbons on her hat flying in the stiff breeze. "Here come our boys!"

Autumn glanced at the field to see the Bliss football team coming out of the locker room. It was easy to spot Maverick. He was a head taller than most of his team, and his blond hair gleamed like spun gold beneath the stadium lights. He stopped and motioned the boys into a huddle around him—something she hadn't seen him do before. Of course, the locker rooms at the Bliss High stadium were in the high school gymnasium so maybe he'd done it there.

She watched as he placed his arms around his team. Whatever he said must've motivated the kids because they let out a loud whoop before they charged toward the field. Which made Autumn angry. How dare Maverick pump the kids up when he didn't really want them to win?

The cheerleaders finally realized that their team was headed to the field. They hurried to unroll a paper banner for them to run through, but it was too late. The only ones left to run through it were Maverick and Waylon. And both coaches chose to walk around the outside, leaving the mascot in the bedraggled bobcat costume to run through it. It took three tries to rip the paper, and on the last try, he had to get help from a stocky cheerleader. Which didn't bode well for the Bobcats' chances of winning. Of course, they had no chance with an arrogant coach who was only there because he'd been forced.

Once the ref whistled for the start of the game, Autumn expected Maverick to do what he always did—stand on the sidelines with his arms crossed while the Bobcats lost. But he didn't do that this time. This time, he looked more intense. More focused. He walked along the sidelines with his team as they moved down the field.

The bully was the quarterback again, which annoyed Autumn to no end. At the other games, she'd secretly cheered when he'd gotten sacked. But he didn't get sacked in this series of plays. His center did an amazing job of protecting him. And she didn't realize until the player got his helmet knocked off during a third-down play that the center was the same boy the quarterback had been bullying. Which made no sense to Autumn whatsoever. Why would Maverick place them so close together? Poor Stuart had to hike the ball to his bully every offensive play. No doubt while Race was calling him super-sized Stewie.

But what was strange was that they didn't seem to be at odds with each other. In fact, when Race threw a touchdown pass to his receiver in the end zone, it was Stuart he high-fived and slapped on the butt. And Race wasn't the only one celebrating. Maverick high-fived or butt-slapped every offense player who ran in after the score.

"Well, it looks like we have a coach," Ms. Marble said with a satisfied smile.

By halftime, Autumn had to agree. Maverick was coaching. And the Bobcats were winning 17 to 7. As she stood in line to get a box of popcorn, she tried to figure out what Maverick had up his sleeve. There had to be some kind of motivation behind his sudden turnaround. While she was trying to figure it out, a little girl spoke behind her.

"Can I have a Skittles with my popcorn, Mama?"

Autumn glanced over her shoulder, but couldn't see the little girl due to a large man standing in line behind her. But she could hear the mother's reply.

"No, you can't have Skittles and popcorn too."

"Cause we don't have enough money?"

"Lower your voice, please."

The little girl loudly whispered. "Cause we don't have enough money?"

The mother sighed.

Autumn couldn't help feeling sorry for the mother and the little girl. She knew what it was like to not have enough money for the extras other kids could afford. There had never been enough money in the Hadley household when Autumn was little. So when she got to the concession stand, she ordered her Coke and a bag of Skittles. After she paid and got her ordered items, she moved out of the way so the large man could step up to the window.

She turned and smiled at the little blond-headed girl behind him. "It just so happens that I bought an extra bag of Skittles. And if it's okay with your—" She cut off when she finally lifted her gaze and saw the woman holding the little girl's hand. "You."

Holt's girlfriend didn't seem to be any happier to see her. She sent her a mean glare before she ignored her. Her daughter didn't do the same.

"Hey, Mama, I think that nice lady is going to give me her extra bag of Skittles."

"We don't want her Skittles," the woman said as she tugged the little girl up in line.

"Yes, I do. I want her Skittles." The little girl looked back at Autumn and smiled. She was an adorable little girl, but that wasn't what struck Autumn the most. It was the shape of her face, her chin, and the curve of smiling lips that reminded Autumn of Dirk . . . and Holt.

Autumn walked back to her seat feeling a little stunned. Maybe she was mistaken. Maybe it was just a coincidence that the little girl looked like Dirk and Holt. The lighting wasn't good around the concession stand. It was possible that Autumn had made a mistake.

But what if she hadn't? What if the woman wasn't just a girlfriend of Holt's? What if she was the mother of his child? That would explain why she was here. She was trying to get money from Holt's other children using her daughter's relationship to them.

Her mind was still reeling by the time she got back to her seat.

"Are you okay?" Summer asked. "You look pale as a ghost."

Autumn wanted to tell her sisters, but she also didn't want to get them upset over just speculations. Until she knew for sure, she decided to keep her mouth shut. "I'm fine. I just should've brought a sweater. It's finally starting to feel like fall." She glanced at the empty bench. "What happened to Dirk and Gracie?"

"The girls were getting fussy so they took them home." Summer tossed her a jacket. "Wear this. I'm too hot."

"You certainly are," Ryker winked at her before his attention was drawn to the people sitting below them. "There's Cord."

Autumn followed his gaze and saw Cord standing up to let two people move into the spot next to him. It was Holt's girlfriend and the little girl. Autumn felt stupid for not putting two and two together. "That's his new assistant?" she asked.

"That's Christie Buchanan and her daughter Carrie Anne," Ryker said. "And let me tell you, that little girl is a pistol. I would bet that Summer acted just like her as a kid."

Autumn wasn't about to bet. Her intuition told

her that the same blood that ran through her sister's veins ran through Carrie Anne's. But there was only one way to find out. She would have to talk to Christie. But not at a football game.

For the rest of the game, Autumn couldn't keep her eyes off the little girl. The more she watched her, the more convinced she felt that Carrie was her half-sister. She didn't know how she felt about that. Part of her wanted to hug the little girl and the other part felt disillusioned. Her father had always been a deadbeat, but the fact that he'd never sired children with another woman had made Autumn feel like her mother had held a special place in his heart. Now that illusion was shattered like all the others.

The Bobcats won the game 27 to 14. Everyone was so excited about the win that they all wanted to head to the Watering Hole to celebrate. Autumn didn't feel like celebrating. She wanted time to absorb the fact that she had a half-sister. But Spring had promised Waylon that she'd meet him at the bar, and she refused to let Autumn go home after they dropped off Ms. Marble.

"Just stay for a little while," Spring begged. "You've been working so hard the last few weeks at the bakery, you can use a night to unwind."

As soon as she and Spring walked into the bar, Summer waved them over to the table she and Ryker were at. Ryker poured them each a margarita from the pitcher on the table. Autumn usually didn't drink. When she did, she always seemed to say or do something that she regretted later—the affair with Maverick being a perfect example. But tonight, she needed a stiff drink to calm all the thoughts that were bouncing around in her head. The icy margarita worked its magic, and after a few sips, she felt herself relaxing.

Some of the tables had been pushed to the side to form a dance floor, and couples were already swinging to the Florida Georgia Line song playing on the jukebox.

Summer got up from the table. "Come on, Computer Nerd, let's see if you can keep from stepping on my toes."

Ryker set down his beer. "The only reason I step on your toes is because you keep trying to lead."

"Then you need to learn to follow." Summer took his hand and pulled him out on the floor. Spring and Autumn couldn't help giggling as they watched their brother-in-law try to keep Summer from taking over. It wasn't until a slow song came on that Summer finally gave up fighting for control and cuddled close to her husband, matching his steps perfectly.

"Who would've thought that our controlling big sister would finally find a man she wanted to surrender to?" Spring poured herself another margarita, then topped off Autumn's. "You want to bet she's pregnant? She didn't take a sip of the margarita Ryker poured her."

Autumn shook her head. "I hate to lose. Do you think Ryker knows?"

"Nope, but I bet he will by tonight." Spring held up her glass. "To our big sister. May she have a healthy, beautiful child . . . who is much less annoying than she is."

Autumn laughed as she clicked her sister's glass. "To Summer and our growing family." Once the words were out, she had to wonder if their family would be growing more than anyone had ever thought. If Carrie Annie was their half-sibling, there was little doubt that the family would welcome her with open arms. Holt's girlfriend would be a different story. Especially if she was out to cause trouble. Autumn started to tell Spring about Christie, but before she could, the people standing by the door started cheering.

Spring set down her glass and smiled. "I think our conquering heroes have arrived."

CHAPTER THIRTEEN

YOU WOULD'VE THOUGHT THAT THE Bobcats had won the Super Bowl the way the townsfolk reacted when Maverick and Waylon walked in the door of the Watering Hole. People started cheering so loudly that Maverick felt guilty as hell for not doing a better job of coaching the first two games.

Emmett from the gas station separated himself from the group and slapped him on the back. "Good job, Coach! Our boys had them from start to finish."

Maverick couldn't argue. The boys *had* done an amazing job and had finally come together as a team. It was all centered around Race and Stuart. They weren't the best of friends, but they weren't enemies either. Race no longer bullied Stuart about his weight, and Stuart was no longer afraid of Race. In fact, Maverick had actually caught Stuart studying Race with sympathy in his eyes.

Maverick knew how he felt. After meeting Race's father, he now understood why the kid had problems. Race wasn't an arrogant bully. He was a scared kid emulating the only role model he had, and Maverick felt guilty that he'd been so hard on the kid. But not anymore. After Sunday, he'd stopped giving Race hard drills to run and started teaching him plays and giving him lots of praise when he executed them.

The kid *was* a gifted quarterback. His performance during the game proved it. His timing was perfect and his throws right on target. He hadn't thrown one interception. Of course, Stuart had given him plenty of time to execute. Not one defensive lineman got past the kid to Race. It was like Stuart had become Race's guardian angel. Which was ironic . . . and pretty damned great.

"A free beer for our winning coaches!" Hank yelled from behind the bar. Everyone cheered again and Maverick and Waylon received numerous whacks on the back as they made their way to the bar. They had just accepted their beers when Spring appeared. She flung her arms around Waylon and gave him a kiss that had Maverick feeling a little embarrassed and maybe a little envious.

He pushed down the feeling and reminded himself that he needed to straighten his life out before he added a woman to the mix. Getting involved with Autumn had proven that women didn't come without strings attached. And Maverick had way too many strings in his life as is.

While he sat at the bar, more and more people came up to congratulate him and talk about the game. After a couple hours of football talk, he decided it was time to leave. It had been a long week, and he was dead on his feet. He made his excuses and headed to the side door. But before he reached it, he spotted Autumn. She was sitting at a table by herself, watching her two sisters dancing with their husbands. She wasn't dressed as matronly as usual. She wore skinny jeans and a pink sweater that hugged her breasts and matched her cowboy boots. Cowboy boots that she was tapping on the lower rung of the barstool in time to the music.

He should've ignored her and kept right on walking. But he couldn't seem to do it. When she saw him, he expected the same frown of disapproval he always got. Instead, her lips took on a sensual tilt that made desire tightened in his gut.

"Well, if it isn't Midas Murdoch," she said. "Does everything you touch turn to gold?"

He took off his cowboy hat and sat down. "You didn't."

She laughed. It had been a long time since he'd heard the husky, throaty sound. The last time had been in a hotel shower. He had been sudsing her up and had accidentally found a ticklish spot. Just the thought of her wet, naked, and laughing had his cock hardening beneath the fly of his jeans. Damn, he should've walked on by.

"I could never be gold," she said. "I'm the dull sister. The one who has no sparkle at all."

He had to disagree. At the moment, she sparkled more than any woman he'd ever met. Her dark curls reflected the multi-colored lights from the jukebox like a night sky filled with fireworks and her eyes twinkled like a clear Montana lake in full sunlight. He glanced at her empty margarita glass. Or like a woman who had too much to drink.

"Are you drunk?" he asked.

She rested her elbows on the table and placed

her chin in one hand, looking adorable and sexy at the same time. "Yep."

He couldn't help smiling. He liked this Autumn. She seemed to be much less uptight than the one he'd gotten to know in the last few weeks—more like the woman he'd met in his hotel rooms in Houston. He picked up the pitcher and refilled her glass. "So are you celebrating the win like everyone else? I didn't realize you were a football fan."

"I'm not." She took a sip of her margarita.

"Then why do you go to the games?" he asked.

Her eyebrows lifted beneath the feathery fringe of her bangs. "How do you know I go to the games?"

It was a good question. One he didn't want to answer. At least not truthfully. He didn't want her to know that whenever he turned to talk to his players on the bench, he always searched the crowd for her. He didn't even like knowing it.

He shrugged. "I just assumed it since there's nothing else to do in this small town on a Friday night."

"That's why I go to the games." He didn't know why he felt a stab of annoyance. Probably because he was kind of hoping she went to see him. Damned if she didn't read him like one of her books. "I hope you don't think I go to see the great Maverick Murdoch."

Since she had read him accurately all he could do was shrug. "I'm going to assume that your crush has worn off."

"Crushes usually do." She leaned closer, and he caught the whiff of tequila and lime, along with the sexy scent of soft, warm woman. It was a heady combination. Which probably explained why his cock refused to relax.

"Be honest." Her voice was low and seductive. "You weren't coaching the team in the first two games because you didn't want them to go to the playoffs."

Obviously, Autumn was a perceptive woman. He could've lied, but didn't. "Can you blame me? Coaching a bunch of teenagers for three months is a pretty stiff penalty for punching a jerk who should've been punched."

He thought she would argue. She seemed to argue with him about everything. But she didn't. "You're right. That was a pretty tough sentence. So what made you decide to pull your head out and start coaching your team?"

He laughed. "I guess I got tired of losing."

"Or maybe you're just using those poor boys to stroke your gigantic ego."

She hadn't lied when she said she was over her crush. It felt like she hated him. Why that would bother him, he didn't know. He didn't exactly like her either. Still, a man could only take so much abuse.

"As always, it wasn't nice talking to you." He started to get up, but she grabbed his wrist and stopped him. She had a firm grip for a woman who wasn't athletic, her fingers pressed firmly against his pulse point. Suddenly, he remembered the time she'd held both his wrists above his head and had her way with him. He could've easily broken free, but he hadn't wanted to.

Like now.

He sat back down on the barstool.

"I'm sorry," she said. "I don't know what gets into me when I'm around you. I'm usually never rude."

"Let me guess. Besides being the sweet, shy, dull sister, you're also the mannerly sister." He studied her. "Funny, but I don't see it. The woman I knew in Houston wasn't sweet or shy or dull. She wasn't rude, but she had no trouble saying exactly what she thought . . . and what she wanted."

Even in the dark bar, he could see her cheeks turn pink. He felt a little warm himself. Why did he have to bring up Houston? But it was too late to go back. And maybe it was best if they rehashed that time and moved on. Although she didn't look like she wanted any part of that. She suddenly looked like a wild animal that was searching for an escape.

She released his wrist and straightened. "That wasn't me."

"Then who was it?"

She looked away from his gaze. "I mean it was me, but I was just playing a part."

He quirked an eyebrow. "The part of your sister? Just so you know, Summer was never that sexually aggressive . . . at least not with me. Which is why I should've figured out your little game. Summer would never have come back to my hotel room. She would've wanted to meet me at the gym and kicked my butt with a sweaty, hard workout. And from her response when I brought up role-playing, I don't think that's her cup of tea either. So it's time for you to be honest, Autumn. You weren't playing a part in Houston. You were playing yourself."

While she sat there in stunned silence, he continued. "Which makes me wonder who the real Autumn is. Is she the shy girl I knew in college who blushed and stuttered whenever I tried to talk with her? Is she the sexually assertive woman who had her way with me? Or is she the feisty woman who rams cakes in jerks' faces, stands up to bullies, and tells me that I'm only winning to stroke my gigantic ego?"

Her eyes snapped with fire. "It's you! You make me do things that are completely out of character. I'm usually the calm, collected, level-headed Autumn who never blushes, or stutters, or goes back to men's hotel rooms, or shoves cakes in people's faces. You're the one who makes me act out of character!"

He smiled. "Or maybe I'm the one who lets you be yourself."

That really got her dander up. "That's the most ridiculous thing I've ever heard. Talk about people being drunk. You've obviously had way too much to drink, Maverick Murdoch, if you think for a second that my real personality is the crazy woman you make me. Ask anyone in my family and they'll tell you who I really am. Now if you'll excuse me, I'm done talking with you."

She got up to leave, but her feet didn't seem to be cooperating. After only two steps, she swayed and landed right on Maverick's lap. A lap that still boasted a major hard-on. Her eyes widened with surprise. All he could do was shrug.

"I guess I have a thing for crazy."

He expected her to jump up and slap him. He did not expect her eyes to darken with passion or her tongue to come out and moisten her lips.

And he sure as hell didn't expect her to wiggle her sweet little ass against the hard length of him until a low moan escaped his throat. For a moment, he forgot he was in a crowded bar. He forgot everything but the woman in his arms. She might be crazy, but so was he.

He lowered his head. But before he could get a deep taste of her moist, sweet lips, Summer interrupted.

"Get your hands off my sister!"

He pulled away to see Summer charging toward them. She tugged Autumn off his lap and pointed a finger in his face. "I've overlooked what happened that day in the bakery because I figured you had gone a little off your rocker after being dumped by the NFL. But that doesn't mean I've forgotten it. And I will not have you playing your creepy role-playing games with my sweet sister."

Spring walked up. She didn't seem to be as angry as Summer. She seemed to be more confused. She looked back and forth between him and Autumn like she was at a tennis match. She opened her mouth to say something, but before she could, Autumn spoke.

"It wasn't Maverick's fault. I had too much to drink and fell on his—" She cut off suddenly. Maverick recognized the green tint to her skin and the wild look in her eyes from having lived through many nights of drunken carousing with his college and NFL buddies. Knowing that time was crucial, he scooped her into his arms and headed for a door.

Luckily, the side exit was only a few steps away. Still, he barely made it outside and set her on her feet before she leaned over and threw up . . . all over his favorite boots.

Spring and Summer hurried out the door. Spring crinkled her nose. "Good Lord, Audie, that is disgusting. If you're going to drink, don't eat nachos before hand."

"It's my fault. I shouldn't have let her drink so much," Summer said. "She never could hold her liquor."

"Well, she's sure not holding it now." Spring looked away from her sister and studied Maverick. "Thanks, Mav."

"No big deal. You want to take over holding her hair so I can look for something to clean off my boots?"

Spring moved closer to help while Summer pointed. "I think there's a water spigot in back." She led him around the building to a spigot that was sticking out of the wall by the back door of the kitchen. She turned it on, then stood there while he stuck first one boot and then the other under the running water. When he was finished, he turned off the spigot and stomped the water from his boots. He turned to see Summer watching him.

"I guess I owe you an apology," she said.

"That makes us even. I certainly owed you one for the way I acted in the bakery." He smiled. "Besides, she's not the first Hadley who's thrown up on my shoes. Remember the time you tried to prove that you could run more laps than I could."

She grinned. "I won."

Summer had always wanted to win. She was as competitive as he was. Which probably explained why they had broken up. Their relationship had been more of a competition than a partnership. In fact, they hadn't even had sex. There were a few times that they'd talked about having it, but they'd never seemed to get around to it. Maverick now realized why. Their relationship had lacked passion. Which was why he'd been so surprised when he'd met Summer in Houston and the sparks had flown.

Of course, it hadn't been Summer who made the sparks fly. It was Autumn. Tonight was proof of that.

Spring came around the corner. "I'm going to go get Waylon so we can take Autumn home."

"Ryker and I are heading out too," Summer said. She glanced at Maverick. "Thanks for putting up with the puking Hadley girls. Come into the bakery anytime and I'll give you a sugar-free cupcake—just a cupcake, mind you. No funny business."

He held up his hands. "The only thing I want from the Hadley girls is friendship."

Summer grinned. "That, you've always had." She socked him hard in the arm before she left. Maverick would've headed to his truck if Spring hadn't still been standing there looking at him with her intense blue eyes.

"Is Autumn okay?" he asked.

"She's fine. She's in the bathroom, but I think the worst is over. All she needs now is a couple aspirins and a good night's sleep."

He nodded. "Good." Not knowing what else to say, he made his excuses. "Well, tell her I hope she feels better and I'll see y'all around." Before he could take a step, her words stopped him.

"You know, Mav, that business with Summer at the bakery never made any sense to me. I mean, why would a man show up after years of not seeing a woman and suddenly want to get straight to the naughty sex? Summer thinks you were drunk, but after tonight, I don't think that's the case at all. You weren't drunk or a little crazy about being shafted by the NFL." A smile spread over her face. A bright smile that was slightly smug. "You just had the wrong sister."

CHAPTER FOURTEEN

THE ONE GOOD THING ABOUT Autumn not being able to hold her liquor is that once it was out of her system, she usually had no after effects. She woke up the following morning with no headache or queasy stomach. What she did wake up with was total humiliation.

She had thrown up on Maverick.

And while that was bad, it wasn't as bad as rubbing against him like a dog in heat.

She squeezed her eyes shut and covered her burning face with both hands. How could she have acted so wantonly? Instead of excusing herself and getting up, the hard feel of him had melted her like butter in a hot skillet.

She lowered her hands as a thought struck her. And why had he been hard? It wasn't like he'd grown hard when she fell on his lap. She'd felt his erection as soon as she landed. Which could only mean one thing: Maverick was as turned on by her as she was by him.

"Good mornin', sweet sister of mine." Spring sailed into the room. She was still in her pajamas, and with her bed head, it looked like she hadn't been out of bed long. Her smile was bright and cheerful as she carried a tray of breakfast muffins and juice over to the nightstand and set it down.

Autumn sat up and smiled at her sister's thoughtfulness. "Thank you, Sweetness, but you didn't have to make me breakfast. I'm fine."

Spring grabbed a muffin and flopped down on the bed, pretzeling her legs in front of her. "I didn't. This is my breakfast." She peeled back the muffin wrapper. "Now start from the beginning." She took a big bite.

Autumn stuffed a pillow behind her back. "There's no beginning. I just drank too much." And became way too chatty . . . and horny. She picked up the glass of orange juice and took a sip.

Spring sent her an annoyed look. "I'm not talking about last night. I'm talking about the affair you're having with Maverick."

Autumn choked and spewed juice out of her mouth all over the comforter and Spring's pajama bottoms.

"Geez, Audie," Spring said as she reached for the napkin on the tray, "try to keep your fluids inside, would ya?"

Autumn grabbed another napkin and blotted the comforter as she tried to collect herself. "Maverick and I? Where would you get a crazy idea like that?"

Spring smiled at her. "You're right. It is pretty crazy. But not as crazy as Maverick showing up out of a clear blue sky and attacking Summer. Now that made no sense at all. Especially when Maverick was such a good guy in college, and when he seems to be such a good guy now. Waylon really likes him, and he's a great judge of character. So I didn't get the entire Summer thing until I saw you sitting on his lap last night, almost setting the entire bar ablaze with your smoldering looks. Then everything started to click." Her smile got bigger. "You did it, didn't you? You pulled the triplet switch on Maverick."

Autumn started to deny it, but then realized it was too late for that. Her dirty little secret was out. Part of her was glad. It was hard keeping secrets from her sisters. She sighed and nodded.

Spring eyes widened. "Oh. My. God. I can't believe you actually pulled the switch. Me and Summer, yes. You, no. You've always been the perfect Hadley triplet, the one who never did anything wrong. Obviously, you were just saving up." She took another bite of muffin and spoke around it. "Now tell me everything. I want to know every detail."

Autumn didn't tell her every detail. There were some things too embarrassing to even tell your sister. But she told her about seeing Maverick in Houston and him mistaking her for Summer, and she told her about going back to his hotel room and meeting him a couple times more before she'd closed the store. After she finished, she didn't know what she expected her sister to do. But it wasn't to let out a squeal and dive across the bed to hug her.

"I'm so proud of you!"

"Proud? How can you be proud of me when I completely ignored the unwritten sister law of never getting with a man your sister dates."

Spring released her and sat back on the bed, giggling. "You did. You totally broke that rule—

numerous times, no less."

"It's not funny."

"Oh, yes it is. I figured that one day you'd have to let off a little steam, but you blew the teakettle apart."

Autumn lowered her eyes and fiddled with the edge of her comforter. "Something I'm not proud of."

"Oh, Audie," Spring squeezed her hand. "You've always been so hard on yourself. Which has given you the most boring life of anyone I've ever met. You've never broken a rule. Not one rule. You don't cuss. You don't drink—at least, not very often. You don't have any bad habits. For that matter, you don't have any good habits. You do what you're supposed to do without complaining and never cause a speck of trouble. Granny Bon used to call you her angel."

"There's nothing wrong with being an angel."

"Yes, there is. Angels spend all their days watching out for humans. They never take time off. They never have any fun. And that's you. You've spent all your life watching out for your family. While Summer took control and became the stern mama who kept us in line, you were the mama who made us feel loved and was always there for us. The one who brought us soup when were sick and gave us hugs when we were sad. The one who did anything we asked you to do without one complaint. You always put everyone before yourself. And that's why I'm so proud of you. This time, you put yourself first. You didn't think about Summer. Or Granny Bon. Or Dirk. Or me. You only thought about yourself and what you wanted." She smiled brightly. "And I say it's about time."

Spring was right. She'd only thought about herself. She hadn't thought about her family or anyone else. Suddenly, she realized that what Maverick had said to her the night before was true. Autumn hadn't been playing a part. She'd been playing herself. For the first time in her life, she'd been doing exactly what she wanted to do. Which meant that beneath her shy exterior was a sexually aggressive woman struggling to get out. That scared the crap out of her.

She shook her head. "I still shouldn't have done it. Especially with Summer's old boyfriend."

"Be honest, Audie. Maverick is the only man living who could've made you do what you did. The only one who could make you put away your lofty morals and take a walk on the wild side. And are you sure you don't want to walk on the wild side again?"

Her eyes widened. "Absolutely not! I'll be thrilled when Maverick leaves town so I can get back to my calm, peaceful life."

"Geez, Audie. You sound like you're eighty instead of in your twenties. Why would you want a calm, peaceful life when you can have a hot, steamy affair with a pro quarterback?"

"Are you crazy?" she asked.

"Occasionally." Waylon walked into the room with Sherlock and Watson trailing behind him. He leaned over and gave Spring a kiss on the lips. "But I'm kinda partial to her craziness."

Spring smiled. "And I love you too." She glanced at his sweatpants. "But those tattered things need to be thrown in the garbage."

Waylon glanced down. "Not a chance. I just broke these in." He winked at Autumn. "I hate to interrupt your sister chat, but I just wanted to let you know that Maverick is coming over to watch the video of last night's game. I didn't want you coming down in your pajamas and getting mad because I didn't warn you that we had a visitor."

Autumn inwardly cringed. The last thing she wanted to do was run into Maverick. She needed to get out of there and fast. As soon as Waylon left, she jumped out of bed. "I better get to the bakery and help Summer."

"You don't need to hurry to the bakery," Spring said. "Ms. Marble is helping Summer this morning. You're running off because you don't want to see Maverick."

Autumn opened a drawer and pulled out a pair of panties. "Can you blame me after what I did last night?"

"That was a spectacular puke session, but I don't think you're running from him because you're embarrassed as much as you're running because you want to hop back in bed with him and you're fighting it."

Autumn slammed the drawer closed and turned to stare at her sister.

Spring was propped up against the pillows eating another muffin. Her eyebrows lifted. "I'm not judging, mind you. I'm just stating what I saw last night. You two have the major hots for each other."

Autumn had a flashback of just how hot Maverick had been and just how melty his zipper steel had made her. "Maybe we do, but I'm not about to repeat the same mistake twice."

"You mean four times, don't you?" Spring set the muffin down on the tray. "Because you already repeated the same mistake three times."

Autumn sent her annoyed look. "I never should've confided in you. And if you tell Summer, I'm going to . . ."

"Smash a cake in my face?"

"Very funny." She grew serious. "Really, Spring. I don't want Summer to know. She would be hurt that I betrayed her trust."

"That's silly. It's not like you were screwing him while they were dating. They hadn't seen each other in years when you ran into him. Which is probably why he fell for the switch. But I'm not going to say anything to Summer." She got off the bed. "I think you should confess to her."

"Me?"

"Yes, you. Take my word for it, secrets always come back to haunt you."

It was a lesson Spring had learned the hard way. She'd kept the secret about their fugitive father being in town and it had almost cost Waylon his job . . . and Spring the love of her life. But Autumn's situation was different.

"This secret isn't going to come back to haunt me," she said. "As soon as Maverick leaves, my secret leaves with him."

Spring scooped up Watson, who was rubbing against her legs, and cuddled the cat. "Whatever you say, sis."

Autumn wasted no time showering and getting

dressed. She peeked out the window to make sure the coast was clear before she opened the door and slipped out to the porch. She was halfway down the front walk when a deep voice made her freeze.

"Good mornin'."

She turned to see Maverick stepping through the opening in the hedge that separated the two yards. He was wearing a pair of faded jeans and a white t-shirt with sleeves that were stretched to capacity by his large biceps. He had switched out his cowboy hat for a cap. She expected the emblem on the front to be from one of the NFL teams he'd played for. Instead, it was a John Deere. Beneath the curled brim of the cap, his multi-faceted blue eyes twinkled.

"Your color looks much better than it did last night."

She willed herself not to blush, but it was a losing battle. "Thank you for getting me outside so quickly."

"No problem. And just so you know, I think Spring has figured things out."

"What did she say to you?"

"Just that she thought I had gotten the wrong sister when I tried to kiss Summer in the bakery."

"She figured it out, so I told her everything."

His eyes widened. "Everything?"

Her cheeks burned hotter. "Not everything. But she knows that I pulled the Triplet switch."

He grinned. "So that's what you call it." The grin faded. "Have you done it before?"

"Of course not. You were the first." She quickly rephrased. "I mean the first time I did it."

He squinted at her. "Because of the crush?"

"Yes. Because of the crush. Now I need to get to the bakery and you need to get to your game film." She went to leave, but he stopped her.

"Autumn." When she turned, he was closer. Close enough that she could smell the scent of soap and musky male. He hadn't shaved that morning. Golden whiskers speckled his chin and jaw. A jaw that flexed as if he were trying to find the words he wanted to say. "Look, I know that the entire sex thing in Houston has made our relationship here in Bliss a little awkward."

"A little?"

He laughed. "Okay, a lot. If we were in a big city, we could avoid each other. But in a small town that's a little unlikely. So what about if we quit trying to ignore the past and accept it?"

It was sad how quickly her mind went to the gutter. All she could think about was what her sister had said about them being hot for each other. Was he proposing that they take up where they'd left off?

It was hard to get the words out of her tight throat. "What do you mean?"

"What happened happened. At first, I wasn't too happy about being tricked, but I'm over it and I want to move on." He flashed a smile. "What say we become friends?"

Friends? She shouldn't have felt disappointed, especially when she had just told her sister that she was over him. But she did feel disappointed. Or at least her body did. Her brain knew that he was right. Bliss was too small to avoid each other, and she couldn't spend the next two months hiding from him. And while she thought they were too different to become friends, they could at least be cordial to each other.

"I think that's a good idea."

"Great." He held out a hand. "So friends it is."

She hesitated for only a second before she took his hand and gave it a firm shake. "Friends." Wanting to make things perfectly clear, she added, "With no benefits."

His gaze lowered to her mouth and heat sizzled through her. "If we must." He turned and headed up the steps of the porch.

Autumn stood there and watched as he disappeared inside. She couldn't help wondering if she'd just made a pact with the devil.

CHAPTER FIFTEEN

"YOU STINK, STEWIE." RACE WAVED a hand in front of his nose as he ran. "You smell like a goat fart."

Stuart, who was doing a damned good job of keeping up with Race and Maverick, didn't even hesitate to come back with a reply. "You're the one who smells like a fart. A cheesy egg fart covered in maggots."

"How can a fart be covered in maggots, you idiot? It's air."

"Maybe because the maggots are filled with farts too and are lighter than air."

Race laughed. "You are so weird." He sidestepped into Stuart and bumped him with his shoulder. Stuart bumped him back and knocked Race into Maverick.

"Quit screwing around, you two," he said, but he didn't really mean it. He liked that his center and quarterback were finally getting along. He also liked that they were winning games for him. If they won two more games, they'd be in the playoffs.

At one time, he'd wanted nothing to do with

staying another couple weeks in Bliss. But now he was pretty damned happy about it. Not only because he was proud of his team, but also because he'd started to enjoy his time in the small town. He'd started having breakfast with Ms. Marble in the mornings and had gotten quite attached to the little old woman. She filled him in on the town gossip while she fed him egg-white omelets with plenty of veggies and lean ham. He spent most of his day at the high school, going over game film and reworking plays. He worked out in the weight room in the afternoon before practice. Occasionally, Waylon would show up and work out with him. He had switched shifts with his deputy during the week so he had his afternoons off to help coach.

Maverick didn't envy many people, but he envied Waylon. Waylon had a job he loved, a wife he adored, a cool old house, and an entire town of friends. Although in Bliss, everyone was your friend.

"Are you going to Boo Night, Race?" Stuart asked.

According to what Maverick could gather, Boo Night was held the Saturday before Halloween on Main Street. Everyone dressed up in costumes and all the businesses handed out candy to the kids. This year, it was scheduled the night right after the first playoff game.

"Yeah, I have to go," Race said. "My little sister has been working on her costume for weeks and I promised I'd go and support her in the costume contest."

"You're not going to wear a costume?"

"Shit, no. That's dorky."

Out of the corner of his eye, Maverick saw Stuart's face fall. As much as Maverick agreed with Race, he couldn't let Stuart feel like a dork. "I'm going and wearing a costume," he said.

Race glanced over at him. "You are? What are you going as?"

He scrambled for a costume idea. When they ran past the Tender Heart museum, he glanced at the cowboy mannequin sitting on the buckboard with his mail-order bride. "A gunslinger."

"Cool," Stuart said. Of course, Stuart idealized him so Maverick could've said he was going as a goat fart and the kid would've thought it was cool. "I was thinking about going as a football player."

Race snorted. "That's stupid. We are football players."

"I don't think it's stupid," Maverick said. "But you can't go as football players. Joanna Daily asked me if the team could work in the museum haunted house as old west zombies."

"Zombies." Stuart grinned. "That's even cooler than a football player."

Maverick should've said he was going as a football player. He could've borrowed a jersey, helmet, and pads from the locker room. Now he had to come up with a gunslinger's costume.

"When are we stopping?" Race asked. "I'm sick of running around this stupid town."

"I didn't ask you to join me," Maverick said. "You were the one who insisted on coming along. More than likely because you saw Stuart running with me and didn't want to let him outdo you."

Race snorted. "As if that would ever happen."

"I don't know. Stuart showed you up pretty good at the last game." Stuart was now playing offense and defense. He was unstoppable on both sides. The running and strength training he'd been doing with Maverick had helped him lose weight and become more agile and quick.

"Just because he caught that interception doesn't mean he played better than me," Race said.

"Don't forget the fumble I recovered." Stuart's smile was smug.

Race rolled his eyes. "You are really becoming an arrogant ass. You know that?"

"About as arrogant as someone else I know." Stuart slowed. "I'm stopping for a donut. I'll see you later, Coach. Hopefully not you, Maggot Fart."

Race turned and jogged backwards. "Same here, Goat Fart." He continued running with Maverick.

"I thought you wanted to quit," Maverick said. "A donut is your opportunity."

Race shook his head. "I can go a little more. Besides, sugar is deadly on an athlete's body."

"Hmm? So the candy bars you bring to practice don't count as sugar?"

Race shot him an annoyed look. "Okay, so I don't want to go back to the bakery after that one triplet threatened me." Maverick laughed and changed directions. "Where are we going?" Race asked as he followed him.

"To the bakery. I can't have my star quarterback scared of a cupcake baker."

"I didn't say I was scared of her."

"Then you shouldn't be afraid to go in and order a donut." Maverick knew the kid's ego wouldn't let him decline, and he was right.

"Fine. But if she starts yelling, I'm out of there." Race pulled open the door of the bakery. But before he could go in, Stuart came running out.

"Fire!"

Maverick didn't wait to get the details. He pushed past Stuart and ran into the bakery. Smoke hung in the air and the fire alarm was going off. He headed around the counter and into the kitchen where he found Autumn standing on a step stool fanning a dish towel at the smoke detector.

"What the hell are you doing?" he yelled above the blaring alarm.

She startled and lost her balance. Maverick made a dive for her and got an arm around her waist fast enough to keep her from cracking her head on the counter. He set her on her feet and assessed the situation. There was a lot of smoke, but it didn't appear to be coming from a fire. It was coming from the batch of blackened burnt cupcakes sitting on top of one of the ovens.

"Holy crap!"

He glanced behind him to see Stuart and Race standing in the doorway.

"Open the window, Stuart," he ordered. "Race, get an oven mitt and carry those cupcakes out back to the trash." They rushed to follow his orders as he climbed up on the stepstool to turn off the smoke alarm. He had to take the battery out to get it to stop squealing. When he came down from the stepstool, Autumn was standing there staring at the oven as if it had somehow betrayed her.

"I checked the time and temperature twice. Fifteen minutes at three fifty. I even set a timer." She shook her head. "I don't know what happened."

"Well, something happened," Stuart said. "My mom has burnt cupcakes before, but never like that."

Race walked in the back door holding the empty cupcake tin with an oven mitt. "He's right. Those things were nothing but lumps of coal."

Autumn's cheeks turned a bright red, and Maverick couldn't help feeling sorry for her.

"That's enough, boys," he said.

"But, Coach, did you see those charred things?" Race waved a hand through the air. "And look at all this smoke. I'm surprised someone hasn't called the fire department." As if on cue, there was the far-off sound of a siren.

Stuart released a whoop. "A fire truck!"

Autumn moaned and covered her face with her hands. She had a right to be embarrassed. The entire town seemed to show up with the fire truck. People circled around the front window trying to get a good view as the firemen rushed in the front door with masks and a hose.

Stuart and Race were extremely disappointed that the firemen didn't get to use that hose. After resetting the fire alarm and checking to make sure the cupcakes hadn't started a blaze in the dumpster, the two volunteer firemen left.

"They didn't even use a fire extinguisher," Stuart grumbled. He glanced at Autumn who was sitting on a stool, looking completely humiliated. "Do you think I could get a donut? I'm starving."

Maverick pulled out his wallet and handed Stuart a twenty. "Take Race over to the diner and have lunch on me. And put the "Closed" sign in the window on your way out."

"Sure thing, Coach," Stuart said. "Come on, Maggot Fart."

Race followed behind him. "Lead the way, Goat Fart."

Once the teenagers were gone, Autumn started to get up. "I can't close early. It's bad enough that I almost burned my sister's bakery down while she took a day off to go to Austin with her husband. I refuse to cost her business too."

Maverick placed a hand on her shoulder. "Sit down. Being closed for an hour so you can let the smoke clear isn't going to hurt anything. And you didn't almost burn down the bakery. You just burned a few cupcakes, is all. It could happen to anyone."

Her expression was completely baffled. "But it happens to me all the time. And I don't get it. Baking should be my thing. It's all about following directions perfectly. And I've always followed directions to a tee. I followed my mama's directions. And Granny Bon's. And Summer's and Spring's. And all my teachers, coaches, and professors." She looked at him and put a hand on her chest. "I'm good at following directions."

That sounded like a whole lot of people handing out directions to Maverick. And he couldn't help but wonder if that's why Autumn had enjoyed giving instructions to him during their nights together in Houston. For once, she wanted to be in control . . . and he had enjoyed giving her that control. Images of Autumn pushing him back against the wall and kissing him popped into his head, but he immediately pushed them back out. He had made a vow to be Autumn's friend—a friend without benefits—and he intended to keep that promise.

"I believe you," he said. "But maybe it's not about following directions. Maybe you just don't like to bake."

She opened her mouth to reply, but then closed it again. She stared at him for a moment before she started to laugh. She laughed until tears dripped from the corners of her eyes, and he worried that she had gone off the deep end.

"Are you okay?" he asked.

She nodded and dabbed at her eyes with the dishtowel she still held. "You're right. I hate to bake. I hate the mess it makes in the kitchen. And I hate the time it takes—time that could be spent doing something else. Like reading. Which is exactly why I burn things. I keep thinking I'll just read one quick chapter on my phone while I wait, but then I get involved in the story and completely ignore timers going off. It took the smoke alarm blaring to get my attention this time."

"So why are you working in a bakery if you don't like baking?"

"Because Summer needs me."

It was such a simple reply, but it spoke volumes about Autumn's personality. She was a giver. And Maverick couldn't help remembering another person who gave unselfishly.

He sat down on the stool next to Autumn. "You sound like my . . . good friend, Robby. Whatever I wanted him to do, Robby did. Even if he hated it." He rested his elbows back on the counter and stared at the smoke that still clung to the ceiling. "Every evening and weekend, we'd go to the stadium by our house and he'd have to put up with me harassing him because he couldn't catch my passes. Or because he was too slow running the patterns I made up for him."

"I pushed him to go out for football in high school, and he ended up warming the bench and being used as a tackling dummy for the first stringers during their practice. He must've been miserable, but he didn't show it." He shook his head. "Talk about a bully. I was worse than Race."

"Summer isn't bullying me," Autumn said. "I want to help her."

He glanced over at her. "Help is one thing. Letting someone take over your life is another."

"She hasn't taken over my life."

A memory struck him. "You used to do Summer's homework for her, didn't you?"

"Only when she had an away softball game. She couldn't be expected to do her homework on a bus. She gets carsick."

The pieces were starting to fall together. "I remember you doing Spring's homework too. And she didn't play softball. And you were the one who typed up my theme paper, weren't you?"

She blushed. "I just like to help."

"Uh-huh. I'm sure you do. But there's a difference between helping and being taken advantage of. Whose idea was it to start the retail store? Let me guess: Spring and Summer's. You just went along because they needed your help."

Her blushing cheeks said it all. "What is your point?"

"You're smart. I think you can figure it out." He glanced around the bakery. "In case, you haven't noticed, your sisters are living their lives. Maybe it's time for you to live yours."

It was obvious that he'd hit a nerve when Autumn's eyes darkened with anger. If a cake had been handy, he figured he'd be getting a taste of it right now. Instead, she just jumped up and got in his face. And he couldn't help thinking how cute she was when she was mad. Or maybe sexy was a better word. He had always liked feisty woman.

"Thanks so much for helping me deal with the smoke alarm and burned cupcakes," she snapped. "But I don't need to be psychoanalyzed by a man who has totally screwed up his own life."

She was right, but he couldn't seem to let it go. He didn't know why it mattered so much to him that she realized what she was doing. Maybe because the situation between her and her sisters reminded him of his relationship with Robby. He wished someone had talked to Robby. He wished someone had stopped him from wilting in his brother's large shadow.

"Maybe I have screwed up my life," he said. "But at least it's my life. You need to quit being bullied by your sisters, Autumn, and stand up for yourself."

"Is that what you told poor Stuart?"

"As a matter of fact, it is. And it looks like it's worked. Race and Stuart are getting along like peas and carrots."

Her eyes widened. "They call each other farts! And I don't need to stand up to my sisters. They want whatever will make me happy."

"Then maybe that's the problem. Do you know what will make you happy, Autumn? Or are you just going to keep trying to make your sisters happy until you wake up one day and realize you're miserable and have no life of your own."

The slap she gave him stung like hell. He didn't know who was more surprised by her actions: him or Autumn. Probably Autumn. She looked like she had just committed a cardinal sin.

"Oh my gosh, I'm so sorry. I've never hit anyone in my life. Does it hurt?" She took his jaw in her hand, the tips of her cool fingers brushing the underside of his chin as she turned his head. Her eyes instantly filled with concern. "I left my fingerprints."

He expected her to rub the welts or maybe run and get some ice. He did not expect her to lean down and kiss his cheek. Her lips weren't as cool as her fingers that still held his chin. They were hot, and he felt like a wick that had just been lit. He caught fire. When she started to step back, he settled his hands on her hips and stopped her. Her twilight blue eyes flashed with confusion. He was confused too. Confused by the control this woman seemed to have over his willpower. He had always been able to resist things that weren't good for him, but he couldn't resist Autumn.

And he was damned tired of trying.

He lowered his head and kissed her.

She tasted like he remembered. She tasted like all the sugary desserts he craved but refused to partake of. He partook now. He partook of the sweetness of her lips and the warm wetness of her mouth like a starving man. And she let him. She slipped her arms around his neck and let him sate his cravings.

But soon kissing wasn't enough. He wanted to gobble up every inch of her. He spread his knees and pulled her closer to the aching need beneath his zipper. He had just gotten her firmly seated against that ache when the sound of a cough had him pulling back. Over Autumn's shoulder, he saw Ms. Marble standing in the doorway.

The older woman didn't seem to be shocked by what she had just witnessed. In fact, if her bright smile was any indication, she was quite pleased.

"I heard that the fire department took care of the fire." Her piercing blue eyes twinkled. "But it looks like it's still burning to me."

CHAPTER SIXTEEN

SPRING'S VINTAGE TRAILER STOOD OUT like a Vegas showgirl at an Amish convention against the backdrop of dark green juniper scrub and brown-leafed oak trees. The hot pink paint and the words *Spring Fling* written in script on the back made Autumn smile, despite being a little nervous.

She pulled her Audi off the dirt road and parked next to an old Chevy Malibu that had seen better days. The back fender was dented and the paint faded and rusted in spots. Before she could even shut off the engine, Carrie Anne came streaking out from behind a juniper bush like blond lightening.

"Hey!" Her smile was bright.

Autumn got out of the car. "Hi, I'm Autumn Hadley." She held out the bag of cookies she'd brought from the bakery. "I brought you some cookies from the Blissful Bakery."

"Cookies!" Carrie Anne took the bag and immediately opened it and looked inside. "Chocolate chip!" She pulled one out and took a big bite, talking with her mouth full. "I remember you from the football game. You are the Skittles lady."

Autumn smiled. "I am."

Carrie Anne took another bite of cookie. "So your name is Autumn?" When Autumn nodded, her eyes squinted. "There are a lot of girls in this town named after seasons. The sheriff's wife's name is Spring—she's the one who loaned us this trailer. And Mama said that a woman named Summer owns the bakery."

"Spring and Summer are my sisters. My daddy thought it was pretty clever to name us after the seasons. Of course, it would've been more clever if he'd had four daughters."

Carrie Anne tipped her head in thought. "Winter? Yuck. That's a horrible name for a girl."

Autumn laughed. "I guess you're right." She glanced back at the trailer. "So is your mom here?"

"Yeah, but she's working. She works for Cord Evans now. He's an old rodeo star. He's got this drawer full of big shiny belt buckles. He showed them to me and let me touch them. And he didn't even care that I got them all smudged up. And he bought mama a new computer and smartie phone to do all his Twittering on." Carrie Anne leaned in closer and put her hand next to her mouth. "I'm not supposed to tell anyone, but my mama doesn't know nothin' about Twittering. Which is why I have to play outside and be so quiet while she figures it out. If she doesn't, Mr. Evans will fire her, and we really need the money 'cause our car broke down and if we want to get out of this two-bit town, we need to fix it."

Autumn was confused. Why would Christie want to leave Bliss if she'd come here to get money from the Hadleys? And if she were after money, why would she need a job? Why wouldn't she just tell people who she was and ask the Hadleys for money? Things just weren't adding up. And she was hoping Carrie Anne might help her figure them out.

"What brought you and your mama to Bliss?"

Carrie Anne finished off the cookie and licked the chocolate from her lips. "We're looking for a new home after my grandma died. We lived with my Mimi after my no-good daddy ran off and left us. He's a rodeo cowboy like Mr. Evans. Which is why my mama wasn't real happy about working for Cord."

Autumn stared at her. "Your father is a rodeo cowboy?"

"Danny Ray Buchanan." Carrie Anne shot her a knowingly look. "We Buchanans have a weakness for bad boys. My great-grandma and grandma, God rest their souls, both fell for losers. And so did my mama. Which means there's not much hope for me." She shrugged. "You can't mess with destiny."

Autumn would've laughed at the little girl's audacity if her mind hadn't been so wrapped up in the fact that Holt wasn't Carrie Anne's father. At least, Carrie Anne didn't think he was. If her mother had a weakness for no-good men, there was still a chance Holt could be her father and Christie just hadn't told her. There had to be a reason she'd gone to see Holt in jail and then come to Bliss."

"Are you married to a bum?" Carrie Anne asked.

"I'm not married," she said. "And I'm a firm believer that you make your own destiny. You get to choose what you want to do with your life and who you want to be with."

An image of Maverick flashed into her mind and, with it, the memory of the kiss they had shared in the bakery. Although it had been more than a kiss. It had been explosive passion unleashed, and she had stayed up all night thinking about it . . . and thinking about what he had said to her before the kiss.

Was he right? Was she living her sisters' life and ignoring her own wants and desires? Was she taking destiny by the reins like she thought she was or letting it lead her where it would?

"I'm never gettin' married." Carrie Anne pulled her from her thoughts. "I'm going to own a big ranch like Cord Evans and raise ostriches."

"Ostriches?"

"Yeah, for boots. Mr. Evans says ostrich skin makes the best boots." Carrie Anne scrunched up her face. "But one thing I can't figure out. That's how they get the skin off the ostriches without hurting them. Do they shear those birds like sheep?"

Before Autumn could think of a reply that wouldn't upset the little girl, the door of the trailer opened and Christie Buchanan appeared behind the screen door. She didn't look happy to see her, and Autumn couldn't blame her. Autumn had been horribly rude to her and for no reason. Christie hadn't been sent by Holt to get money or cause trouble. She'd come looking for a home after her mother had passed away. Having lost her own mother, Autumn understood how adrift you felt when you no longer had a mom.

She pinned on a smile and glanced down at the bag Carrie Anne held. "I just stopped by to bring some cookies." She paused. "And to apologize for the way I acted the other day at the bakery."

"You're the mean lady from the bakery who wouldn't hire my mama?" Carrie Anne asked. Before Autumn could answer, she threw down the bag. "I don't want your stupid cookies then." She crossed her arms and glared.

Christie came out the door. "Carrie Anne Buchanan, you apologize this instant. Just because a person is rude that does not give you the right to be rude back. Good manners are good manners."

Talk about being put in her place. Autumn had just received a setting down better than Granny Bon gave.

"Maybe I don't want to have good manners," Carrie Anne said. "You and Mimi always had good manners and it didn't get you anything but hard luck and bad boys." She jutted out her chin and stomped back to the trailer, slamming the screen door behind her.

When she was gone, Christie shook her head. "Some days I wish I believed in spankings."

"She has every right to be mad at me," Autumn said. "And so do you. I shouldn't have acted the way I did at the bakery. After I saw you at the jail with Holt, I thought he sent you here to cause trouble or ask for money."

Christie stiffened. "I'm not here to cause trouble. And I don't want money. I don't want anything from the Hadleys."

"How do you know Holt?"

"I don't know him. At least, I didn't know him

before I met him at the jail. He was a friend of my mother's and I just stopped by to tell him that she had passed away."

"I'm sorry. I lost my mother too, and I know how hard it is."

Christie nodded. "I couldn't stay in Cheyenne. It held too many memories. I wanted a fresh start for me and Carrie Anne."

"Why Bliss?"

"Holt mentioned that his daughter ran a bakery here. I thought . . ." She shook her head. "It doesn't matter what I thought. I'm going to work until I can pay to fix my car and then you'll never have to see me again."

Autumn knew what she'd thought. She'd thought that Bliss sounded like a perfect place to make a home for her and Carrie Anne. And Autumn had ruined that dream by refusing her a job and treating her so badly.

She picked up the bag of cookies and held it out. "They might be a little crumbly, but they're still edible. Carrie Anne seemed to love them."

Christie took the bag. "Thanks, now I better get back to work." She turned and went back inside the trailer.

Autumn stood there for a moment, feeling like the worst person in the world. In the last month, she had been rude to a single mother who had only wanted a job and slapped Maverick. She had to wonder if Maverick was right. Maybe she wasn't the kind-hearted, shy Hadley triplet. Maybe she had a mean streak like her daddy.

She started to leave when Christie's voice came out the screen door of the trailer. "What have you done, Carrie Anne Buchanan!"

"I'm sorry, Mama. I was just trying to help. I didn't mean to mess up your Twittering."

Autumn walked over and peeking in the screen door. Christie was sitting at the small table staring at the screen of her laptop with a look of horror on her face.

"Can I help?" Autumn asked.

Christie glanced over at her. "Only if you know how to delete my daughter's tweet about her favorite super hero from Cord Evans' twitter feed."

Autumn opened the door and stepped into the trailer. "As a matter a fact, I do." She sat down on the opposite side of the table and turned the laptop around so she could see the screen. She laughed when she read the tweet about Wonder Woman being the greatest super hero ever. "I'm not sure you want to delete this."

"What?" Christie looked at her like she was crazy.

She turned the laptop. "It's already gotten five likes."

Carrie Anne bounced in the booth. "See, Mama, people know Wonder Woman's the greatest."

Christie looked confused. "But I don't understand. It got likes and the posts I made about Cord Evans boots haven't gotten any."

"Can I have a look at your past tweets?" Autumn asked. When Christie nodded, she turned the laptop back around. After spending a few seconds scanning the tweets, she knew what the problem was. "You're hard selling."

"I'm what?"

"You're acting like a car salesman who needs to meet a quota. People don't like that. If people are following Cord Evans, they already know he sells boots. They probably already own a pair or two. They are following him because they want to know more about him and what a retired rodeo star does during the day. Can you occasionally slip in an ad about his boots? Of course, selling boots is part of who he is. If he has a new style of boots out or is having a sale, people what to know. When I did social media for Seasons, the clothing store I owned with my sisters, I always posted when we were having a sale or got a new line of clothing in. But the majority of my posts were about owning a business with my sisters. I'd post pictures of us working late and eating takeout. Spring chatting with a customer and making them laugh. Summer on the phone haggling with a wholesaler. My morning latte sitting amid a pile of sales receipts and my calculator. Just everyday things that made people feel like they were part of our lives."

"I don't have sisters," Carrie Anne said. "I don't have a brother either. I had a hamster, but I had to give Jitters away when we left Wyoming." She sent her mother a resentful look. "And I bet he misses me a lot."

"I'm sure he's doing just fine with your friend Mia." Christie turned to Autumn. "The feeling I get from Cord is that he's a private man. I don't think he'll want people knowing too much about his life. Which is why he's not very good at social media and hired me to become his assistant." She glanced at the laptop. "Unfortunately, I made him believe I'm better at this stuff than I am because I needed a job."

The reason Christie needed a job was because

Autumn had refused to give her one at the bakery. That being the case, she needed to make sure she kept this one.

"You don't need to post everything about Cord's life. Just little bits and pieces. A picture of him working around his ranch. Riding his horse. Sitting on his porch. Even pictures of what's going on in his town." A thought struck her. "I bet his demographic would love to see pictures of some of the old cowboy artifacts in the museum. It's all about figuring out his brand and using it to connect with people who love the same thing."

Christie looked a little stunned and overwhelmed.

Autumn tried to ease her fears. "It's not as hard as it sounds. I'd be happy to help you. It's the least I can do after being so rude to you at the bakery." She paused. "And speaking of the bakery. Would you still be interested in the job? I know you're working with Cord, but it sounds like it's just a part-time position. Maybe you could work at the bakery when you're not helping him."

"I'm not sure that's a good idea."

"Yes, it is, Mama!" Carrie Anne piped up. "If you worked at the bakery, I bet you could get free cupcakes and donuts whenever you wanted."

Autumn laughed. "She does have a point."

"I'll have to think about it."

"Why do you have to think about it, Mama? You said that we need money. Wouldn't that give you more money?"

Christie blushed, and Autumn was glad that she wasn't the only one who had that affliction.

"It would certainly help me out," Autumn said. "And my sister Summer. She desperately needs someone to help her with the baking. I've decided to give baking up for good after I set off the fire alarm and the fire department came."

"A fire truck came?" Carrie Anne almost jumped out of her seat. "Did they use the ladder?"

"No, they just gave me a warning about being more careful when I'm baking and talked football with Coach Murdoch."

"Coach Murdoch came? He asked me to help him coach, but Mama wouldn't let me do it. She said he was just being nice."

Maverick was nice. Much nicer than Autumn had realized. Not only had he been kind to Carrie Anne, he'd also been aware of Stuart getting bullied and fixed it much better than Autumn had. And every time she looked out her window, she saw him doing handy work for Ms. Marble, blowing her leaves or cleaning out her gutters or helping the older woman hang a fall wreath on her door.

At one time, she'd put him in the same category as her daddy—just one more selfish man who cared only for himself. And maybe that's why she'd been so attracted to him: she'd been searching for her father's love. But now she realized that Maverick was nothing like her father. He was single-minded and dedicated to becoming a professional football player, but when he'd been forced to coach the high school team, he hadn't shirked his responsibility like her father would've. He'd become a beloved coach to those boys and a beloved resident of the town.

"I don't think Coach Murdoch would've made the offer if he didn't think you would make a great assistant coach," Autumn said.

"See, Mama," Carrie Anne said. "I told you."

Christie shook her head. "No coaching. You need to concentrate on your homeschooling."

"You homeschool her?" Autumn asked.

"Without a car, it's hard to get her to school in town. Cord offered, but he's already done too much."

"I hate being homeschooled." Carrie Anne said. "I'd rather go to a school that has playground equipment and recess." Autumn thought about offering to drive Carrie Anne, but it seemed that Christie didn't like taking help from anyone. Which meant that Autumn would have to be like Spring and become a little sneakier with her help.

"Are you going to Boo Night?" Autumn asked.

Carrie Anne stuck out her bottom teeth. "I'm going as a bloody vampire."

"Not bloody," Christie said. "Just a vampire."

"Still, vampires are pretty scary even without the blood," Autumn said. "And I'll be there too. The bakery is going to have a special booth, and I'll make sure to have Summer decorate a vampire cupcake just for you." She picked up the pen lying on the table and wrote her number down on the notepad. "And if you need any more help with social media, Christie, just call me." She sent Christie a beseeching look. "I really am sorry for assuming something that wasn't the case."

When Christie only nodded, Autumn got up and headed for the door. On the way to her car, she glanced back to see Christie and Carrie Anne standing in the doorway of the trailer. Carrie Anne smiled and waved. Christie just stood with her arms crossed and a frown on her face. They had obviously gotten off on the wrong foot, but Autumn intended to fix that. Christie was in desperate need of a friend, and she was going to get one.

Whether she liked it or not.

CHAPTER SEVENTEEN

∽

"ARE YOU SURE YOU DON'T mind me borrowing these? They look pretty old." Maverick took the stack of clothes Ms. Marble was offering him.

"They are old. They belonged to my grandfather. He was quite the cowboy." She handed him the grocery bag slung over her arm. It was heavy. "And a bit of a gunslinger himself. This is his Colt."

He opened the bag and glanced in at the old gun and leather holster. "I couldn't borrow your grandfather's gun."

"Why not? If you're going to be a gunslinger, you need a gun."

"But not a gun that belongs in the Tender Heart museum."

"Where do you think I got them?" She flapped a hand. "Now quit being silly and go try them on for me. If they need to be nipped and tucked, I'm just the girl to do it."

A few moments later, he walked out of his bathroom.

Ms. Marble's almost non-existent eyebrows

lifted. "I knew you were close to my granddaddy's size, but I didn't realize how close until now." She walked around him. "That's about as perfect a fit as you can get. Did you realize that those are some of the first Levi jeans ever made?" She moved behind him. Maverick had to admit that the fit was good, but it was a little embarrassing to have the old gal checking out his butt. "Sorry I don't have Granddaddy's old boots, but he was buried with them on like any good cowboy." She came back around. "Of course, yours look just fine with the outfit. All you need is a horse and a mail-order bride to complete the picture."

"I wouldn't mind a horse, but I can do without a bride," he said.

She smiled. "Yes, you've made it clear that you're not a man who believes in soul mates and happily-ever-afters."

Before he came to Bliss, he would've agreed wholeheartedly. But after being around all the happily married couples in the town, he'd started to rethink his position. Maybe there was such a thing as a soul mate. And maybe one day, he would find his.

He didn't know why an image of Autumn popped into his head. Autumn certainly wasn't his soul mate. He desired her. The kiss they'd shared in the bakery was a perfect example. And he liked conversing with her. Every day, he ran past the bakery around the time she got off work and stopped to talk for a while. He'd talk about town gossip and the football team. She'd talk about some book she was reading and the customers that came into the bakery. He wished she would stand up to Summer and tell her that she didn't want to work at the bakery anymore, but he knew it was something she'd have to do for herself.

"I'm sorry I couldn't use my matchmaking skills on you," Ms. Marble said as he strapped on the holster and gun. "But there are plenty of other people in town who need to find the right partner. In fact, I'm working on getting the perfect couple together as we speak."

Maverick quick drew and pointed the gun at the guy in the painting over the bed. "Who are your new guinea pigs?"

"Cord and Autumn."

Maverick dropped the gun on his foot. It was a good thing that he had on boots or he'd be sporting a broken toe.

Ms. Marble gave him a stern look. "After witnessing the kiss in the bakery, it became obvious that you're planning on having a little dalliance with her while you're here in town. But I'm afraid I can't allow that. Autumn isn't the type of woman who can give her body without first giving her heart."

Obviously, Ms. Marble didn't know Autumn very well. She did, however, know him. He *had* been thinking more and more about having "a dalliance" with Autumn. She wasn't as crazy as he'd once thought. She had just been suffocated by her sisters and was a little confused about who she really was. But he could deal with a small personality disorder for a night of raunchy sex like they'd had in Houston.

What he couldn't deal with was the thought of her being paired up with Cord Evans. He was

Ryker's father, for God's sake. Which meant he was old enough to be Autumn's dad. That was just creepy. And Autumn probably thought so too. She was just going along with it so she wouldn't hurt Ms. Marble's feelings.

But Ms. Marble cared nothing about hurting his feelings. "I like you, Maverick," she said. "You're a good man. And if I thought for a second that you were the type of man who would make Autumn happy, I'd never let you get out of Bliss." She shook her head. "But sadly, you aren't that man. She wants a home and family, and you don't. You still have some wild oats to sow. Now, Cord Evans, on the other hand, has sowed all his wild oats and is ready to settle down."

"Because he's old," he snapped.

Ms. Marble raised her eyebrows. "Not so old. According to Spring, Autumn has a major crush on him."

That did it. Maverick was just annoyed before. Now he was out-and-out pissed. "A crush? Are you kidding me?"

Ms. Marble did not look like she was kidding or amused. "Watch your tone, young man. I never kid. Cord and Autumn are on Waylon and Spring's front porch as we speak." She headed for the door. "Now if you'll excuse me, I have some marshmallow ghosts to make for Boo Night."

Once she was gone, Maverick stared at the closed door and tried to process the fact that Autumn and Cord were together. But he couldn't. He couldn't think about Autumn being with anyone but . . . him.

He jerked open his door and took the stairs two

at a time. When he reached the bottom, instead of heading around the front of Ms. Marble's house, he slipped around the back. There were no fences or hedges dividing the backyards so it was easy to get to Waylon and Spring's house.

It was dark outside. Only a sliver of moon hung in the sky. Maverick tripped over a hose and almost went down before he regained his balance and pressed against the side of the house. He moved to the edge of the porch, then leaned around the corner. The porch was elevated so he had to look through the slats of the railing in order to see anything.

Sure enough, Cord and Autumn were sitting on the porch. They weren't cuddled together on the porch swing. Autumn was sitting on the swing and Cord was sitting in a chair. Still, they seemed to be having an intimate conversation. They leaned close to one another and were talking in hushed voices. Which pissed Maverick off even more. He tried to justify his anger as simply being protective of a college friend. The old guy had to be a good twenty years older than Autumn.

Of course, he didn't look that much older. His body looked fit, and there was just a touch of silver at his temples—something that women probably found attractive. And he *was* a major celebrity.

That would explain why Autumn had a crush on him. She seemed to have a thing for celebrities. And Maverick knew exactly what happened when Autumn had a thing for you. Just the thought of her playing naughty pony and horse trainer with the guy made Maverick want to punch his fist through the side of the house.

A deep growl had him glancing down. The droopy hound dog that looked so laid-back and nonthreatening when sleeping on Waylon and Spring's porch looked pretty intimidating in the dark with his teeth bared.

"Easy boy," he whispered.

The dog's growl grew even lower and more threatening. Before Maverick could take a step, he was attacked. Not by the dog, but by a little gray cat with really sharp claws.

"Shit!" He shook his leg, but the cat held on. The dog had stopped growling and was watching as if he thought it was all pretty funny.

"What are you doing?"

Maverick stopped shaking his leg and glanced up to see Autumn leaning over the railing of the porch. Cord Evans stood behind her with a big smile on his face.

"Evenin', Coach," he said with a deep drawl. "Looks like you got a cat problem. I hope you're not going to shoot it with your six-shooter."

Maverick hadn't even realized that he'd run out of his apartment in his gunslinger outfit. Now he really felt like a fool. Trying to ignore the searing pain in his calf, he reached down to scratch the cat's head. "Nope. No problem." The cat released him and dropped to the ground, but the dog continued to growl.

"If you'll excuse me for a minute, Cord," Autumn said. A second later, she was striding around the corner of the house. She scooped up the cat and patted the dog on the head until he stopped growling. "What are you doing, Maverick?"

"I was just . . . cutting across your lawn to go for

a run."

She gave him the onceover. "In jeans and boots? And what's up with the gun?"

He ignored the questions and got to the one that was eating him alive. "Do you like that guy?"

She blinked. "Cord? Of course. He's an extremely nice man."

"He's old."

"He's in his mid-forties. That's not old."

"It is if you're in your late twenties. He probably can't even get it up."

The sound of a throat being cleared had him glancing back at the porch. Cord was still standing there. "Things are working just fine, son." He put on his cowboy hat. "But I can see that you and Miss Hadley have some talking to do." He nodded at Autumn. "I'm glad you called me. We'll talk later."

Maverick was about to say "Over my dead body" when Autumn cut him off. "I'm sorry for the interruption, Cord. Thank you so much for coming. Between the two of us, we should be able to figure something out."

"That might be harder than you think. That little gal is as skittish as an abused filly." He winked. "Good thing those happen to be my forte." He glanced at Maverick and grinned. "You might want to stick to the sidewalk when you're running, Coach. It's a lot less dangerous—of course, you can't really eavesdrop from the sidewalk."

Maverick cringed. As soon as Cord was gone, Autumn turned to him. "You were spying on us?"

When he couldn't come up with a good lie, he took the offensive. "I figured turnabout was fair play. You spied on me the other day while I was cleaning up Ms. Marble's yard."

"That was because you were half—" She cut off, and Maverick smiled.

"Naked?"

Even in the dark, he could see her cheeks brighten. "Don't try to change the subject. Why were you spying on us?" She must've figured out the answer because her breath caught. "You're jealous?"

His answer came out sounding like a twelve-year-old girl. "Not." He quickly changed the subject. "What do you need to figure out with him?"

She stared at him for a long moment, and he thought she was going to push him on the jealousy issue. Instead, she let it drop. "Christie Buchanan. She's the woman who came to the bakery that day I was getting on you about Race's bullying."

"The one you refused to hire."

"My mistake. Hopefully, one I can fix." She turned and headed back to the porch, and both he and the hound dog followed.

"So you want to offer her a job at the bakery?"

"I already did, but she's as stubborn as my sister Summer." She sat down on the porch swing and placed the cat on her lap. "I'm hoping Cord can help me convince her."

Maverick could've sat in the same chair as Cord had been sitting in, but instead he sat down next to her on the swing. "I thought she was working for Cord."

"She is, but only part-time. She'd make a lot more working full-time at the bakery."

"And it would take some of the baking responsibilities off you."

She smiled. "Exactly. Maybe I could take her place working for Cord."

The thought of her spending every day with some rodeo star did not sit well at all. "I don't think you should work for Cord." When she glanced at him, he shrugged. "I mean, haven't you had enough of being someone's assistant?"

She sat back against the swing. "You're right. Besides, I did more than enough online marketing and social media when we owned the store. But I do think Christie would like working at the bakery. And if she worked at the bakery, she could drop Carrie Anne off at school on her way and Carrie Anne could walk to the bakery after school."

"That little girl is quite the character." He pushed the swing with his foot. "She wants to be part of the football team."

"Not anymore. Now she wants to have an ostrich ranch."

He laughed. "An ostrich ranch? Where did she get that?"

"Cord Evans."

His laughter died. "Football is cooler."

She glanced over at him and grinned. "Not than an ostrich ranch."

"Yeah, you're right. An ostrich ranch would be pretty cool. So I guess Carrie Anne and you both have a crush on an old rodeo dude."

She stroked the cat's back. The cat looked like he was thoroughly enjoying it. Maverick could relate. He'd thoroughly enjoyed being touched by her too.

"I don't have a crush on Cord. Or you," Autumn

said.

The tension in his shoulders released, but he still felt a little annoyed. Or maybe disappointed. "I kind of got that when you hauled off and slapped me."

"I'm sorry. That was uncalled for."

"I deserved it. What you do with your life is none of my business."

They swung for a while before she spoke. "You were right. I do need to become my own person. But it's hard to become your own person when you don't know who you are."

He should've kept his mouth shut. He'd just got finished saying that her life was none of his business. But damned if it didn't feel like his business. "I think you know who you are, Autumn. I think you're just afraid of letting your family see that person. Afraid that they won't love someone with flaws as much as they love the perfect person you've tried so hard to be. But I think you're wrong. The Hadleys seem like the kind of people who love unconditionally." Unlike his family who struggled with love. Except for Robby. Robby had loved unconditionally.

A cold breeze kicked up and sent a dry leaf tumbling across the porch, and Autumn shivered. Without much thought, Maverick placed his arm around her shoulders. She tensed for just a second, then relaxed against him.

He continued to push the swing, and they glided back and forth as the sliver of moon made its way through the star-filled sky. Crickets kept time with the creak of the porch swing and the symphony was soothing and relaxing. A breeze fluttered Autumn's hair against his arm and filled the air with the scent of shampoo and cookies.

For the first time in a very long time, Maverick felt at peace.

CHAPTER EIGHTEEN

BOO NIGHT TURNED OUT TO be a big success. All the businesses on Main Street decorated the front of their shops with strings of orange pumpkin lights and their windows with lit jack-o-lanterns and ghosts and ghouls. There were groupings of pumpkins and cornstalks beneath every streetlight. And the hanging flower planters were filled with bright yellow mums.

One of the farmers had made a maze in his cornfield and was shuttling people to it in his horse-drawn wagon filled with hay bales. A Frankenstein-themed bounce house had been set up in the parking lot of the First Baptist Church and a country and western band and dance floor had been set up in the parking lot of the Watering Hole bar. Lucy's Place Diner had a special of Bloody Brains (meatloaf covered in ketchup) and Green Monster Pie (key lime pie with candy eyeballs). The Tender Heart Museum had been turned into a haunted museum with the football team dressed as Old West zombies who scared people as they walked through. And at the bakery, there were dozens of cupcakes and cookies decorated like ghosts, spiders, and jack-o-lanterns, and a huge cake that looked like a miniature haunted house.

Autumn had helped frost all the baked goods, but she'd left the baking and detailed decorating to Summer and her new assistant. Autumn and Cord had finally worn Christie down, and she'd accepted the job at the bakery. She'd also enrolled Carrie Anne in school and let Cord help her fix her car—but only if he let her keep working as his assistant to pay him back. She seemed to be able to handle her job at the bakery and social media for Cord too.

But Autumn flat refused to let Christie work the bakery for Boo Night. She didn't want Carrie Anne missing out on all the fun. Besides, Spring had offered to help work the counter so that left Autumn to mingle on the street, handing out mini-muffins to anyone who wanted them. The weather was perfect. There was just enough chill in the air to feel like fall, but not one cloud to cover the big harvest moon and scattering of stars.

"Are those Maybelline Marble's cinnamon-swirl muffins?"

Autumn turned to find Emmett Daily sitting on a bench. He was dressed as a scarecrow. He had painted triangle patches around his eyes and on his nose and real straw stuck out of his flannel shirt and the straw hat on his head.

"No, they're pumpkin." She held out the basket. "Would you like one?"

"Don't mind if I do." He took a mini-muffin and popped it into his mouth. Once he'd chewed and swallowed, he helped himself to another. "These are almost as good as Maybelline's. Did you make them?"

"No. I've retired from the kitchen after I almost burned down the bakery."

He grinned, showing off his chipped tooth. "That was quite the ruckus. I watched the entire thing go down while I was sitting in front of the gas station playing dominos with Old Man Sims." A pile of straw slipped out of his shirt, and he picked it up and stuffed it back in. "Good thing I have on my long johns, this straw is itchy as heck."

"I'm going to assume you're the scarecrow from the Wizard of Oz since your wife is dressed like Dorothy," she said.

He scowled. "She wanted me to go as Toto, but I flat out refused to dress up in a furry suit with pointy ears. A man has to keep some kind of dignity." He studied Autumn's costume. "Usually, I can tell you girls apart by your hair. But with it tucked up in that calico bonnet, I'm at a loss."

He wasn't the first person who didn't know which triplet she was. Which wasn't surprising since she and her sisters were dressed in almost identical 19th-century clothing—long dresses with petticoats and bonnets. Summer had wanted to go as female superheroes, but Spring had thought it fitting for Lucy's great-granddaughters to go as mail-order brides.

"I'm Autumn," she said.

He nodded. "The shy, reserved one."

A few weeks ago, the description wouldn't have bothered her. But it bothered her now. And it was all Maverick's fault for pointing out that she didn't know who she was or what she wanted out of life.

She had yet to find the answer, but she did know that she didn't want to be thought of as the shy, reserved triplet anymore.

"I wouldn't say I'm shy or reserved. I just don't talk unless I have something worth saying."

"Then I'd say you're the smart one. Which is probably why you've caught our coach's eye."

"Excuse me?"

Emmett grinned sheepishly. "The entire town has noticed him stopping by the bakery on his runs. And since he doesn't eat sweets, I'm pretty sure he's sweet on something else."

She shook her head. "I'm sure he's just checking to make sure that his team isn't eating too much sugar."

Emmett lifted an eyebrow. "You're not interested in our coach, I take it?"

She was too interested. That was her problem. Since they had cuddled on the porch swing, he was all she could think about. She should've run into the house and never looked back. She shouldn't have snuggled into his arms and started to dream about something that was never going to happen. Her mama had taught her the problem with putting your hopes in the wrong man. She wasn't going to do that. She was too smart to fall for a man like Maverick Murdoch. A man who had his heart set on leaving.

"No, I'm not interested," she said.

"That's probably a good thing. I like Maverick, and he's sure done a good job of coaching our boys to victory—last night, they beat the socks off the opposing team in the first playoff game. But I'm not so sure he's gotten over his past. Of course, losing a brother is a hard thing to get over."

She was stunned. Maverick had never mentioned having a brother. "He lost his brother? When?"

"Right after he got drafted by the Chicago Bears. There was a brief mention of it in an article I read about rookies."

No wonder he hadn't done well with the Bears. He'd been grieving. "I didn't know," she whispered. "He never said a word."

"I guess some pain hurts so much that you just can't talk about it. I couldn't talk about what happened in Vietnam for years after I came back. I buried all the pain deep inside until it came out in other ways—sudden angry outbursts over nothing, nightmares, panic attacks. Joanna was the one who saved me. She kept after me until I went to a therapist and joined a group of veterans who were suffering from PTSD. Still, it took months before I could talk about the atrocities I witnessed. And if Maverick didn't ever mention his brother, it sounds like he's doing the same thing. Which might explain why he choked in the NFL."

Autumn tried to imagine what she would do if one of her siblings died. She'd be devastated. Completely lost. And that was how Maverick had looked when she had seen him walking down the street in Houston. He had looked lost. When she'd said his name, he'd looked relieved. Not because he still had a thing for Summer, but because he had hoped that an old friend might help him get found. Instead, all Autumn had done was trick him and use him. She had thought Maverick was the shallow, selfish one. But it turned out that it was her.

"I need to go." She got up from the bench. "Thank you, Mr. Daily. Thank you for your service and for sharing your story with me." She turned and hurried back to the bakery. There was a long line of people waiting to place an order with Spring. Autumn should've moved behind the counter and helped her sister. Instead, she headed into the kitchen where Summer was decorating cupcakes.

"How did everyone like the pumpkin spice muffins?" Summer asked.

"They loved them." She set the basket on the counter. "Did Maverick ever mention his brother?"

Summer sent her a confused look. "What?"

"Maverick. Did he ever mention his brother?"

Summer went back to decorating. "Umm, I don't know. Yeah, I think he did. A younger brother who played high school football. Robby, I think."

Robby. The story Maverick had told her wasn't about his friend. It had been about his brother.

Summer held out a knife and a bowl of frosting. "I'm not going to let you near an oven again, but you can help me frost."

Normally, she would've taken the knife, but there was someone else who needed help more. "I can't. There's something I have to do." She turned and headed for the back door.

She searched the crowd from one end of the Main Street to the other for Maverick. When she saw zombie cowboys Stuart and Race coming out of the Tender Heart Museum, she hurried over to them. Before she could reach them, Race saw her and took off.

Which Stuart thought was hilarious.

"A zombie is scared of a mail-order bride."

She would've laughed too if she wasn't on a mission. "Have you seen Coach Murdoch?"

"Yeah. He came into the haunted house a little bit ago to make sure the team wasn't screwing around and breaking anything. He was pissed when he found Race and me horsing around."

"Is he still in the museum?"

Stuart shook his head. "He left with Carrie Anne and her mom. Carrie Anne challenged him to a bouncing contest in the Frankenstein house."

She found Maverick bouncing with Carrie Anne in the Frankenstein bounce house. The little girl was dressed like a vampire, her black cape flapping behind her as she jumped. Maverick was dressed in the same outfit he'd been wearing the other night—minus the gun, boots, and cowboy hat. In the jeans and a bib front western shirt, he looked like a young John Wayne.

When he glanced over and saw Autumn, he smiled his devastating smile. "That *Little House on the Prairie* hat suits you, Autumn Layne."

She didn't know why tears filled her eyes. Maybe because he recognized her when most people couldn't. Or maybe because he knew her middle name. Or maybe because she realized how very wrong she'd been about him. She hadn't used a bad boy quarterback for her little sex games. She'd used a good man who'd been hurting.

He must've read her sad expression because he stopped jumping. "What's wrong?"

Her intentions had been to apologize and tell him how sorry she was about his brother. But now she realized that it was a stupid idea. Maverick wouldn't want her apology or her sympathy. If he'd wanted her to know about his brother, he would've told her.

"Nothing's wrong," she said. "I was just watching you and Carrie Anne jump."

"Don't just watch, come on in. It's more fun than I remembered."

"I should get back and help at the bakery."

He squinted his eyes and tipped his head. "Is that what you want to do or is that what you think you should do?"

She thought for only a second before she sat down on the little bench outside the bounce house to take off her cowboy boots. As she was tugging the first one off, Maverick knelt in front of her to tug off the other one.

"I didn't realized that mail-order brides wore pink cowboy boots," he teased.

"Joanna Daily loaned me and my sisters these authentic mail-order bride costumes, but the shoes didn't fit so we had to improvise."

He lifted the boot and his gaze narrowed on the C and E branded into the stacked leather of the heel. "Cord Evans?"

She nodded. "He made boots for all Summer and Ryker's bridal attendants."

"Hmm?" He carelessly tossed the boot to the ground before he took her hand and helped her up from the bench.

It wasn't easy getting into the slit opening of the bouncer in a long dress. After three failed tries, Maverick finally gave her some help by placing a hand on her butt and shoving. She landed inside in a tangle of calico skirts and petticoats.

"Hey!" Carrie Anne squealed as she jumped over Autumn.

Maverick laughed as he crawled in. "She's quite the kangaroo."

"Kangaroo! Kangaroo!" Carrie Anne bounced by, barely missing Autumn's head.

"Is it okay if she jumps?" Autumn asked. "Christie mentioned that she had asthma."

Maverick got to his feet. "Her mom said that her new insurance is paying for a medication that seems to be working better at controlling Carrie's asthma." He lifted an eyebrow. "I didn't realize bakeries had such good employee health insurance."

Autumn grinned up at him. "I convinced Summer it was essential to offer good benefits if she wanted good employees . . . ones who wouldn't burn down her bakery."

He laughed, and then held out a hand. "I've learned that if you don't want to get jumped on, it's best to stay on your feet."

That was easier said than done. Autumn had trouble keeping her balance in the long dress and ended up on her butt more times than she could count. Maverick and Carrie Anne thought it was pretty funny. Frustrated and more than a little annoyed, Autumn finally gathered the hem of her dress and petticoat and pulled them through her legs, tucking them into the sash around her waist. She knew she looked ridiculous, especially with her polka-dotted boot socks, but she didn't care.

Once she was free of her skirts, she could bounce as high as Maverick and Carrie Anne. It *was* fun. In fact, it was more fun than she'd had in a long time. Even when she was a child, she couldn't remember enjoying something so much. She had been too busy trying to be the perfect kid who never got too rowdy.

"I'm bouncing higher!" Carrie Anne yelled.

"No, you're not," Maverick said. "I've got you by a good foot."

"And I've got you by another foot." To prove it, Autumn jumped closer to Maverick. Unfortunately, she got caught in the rebound of his last bounce and ended up sailing right into him. They both went tumbling. Maverick ended up on his back with her sprawled on top of him. When she lifted her head, their gazes locked.

"I feel like we've been here before," he said. "If I remember correctly, you prefer being on top."

Her cheeks heated, but she didn't look away from those teasing blue eyes. "And if I remember correctly, you preferred it too."

A flash of surprise registered on his face before he smiled a slow, sexy smile. "You remember correctly." His gaze lowered to her mouth, and for a just a second, she thought he was going to kiss her. Instead, he lifted her off him and got to his feet.

They continued to jump until other kids showed up and the bounce house got too crowded.

"Come on, Kangaroo," Maverick yelled to Carrie Anne. "Let's go find your mama."

They ran into Christie on Main Street, juggling three cups of apple cider. "Hi, Audie," she said as handed off the drinks to Maverick and Carrie Anne. "Did you need me to relieve you at the bakery?" She held out the last cup to Autumn, but Autumn shook her head.

"No, thank you. And the crowds have dwindled

down so you don't need to help." She smiled at Carrie Anne. "But you might want to stop by and get the Dracula cupcake I saved for you."

"Yippee!" Carrie Anne hopped around, sloshing cider out of her cup. "Can we get it tonight, Mama? Ple-e-ease!"

Christie took her daughter's cup. "Okay, but you can't eat it tonight. You've had enough sweets. Now thank Coach Murdoch for keeping an eye you and Autumn for saving you a cupcake."

"She doesn't need to thank me," Maverick said. "I had as much fun as she did."

"It's true, Mama." Carrie Anne shrugged. "'Course, I don't think he liked jumping as much as watching Autumn's boobies bounce."

Autumn's face burned as Maverick choked. Even Christie looked stunned. She quickly recovered and took her daughter's hand. "If you'll excuse us, my daughter needs a reminder on what is and isn't appropriate to say." She pulled a confused Carrie Anne down the street with her.

When they were gone, Maverick looked at Autumn.

They both burst out laughing.

CHAPTER NINETEEN

AUTUMN LAUGHED UNTIL TEARS CAME to her eyes and her sides hurt. When she finally stopped laughing, she glanced over to see Maverick standing there watching her with a big smile on his face.

"You're a belly laugher."

"What?"

"A belly laugher." He took a sip of his apple cider. "You laugh from deep down in your belly. And don't look so offended. It's a good thing. It means you're thoroughly enjoying life. Robby used to laugh like that."

Her heart tightened. She started to tell Maverick that she knew who Robby was, but then she remembered what Emmett had said about it being hard to talk when you were in so much pain. She hadn't been able to talk about her mother after she passed away, no matter how much the school counselors had tried to get her to. But if Maverick couldn't talk about his brother, maybe he could talk about his friend.

"You mentioned your friend Robby before."

Trying to act nonchalant, she pushed her bonnet off her head and smoothed her hair. "It sounds like you two were close."

She watched his smile fade and his eyes fill with so much hurt it took her breath away. "We were." He finished off his cider before tossing the cup in a nearby trash can. "Look, I'm pretty tired from all that bouncing so I'm going to head back to Ms. Marble's."

She should've let him go, but that was no longer a possibility. "Mind if I walk with you? I'm pretty tired myself."

He didn't say anything as she fell in step next to him. They headed down a side street away from the crowds. The moon looked brighter away from the town lights. It hung in the sky like a huge glowing white pumpkin. The wind had kicked up, and she rubbed her arms.

"You said 'were.' Is Robby no longer your friend?"

Their cowboy boots clicked against the sidewalk for what felt like hours before he answered. "He died." There was a lifetime of pain in the two words. A lump formed in her throat, and they walked for a good two blocks more before she was able to talk around it.

"My mom died when I was eleven. Even though I knew she had cancer, I was completely blindsided. I thought my mom would get better. She was strong like Summer, vivacious like Spring, and gregarious like Dirk. When she held you, you felt completely safe. Like nothing in the world could ever harm you. She used to rock and sing us to sleep every night—even as we got older. My siblings would fall asleep quickly, but I only pretended to be asleep. I wanted to listen to her singing until the very last verse of the song." She smiled at the memory. "No one will ever love me like she did. She loved me, whether I was perfect or not."

They continued to walk, his stride shortening until their boots clicked as one against the cement. "Robby loved me like that," he said in a voice almost too low to hear. "He thought I was a god. He never saw any of my flaws."

"You don't seem to have many."

He glanced over at her. "Thus says the woman who called me self-centered and selfish."

"I was just mad."

He shook his head. "You were right. I am selfish. Too selfish to read the signs. Too selfish to realize that my brother needed help." If he recognized his slip, he didn't correct it.

"Why did he need help?"

They walked another block before he answered. "He had bulimia. Something I didn't even know boys could get. I thought only girls got it. When Robby got skinnier and skinnier, I just thought he was working out and trying hard to get in shape. I didn't realize he was using diet pills and laxatives and purging after he ate."

Autumn felt as if her heart was breaking. She reached out and took his hand. He didn't pull away. Instead he linked their fingers and held tight—as if he was worried she might slip away. She wasn't going anywhere.

"He died of cardiac arrest." He took a deep breath and released it. "How can a twenty-year-old die of heart failure? It doesn't make any sense.

Twenty-year-olds don't die. They finish college and get jobs and fall in love. They have kids and a couple of dogs and mortgages. They don't die and get buried in the cold ground."

Autumn couldn't help the tears that leaked from her eyes as he continued. "But Robby did. He died in his college dorm room all by himself—his parents were on a cruise and his brother was off trying to be the best quarterback who ever lived. When I heard, I felt like I was being sucked into this black hole of grief and disbelief and the only way to keep from disappearing was to pretend like it was just a bad accident that I had nothing to do with."

He stopped and lifted his face to the moon, his perfect features bathed in golden light. He had never looked more handsome or more heartbreaking. "But I had everything to do with it. I was the one who gave him a superstar big brother to emulate. I was the one who ranted on and on about the importance of diet and exercise. And for what? So I could throw a football farther than anyone else? So people would say that I was the best NFL quarterback who ever lived?"

His fingers tightened almost painful on her hand. "Who gives a shit? I don't care about throwing a stupid football. I don't care about the NFL. I care that my brother isn't here anymore. That I'll never get to hug him, or play catch with him, or hear his belly laugh. That's all I fuckin' care about."

Autumn wanted to say something to ease his pain. But she knew there was nothing to say that would make the pain go away. He had to go through it, just like she'd had to go through it. But he didn't have to go through it alone. She released his hand

and put her arms around his waist, pressing her head to his hurting heart. "I'm so sorry, Maverick. I'm so sorry."

He stood there for a moment before his arms tightened around her. She could feel his heart beating beneath her cheek, his breath fanning the hair on the top of her head. Wrapped in his arms, she took his grief as her own and accepted what she had fought so hard against.

She had a connection with this man. A connection that went beyond crushes . . . and even love. Her soul had recognized its other half the moment Summer had introduced them. Her body had recognized its other half the moment he'd first touched her in Houston. And her spirit recognized its other half right now. At this very moment, she realized that Maverick was the only man she would ever love with everything she had. The realization was overwhelming and a little terrifying. Especially when she knew he didn't feel the same way.

He stiffened in her arms. "Are you crying?"

She hadn't realized it, but tears were trickling down her cheeks and wetting his shirt. "No." A sob broke free.

He drew back and lifted her chin. "Oh, Autumn, I didn't mean to make you cry. I shouldn't have told you about Robby. I've kept it in this long, I should've continued to keep it in."

She blinked back her tears. "No, I'm glad you told me. You need to talk about it. And you're wrong to blame yourself for Robby's death. There's a difference between watching your diet and exercising and what Robby was doing. He had an illness, Maverick."

He dropped his arms. "And I should've gotten him help. I should've known."

"I did the same thing after my mom died. I blamed myself for not being a nicer kid. I thought that if I'd just been better behaved, God wouldn't have taken her away from me."

"But I thought you *were* the sweet, well-behaved triplet."

"Not when I was little. According to Granny Bon, I was the one who threw temper tantrums when I didn't get my way, bit Summer for taking my favorite teddy bear, and told my mom to take Dirk back and exchange him for a girl when she first brought him home from the hospital."

Maverick studied her. "So it was only after your mother died that you became the good triplet?"

"Guilt can do that to you. Plus, I didn't want to be an added burden to my grandmother."

He smiled. "You still throw tantrums with me."

"There are a lot of things I do with you that I don't do with anyone else." She wanted the words back as soon as they were out, but it was too late.

He lowered his gaze to her mouth. "Like having naughty affairs?" There was a sparkle of possessiveness in his eyes when he lifted them that made her knees suddenly feel like melting butter.

She cleared her throat. "I'm not that naughty."

He stepped closer and pulled her back into his arms. "It's okay, Autumn." He lowered his head and spoke against her lips. "I promise I won't tell a soul ..." He sucked her bottom lip into his mouth, then released it. "If you should want to get naughty with me again."

She should pull away and run for home. Nothing

good would come from having sex with Maverick again. Especially when it would just be sex to him and much more to her. And if she had learned anything from her mama it was that an imbalance of love in a relationship only caused pain.

But she didn't run away. Instead, she slid her hands into his hair and kissed him. The heat they'd been holding back flared to life at the first touch of their lips. He moaned and pulled her closer as the kiss became deep . . . and wet . . . and completely inappropriate for the middle of the street on Halloween night when little costumed kids were wandering around.

She pulled back. "We can't do this here in the middle—"

Before she could finish, he had her hand and was pulling her down the street so quickly she had to run to keep up. They bypassed Waylon and Spring's house, and when they reached the stairs that lead to his apartment, he scooped her up in his arms. On the way up the stairs, he kissed her again—a long, lazy kiss that tasted of spicy apple cider. He didn't stop kissing her until they were inside his apartment with the door closed.

It was dark, the only light coming from the moon that shone through the thin curtains. Autumn was thankful for the lack of light. It was silly, but she suddenly felt nervous. All the other times they'd been together, she'd been playing a part. The part of an assertive, confident woman who knew what she was doing in the bedroom. But now that she was herself, she didn't feel confident. She felt inadequate. What if she was awful in bed? What if Maverick was disappointed?

While her stomach jumped with nerves, he kissed his way down her neck, untied her bonnet and tossed it aside, and then slowly unbuttoned her dress. He slipped it off her shoulders and the yards of calico pooled around her feet as his hand reached for her bra. He froze when he came in contact with her undergarments. "What in the hell do you have on?"

"A chemise, corset, and petticoats."

There was laughter in his voice. "This I've got to see." He reached for the light switch, but she stopped him.

"Leave it off . . . please."

He hesitated for only a second. "Okay, but I'll want to see them on you later. Especially the corset." He pulled her into arms and kissed her. She tried to concentrate on kissing him back, but it was impossible when her mind was filled with self-doubt. After only a second, he drew back. "Okay, what's wrong? Have you changed your mind?"

She cleared her throat. "I'm a little nervous."

She thought he would point out how crazy that was, but he didn't. Instead, he released her. A second later, she heard a boot dropping to the floor, followed by the other one. There was the muffled sound of clothes being removed before the lamp on the nightstand came on. Maverick was lying on the bed completely naked except for his cowboy hat.

His gaze slid over the old fashioned undergarments she wore as he tucked his hands behind his head. "I purchased you, pretty mail-order bride, but I'm not going to keep you if you don't show me the goods."

She blinked. "Excuse me?"

"Strip off them undies."

She suddenly realized that Maverick was giving her a chance to be someone other than the sister who had to be perfect. She could be whoever she wanted to be with him. He was okay with it.

Her nerves evaporated, and she slowly and seductively started to remove her undergarments. It took a while, but Maverick didn't seem to mind. He lay on the bed with his hands tucked behind his head and his gaze intent as each piece of clothing fell to the floor.

Once she was naked, she placed her hands on her hips. "Will I do, cowboy?"

His gaze was hot and thorough. "I think you'll do quite nicely. Now come here."

She walked to the bed, expecting him to reach for her. But he kept his hands behind his head, giving her unspoken permission to do what she would. In Houston, she'd rushed their time together so he wouldn't recognize her identity—and so she wouldn't see their relationship as anything more than sex. Now that she'd accepted her love for him, she wanted to slow everything down. She wanted seconds to become minutes and minutes to become hours.

She sat down on the bed and touched him. She could've touched any of his perfectly sculpted muscles. Instead, she touched the pale skin on the underside of his arm. Most of his skin was tanned and scarred from being exposed to the sun and hard football hits. But this skin was soft and vulnerable—like his heart. She used one finger to trace a thin blue vein along its crooked path to the dark blond hair of his armpit. Before she could reach it, his muscles jumped.

"I'm ticklish," he said, but he didn't lower his arms from beneath his head. He just bit his bottom lip as if preparing to endure her tickling. She didn't know why that turned her on. Maybe because he was offering up the most vulnerable parts of himself. He'd done the same thing by telling her about Robby. He might not love her, but he trusted her. And for a woman whose father had given her major trust issues, trust was huge.

She bypassed his ticklish armpit and ran her fingertips over his broad shoulder and along his collarbone. Who would've thought that a collarbone would be so beautiful? But it was, and so were the swells of his pectoral muscles with their brown penny-sized nipples. And the indention between his ribcage. And the ripples of his stomach. And the dip of his navel. But what was more beautiful that anything else was the muscle that jutted out from the nest of dark golden hair. Its length and hardness spoke of his desire.

For her.

Autumn.

She traced one finger up the velvety length before she fisted him and stroked from base to tip. A moan came from deep in his throat, but he remained perfectly still beneath her hands. She rubbed her thumb over the tip and spread the drop of moisture before stroking him again. His stomach muscles spasmed as she lowered her head and took him into her mouth. His breath rushed out and his hands tangled in her hair as his hips lifted off the mattress to meet her mouth on the down stroke. She continued until she glanced up and saw his head thrown back and his teeth gritted. She knew he was close, and she wanted to send him over the edge. But she also wanted to share the moment of release with him. Especially the first time of loving him as herself.

After one more deep pull, she moved over his body and straddled him. It took only a slight adjustment before she had him completely sheathed inside her. His passion-filled gaze locked with hers as he settled his hands on her hips, holding her as if he never wanted to let her go. She knew how he felt. She didn't want to let him go either.

The first lift and downward thrust was like coming home. And with each thrust after, the truth became clearer and clearer. This *was* her home. Her other half. Her missing puzzle piece. Her soul mate. And suddenly she understood why her mama had always taken her daddy back. It was this feeling of wholeness—this feeling of total and complete rightness.

Their gazes remained locked as their bodies found the perfect rhythm to feed the desire that consumed them. When they came, they came together. A chain reaction of intense orgasms that had words of love trembling on Autumn's lips.

But before she could say them, Maverick spoke. Not words of love. Just a name. A name that made her heart smile and her soul sing.

"Autumn."

CHAPTER TWENTY

"I NOW GET WHY EVERYONE GOES crazy over Ms. Marbles' cinnamon-swirl muffins. These things are amazing." Maverick polished off his second muffin and took his time licking every last moist crumb from his fingers.

When he was finished, he glanced over to see Autumn studying him exactly how she used to study him in college. The intensity of her gaze used to make him feel uncomfortable. Now, it made him feel special. Like he was something worth looking at. It had been a long time since he'd felt worthy. After Robby's death, he'd felt worthless. Which was probably why he'd lost his football mojo. He no longer believed in his ability to win.

At the moment, he felt like a winner.

Autumn sat cross-legged in his bed with the sheet draped over her lap. The morning light filtered in through the crack in the curtain and spilled over her pretty pink nipples and her sexy, mussed hair. Right after they'd made love last night, she had insisted on going back to Waylon and Spring's so her sister wouldn't worry. He thought she wouldn't return. But only thirty minutes later, she'd knocked on his door wearing a trench coat and carrying a plate of Ms. Marble's muffins. Under the coat she'd worn nothing but the old-fashioned corset. Which explained why they hadn't gotten any sleep that night. And why he was so hungry the following morning.

"For a man who hates sugar, you certainly enjoy it," Autumn said with a slight smile.

"It's all your fault. I could've lived without Ms. Marble's muffins if you hadn't brought them into my apartment and enticed me."

Her eyebrows lifted. "Enticed you? All I did was eat one."

"That was enticing." He leaned over and kissed her lips. She tasted of cinnamon, sugar, and Autumn. It was a heady combination. "As was the trench coat." He drew back. "How did you sneak passed Spring?"

"I didn't sneak. I told her and Waylon where I'd been and where I was going."

"And she was okay with that?"

"I didn't ask her. I'm a big girl. I think I can make my own decisions."

He grinned. "It's about time you realized that. So you just grabbed a plate of muffins and said I'm heading over to have hot sex with Maverick?"

She playfully swatted him. Which made him realize that Carrie Anne was right. He did like to watch Autumn's boobies bounce. "No. I just told her I wasn't going to be home until this morning. And I didn't get the muffins from Waylon's and Spring's. I found them on your doorstep. I guess Ms. Marble dropped them by."

"That's funny. Ms. Marble knows I don't eat sugar." He gave her another kiss. "But I'm thinking that maybe it's time to put a little sugar into my diet. I like sweet much better than I thought."

He assumed the compliment would make her happy, but her brow knitted in a frown. "I'm not sweet. I have a temper. It's not as hot as Summer's, but it's there." She paused. "And I've also accepted that I have a wild streak."

He bit back a smile. "Really? I never would've guessed."

Her forehead wrinkled. "Don't laugh at me. It's not funny. Last night when I was talking about my mom dying, I realized just how long I've been keeping up this charade of being the sweet Hadley triplet. I did it for so long that I actually started to believe it. And it's terrifying to realize that the person you thought you were isn't who you are at all."

He brushed a strand of hair behind her ear. "Just because you have a temper and enjoy sex doesn't mean you aren't sweet, Autumn. You are one of the sweetest women I know. You would do anything for anyone. You worked at two jobs that you hated for your sister Summer. You helped Christie get a job and insurance and Carrie Anne get enrolled in school. And you helped a screwed-up quarterback finally face his brother's death. That's pretty darned sweet, if you ask me. Just because you're a triplet doesn't mean you have to fit into a certain groove. If Spring and Summer have certain traits that doesn't mean you can't have them also. And you can have traits that are solely Autumn." He leaned over and touched the birthmark at the corner of her eye. "Like this birthmark."

She rolled her eyes. "Yes, I'm the only one with an ugly birthmark."

"It's not ugly. It's cute. It looks like a tiny little heart. It was what gave you away that day in the bakery." He slid his finger down her cheek. "That and your soft skin." He leaned in and kissed the spot behind her ear, his tongue brushing across her sweet tasting skin. "Did you know that you taste like vanilla? Like my mom's sugar cookies."

She pulled back with concerned eyes. "You never talk about your mom. Is she still alive?"

"Yes. She and my dad moved to Phoenix after Robby death. I'm sure they're still fighting away in the hot desert sun."

"You don't talk to them?"

He stacked some pillows behind his back and reclined. "I tried calling them a few times after Robby died, but we really don't have anything to say to each other. I think I remind them of Robby, and they'd just as soon forget him."

She snuggled close to his chest. He liked having her there. She felt like a cozy blanket of comfort. "I don't believe that. They're probably just hurt." She kissed his chest like she was kissing his heart. "Like you are."

It was funny, but he didn't feel as hurt anymore. He would always miss Robby, but his life didn't feel as empty and useless as it once had. It was hard to feel empty when you had a beautiful, caring woman in your arms.

"You need to try calling them again," she said. "You can't give up on family."

He could give her about a thousand reasons why that was a bad idea, but he knew that no matter how many reasons he gave her, she wouldn't concede. Probably because no matter what her family did, she would never give up on them. It was just one more thing he admired about her.

"Fine," he said. "I'll call them."

She leaned up on his chest and gave him a kiss that made him horny and happy at the same time. She drew back and smiled. "And some people think you're just a dumb jock."

He laughed. "I am a dumb jock. A dumb jock who will do anything for a pair of pretty blue eyes."

Her eyebrows lifted. "Anything?"

"Don't tell me you want to play naughty pony and—" A loud banging on the door cut him off.

"Hey, Coach! You awake?" Stuart's voice came through the door.

"Of course, he's not awake, dumbass," Race said. "Otherwise, he'd answer."

"Don't call me an dumbass, dumbass." There was the sound of scuffling.

Autumn sat up. "What's happening?"

"My two best players have decided to bug their coach on a Sunday. Just ignore them and they'll go away." He tried to pull her back in his arms, but she wouldn't allow it.

"But it sounds like they're killing each other."

"They're just having some fun. Now where were we?" He leaned up to kiss her neck when a loud crash had him sighing. He rolled to his feet and grabbed a pair of sweats off the chair. When he opened the door, Stuart and Race were staring down at a broken flowerpot that had been on the landing. "What the hell do you two think you're doing?" he asked.

They pointed at each other and spoke at the same time. "He did it." They looked at one another, and then burst out laughing. Maverick was too annoyed at having his morning with Autumn disrupted to join in.

"Well, don't just stand there," he said. "Go ask Ms. Marble for a broom and dustpan and clean this mess up."

They clomped down the stairs like only two rowdy teenage boys could, pushing and shoving each other as they went. Maverick closed the door and turned to find Autumn in her trench coat and high heels.

"Are you going somewhere?" he asked.

"You need to deal with your football players and I need to go to church."

He caught her around the waist on her way past. "To confess all your sins?"

She laughed. "You want to come too? That way, we can cover all our sinful bases."

"I'm not much on church . . . or confession. Besides, I need to run off those muffins I ate. Why don't you be wicked and skip church and run with me?"

"I don't run. That's Summer's—" He arched an eyebrow, and she cut off. "Fine. I'll try running if you try church."

He wasn't a church kind of guy. His parents had taken him and Robby to church every Sunday, but it was all for show—to keep up the image of a perfect family. As soon as they got back home, his parents' fighting had started again. Still, if going to church meant Maverick got to spend more time with Autumn, he was willing to go.

He kissed the tip of her nose. "Deal."

"I told you that he left Boo Night with the mean triplet, Stewie."

They both turned to see Race and Stuart standing in the doorway. Race was holding a dustpan and Stuart the broom. Maverick thought Autumn would be offended by Race's comment or embarrassed about being caught in his room, but she didn't seem to be either. With a slight lifting of her chin, she strutted toward Race and poked him in the chest with her finger.

"And don't you ever forget it." She walked out the door with the click of high heels and a sassy wiggle that had both boys' eyes widening in admiration.

"Wow," Stuart said. "She's hot."

Maverick smiled. "And she's all mine."

After they cleaned up the broken pot, Maverick gave them the leaf blower and had them clean up the rest of the leaves in Ms. Marble's yard while he got showered and changed for church. He didn't have any Sunday clothes, but he polished his boots and pressed his western shirt and jeans. When he walked around front to see how the boys were doing, he found the lawn cleared of leaves and the boys sitting on the porch drinking lemonade and eating cookies with Ms. Marble. Maverick didn't know if the old gal had gotten after them or they just knew a strict teacher when they saw one, but they seemed to be on their best behavior.

"These fine boys have agreed to help me with my lawn when I need it," Ms. Marble said. "Isn't that right, boys?"

"Yes, ma'am," they muttered in unison.

Maverick smiled. "I'm glad to hear it. Now if y'all will excuse me, I need to get to church."

Ms. Marble got up from her rocker. "I'm headed there myself." She adjusted her big hat before she picked up her white gloves from the table and pulled them on. "You boys take your time eating the cookies and lemonade. Just leave the plate and glasses, I'll get them later. But you can put those bags of leaves out by the curb for the trash man to collect tomorrow."

"Yes, ma'am," they said.

Maverick bit back a grin as he walked over to the porch steps and helped Ms. Marble down. "Would you like a ride to church, Ms. Marble?"

"No, thank you," she said. "I need to stay after church and organize the election-day volunteers. Although it won't be much of an election. Everyone already knows that Dirk Hadley is going to be our next mayor. He's a good man who will do a fine job." As they walked to the driveway where their cars were parked, she glanced over at him. "And speaking of that, you've done a fine job of mentoring those two boys. With the fathers they have, they needed a good role model to look up to. And I think it's a shame that you'll be leaving as soon as the season is over."

A month ago, he wouldn't have thought it was a shame. He would've thought it was a blessing. But now he felt a stab of regret that he wouldn't be there for Stuart and Race. He wouldn't be able to run with them and listen to their horseplay. He wouldn't get to watch their friendship develop or their football skills. He was surprised by how much he was going to miss the two ornery teenagers when he left. And he'd miss Ms. Marble too. He'd miss their breakfast chats and sitting by the fire with her in the evenings and sipping hot tea.

But mostly, he regretted not being here with Autumn. It wasn't just about the sex. It was about liking the man he became when he was with her. Not a superstar, but just a man he could admire.

As if reading his mind, Ms. Marble spoke. "And it's a shame you'll be leaving such a sweet girl as Autumn Hadley . . . and ruin my perfect matchmaking record."

He turned to her. "You've been trying to match me with Autumn? But I thought you didn't want us together. I thought you were trying to fix her up with Cord Evans."

The older woman tugged on her white gloves. "I just told you that to make you see that you have feelings for the girl. Cord and Autumn would be a terrible match. Not because he's too old for her, mind you, but because Autumn has already given her heart to you."

Maverick was too stunned to speak. Not over Ms. Marble having played him, but over her statement that Autumn had given him her heart. Elation warred with sheer terror. There was nothing he wanted more than Autumn's heart . . . and nothing he wanted less. He wasn't a person anyone could trust with their heart. Robby had proven that. And Maverick couldn't stand the thought of hurting someone else. Especially Autumn.

"No," he said with a shake of head. "We're just friends."

Ms. Marble patted his cheek with her gloved hand. "You'll figure it out soon enough, dear. Let's hope when you do, you'll be smart enough to make the right decision." She got in her car.

Maverick denied Ms. Marble's words the entire way to his truck. There was no way Autumn had given him her heart. She'd just started to like him. And the right decision wasn't to stay in Bliss. The right decision was to become a professional football player. It was his dream. He couldn't just release it like a helium balloon and let it drift away. He had worked too hard to achieve it.

By the time he climbed into his truck, he had convinced himself that Ms. Marble was going through the early stages of dementia. But as he drove down Main Street and saw all the signs in the windows cheering the Bobcats to victory, he couldn't help wishing that he could have it both ways: Stay in Bliss and play professional football.

As he stopped at the stoplight, a thought struck him. Why couldn't he have it both ways? Why couldn't he stay in Bliss until he got picked up by a team? He had been traveling from town to town living out of his suitcase, but wouldn't it be better to have a home base—a friendly place to come home to with nice townsfolk and a woman who made all the tattered pieces of his life come together?

As for Autumn's heart, he would protect it and guard it better than an offensive lineman guards his quarterback. He wasn't going to let Autumn get hurt.

Feeling pretty damned confident that he'd figured everything out, he pulled into the church parking lot and hopped out of his truck. Autumn was waiting in front for him, her hair windblown and her cheeks pink from the cold. When she saw him, a smile lit her face. A smile that punched Maverick right in the chest with an emotion he'd never felt before.

Suddenly, he wasn't just worried about protecting Autumn's heart.

CHAPTER TWENTY-ONE

AUTUMN DIDN'T LIKE RUNNING. IT was hard. After only a few blocks, her shins started to ache and her side cramped. And she wasn't even running. The pace Maverick had set was more like a slow jog. Obviously, he felt like she couldn't keep up with a run. Which was true, but still humiliating . . . and annoying. As was his constant checking on her.

"You doing okay?" he asked for about the hundredth time. He wasn't even breathing hard while she was puffing like a steam-powered train.

"How far have we gone?" she asked. "A mile?"

He glanced at the Fit-bit on his wrist. "Not quite."

"How much do we have left?"

He hesitated. "A little over three quarters of a mile."

"You mean we haven't even gone a quarter of a mile?"

He sent her an encouraging smile. "No. But you're doing great. And isn't this fun?"

It wasn't fun, and it didn't look like he was having fun either. He looked like a dog on a leash that couldn't wait to break free. Autumn finally brought an end to their torture and stopped.

Maverick was instantly concerned. "Are you okay? Do you have a cramp?"

She bent at the waist and tried to catch her breath. "No, I just need a break from running." She panted. "Like forever."

There was a pause before Maverick laughed. "So I guess we've figured out that running isn't something Autumn Hadley likes to do. Okay, we'll do something else. We could take a drive and look at the changing leaves or we could go check out this little white chapel that everyone keeps talking about."

Even while struggling for oxygen, she couldn't help smiling. He was trying his darndest to please her. And it was sweet and endearing, but she couldn't let him give up his beloved exercise routine for her.

She straightened. "We can do those things later. You go ahead and run. I don't want Ms. Marble's muffins settling on your amazing abs."

"Amazing?" His look was pure male arrogance.

She rolled her eyes. "As if you didn't know."

"A man still likes to hear it from his woman." Just the thought of being Maverick Murdoch's woman made her heart thump in overtime. It thumped even faster when he winked at her in that sexy way of his. "And for the record, I think your body is pretty amazing too." Then he brushed a kiss over her lips right there in the middle of town with people walking by.

When she blushed, he smiled. "Don't think

you're getting away from me for long, Miss Hadley. I'll stop by Waylon and Spring's when I'm done." He turned and took off down the street. She stood there and watched him as a thousand butterflies filled her tummy with happy flutters. Maverick Murdoch was her boyfriend.

Not Summer's.

Or some beautiful model's.

Or some talented celebrity's.

Hers.

She turned and headed home with a major stitch in her side, but a bright smile on her face. That smile faded when she stepped in the door of Spring and Waylon's house and saw her sisters sitting in the living room. Summer had eyeballed her and Maverick all during the pastor's sermon, and Autumn knew she was starting to put two and two together. This was confirmed when Summer jumped on her as soon as she stepped into the room.

"What in the world are you doing, Autumn Layne Hadley?"

She hedged around the question. "I went for a run, but I've discovered that I'm not very good at running." She flopped in the chair across from the couch her sisters sat on and leaned down to scratch Sherlock's ears. "Running is a lot easier when you're young. Don't you agree, Sherlock?"

"I wasn't talking about you going for a run," Summer said. "I was talking about you being with Maverick Murdoch. Granny Bon gave me a stern lecture on leaving you and Spring to live your own lives, but I will not allow my sister to get into a relationship with a professional quarterback who likes to play kinky sex games. From what I saw in church, that's exactly what he has in mind for you. The man has no moral code whatsoever. He was lusting after you right there in front of God and the entire congregation."

Autumn had hoped she'd never have to tell her sister about what had happened between her and Maverick. She had hoped he would leave and Summer would never be the wiser. But now she didn't want Maverick to leave. She wanted him to stay. In fact, she had even said a prayer in church that morning that God would let the Bobcats win the semi-finals so Maverick would stay in Bliss for just a little longer. If he stayed, she intended to spend every second she could with him. Which meant she couldn't have Summer thinking he was a pervert. Still, it was hard to find the words to tell your sister that you'd seduced her old boyfriend.

"The thing is . . . you see . . . Maverick and I . . . we sort of—"

"Good Lord, Audie," Spring said. "It's not that big a deal." She looked at Summer. "Autumn's already had kinky sex with Maverick."

Summer's eyes widened. "That bastard!" She jumped up. "I'm going to string him up by his balls for defiling my sister."

Spring had a major laughing fit as Autumn quickly got up to stop Summer from leaving. "Calm down, Summer. He didn't seduce me. I seduced him."

Summer stared at her. "What?"

She released her breath. "I should've told you this a long time ago, but ever since college, I've had a major crush on Maverick."

Her sister didn't look surprised. "I think any idiot

could've figured that out, Audie."

"You knew? Why didn't you say anything?"

"Because it was harmless." Her eyes narrowed. "Unless you two were doing it behind my back in college."

"Of course not! I never would've done that while you were dating him. But six months ago I ran into him in Houston." She swallowed hard. "And well, he thought I was you, and I sort of played along."

Summer's eyes widened. "You pulled a triplet switch? So when Maverick walked in to the bakery and tried to kiss me, he wasn't crazy or drunk. He thought I was you. Or he thought I was me." She waved her finger in a circle. "But I was really you." Her eyes got even bigger. "You were the one who played horse trainer and pretty pony with him?"

Autumn's face burned with guilt and humiliation when Spring stared at her. "Horse trainer and pretty pony? Why, Audie, you naughty little girl. I didn't get those sordid details."

Summer turned on Spring. "You knew about this and didn't tell me?"

"Yes, but don't get your panties in a bunch, Sum. It wasn't my place to tell you. It was Audie's."

Summer looked at Autumn and crossed her arms. "So tell me."

It didn't take Autumn long to tell her sister about what had happened in Houston. When she was finished, she gave Summer a long-overdue apology. "I'm sorry. I'm sorry I pulled a triplet switch. And I'm sorry I didn't confess when Maverick showed up in town. But mostly I'm sorry that I broke the golden rule of sisterhood."

"What's the golden rule of sisterhood?" Summer

asked.

"Never date your sister's boyfriends."

Watson came into the room at that moment and jumped up on the couch between Spring and Summer. Spring pulled the cat over to her lap and stroked his fur. "I think that rule applies to serious relationships, Audie. And Maverick and Summer never had a serious relationship. They were two jocks who like to run and work out." Her eyes twinkled with humor. "Or were you his pretty pony, Summer?"

Autumn didn't find that amusing and neither did Summer. "Shut up, Spring," Summer said. "But you're right. Maverick and I were more friends than boyfriend and girlfriend. So I'm not mad at you, Audie, for breaking some stupid sister rule. I'm mad at you for dating a man who will never commit. And believe me, I know a non-committer when I see one. I was the exact same way. That's one of the reasons I dated Maverick. I knew he wasn't going to get too attached to me, just like I wasn't going to get too attached to him. Our hearts were too hard to get broken." Concern filled her eyes. "But you don't have that problem, Audie. Your problem is that you get attached too easily. And I don't want you to get hurt."

That had been Autumn's fear ever since she'd fallen for Maverick. And she had done everything she possibly could to avoid being hurt. Including setting up a sex-only affair and trying to pretend that all she wanted from Maverick was his body. But she had always wanted more. Now, she realized that she wanted everything. She wanted the bigger-than-life football hero who refused to give up his dream. The abused son who struggled to forgive. The mourning brother who searched for redemption. And the caring coach who loved his players. But mostly she wanted the man who had touched her heart and turned a simple crush into a deep love that she would carry with her long after he was gone.

And he would leave. She knew that. He had too many demons left to fight. Too many dreams to fulfill. But for now he was hers, and she was going to enjoy him for as long as she could. But it was best if she didn't share her love for Maverick with her sisters. It would only make them worry.

"I won't get hurt," she said. "This is just a fling. I'm smart enough to realize that Maverick isn't husband material."

Summer studied her for a long moment before she nodded. "Good. But I'd be a little careful about looking at each other the way you were looking at each other in church today. Granny Bon is coming next week and nothing gets past that woman. If she catches you, she'll give you a lecture and a half on appropriate behavior."

"Aww, why did you have to go and warn her, Sum?" Spring said. "It's about time Audie got a lecture. We've gotten dozens over the years, and our perfect sister has never gotten one. Of course, it turns out she's not so perfect after all." She winked at Autumn before she turned to Summer. "So are you going to tell us or do we have to wait until you start showing?"

Summer looked surprised for only a second before a bright smile spread over her face. "Ryker and I are going to have a baby."

The declaration was followed with a lot of hugging and tears. Even Summer cried, and she was not a crier.

"I'm so happy for you," Autumn said. "How did Ryker take it?"

"He's over the moon. He's already planning the baby's room. He wants to paint it pink. He's convinced I'm having a girl. He also wants me to cut my hours at the bakery. Which isn't a problem now that Christie is working there. She can bake while Audie waits on customers."

Autumn wanted to help her sister. Especially now that she was pregnant. But as much as she loved her family, it was time she had her own life.

"I'm sorry, Summer," she said. "But I'm quitting. I'll help until you find someone else, but after that I'm not going to work in the bakery. It's not my dream. It's yours."

Summer looked hurt and confused. "Why didn't you say something sooner?"

"The same reason that I didn't tell you about Maverick. I don't like to disappoint my sisters. You were so happy about us working together, I wanted you to continue to be happy. Even when I was miserable."

There was disappointment in her sister's eyes. "I always thought we'd be close forever, but things just aren't working out that way."

Autumn got up, and her sisters scooted over so she could join them on the couch. "Just because we aren't together twenty-four-seven doesn't mean we can't still be close. I'm not going anywhere. I love Bliss. I want to live here. I just don't want to work at your bakery."

"What do you want to do?"

"I've been thinking about it a lot lately, and I think I might have an idea. The last job I loved was working at the bookstore in Waco."

Summer pointed a finger at her. "I knew you wanted to open your own bookstore. And I think it's a great idea. I'll talk to Dirk and Ryker about helping you with some start-up money and I know just the building you should—"

Autumn held up a hand. "Stop. I don't want to own a bookstore. I've had enough experience running businesses to know that I don't want one of my own. But I do want to work around books. The new library will be open by the first of the year, and every library needs a good librarian. It looks like all those library science classes I took are finally going to come in handy. It shouldn't take me anytime to get my masters degree. And Joanna doesn't see a problem with me working there while I'm getting it."

Spring hugged her. "I think that's the perfect job for my bookworm sister."

Summer wasn't as excited. "It sounds boring to me, but if it makes you happy." She got up. "I guess I'll go put up a new ad for someone who will like working in a bakery. I'll talk to y'all later." She had no more than left the room when a knock sounded on the front door. It was quickly followed by Summer's greeting. "Hey, Mav. I hear you're dating my sister."

Maverick cleared his throat. "Uhh . . . yeah. Is that okay?"

"Would you stop seeing her if it wasn't?"

There was only a slight hesitation before Maverick answered. "No." Spring gave Autumn a thumbs up, and Autumn couldn't help grinning like an idiot. But her smile faded when Maverick yelped.

"Oww! What did you punch me for?"

"Just a friendly warning to be careful. Be very, very careful." Summer yelled into the living room. "Audie! Your boyfriend's here."

CHAPTER TWENTY-TWO

MAVERICK PACED THE SIDELINES OF the football field like a caged animal. Something wasn't right. The week before, in the playoffs, they'd won by twenty points. Tonight, in the semi-finals, they were losing by two touchdowns and it was already the third quarter. His receivers couldn't catch a ball to save their souls. His offensive lineman couldn't hold the defense. And Race was hurrying his passes. He'd already thrown three interceptions.

"What the hell is going on out there?" Waylon voiced Maverick's exact concerns. "In the first half, I thought it was just nerves."

"I did too." Maverick shook his head. "Now I don't have a clue. But those boys better pull their heads out or our chances of going to state are over."

Maverick didn't realize how much he wanted that state title until now. He wanted it badly. Not for himself, but for the determined group of boys who had worked so hard in the last few months to become a team. They deserved the trophy. And he was going to do everything in his power to make sure they got it.

He signaled for a timeout. As soon as his team ran in, he grabbed Stuart and Race by their shoulder pads and pulled them to the side. "What's going on?"

Race jerked off his helmet. "Stewie isn't doing his job of protecting me worth shit because he's too busy watching his cheerleader girlfriend."

"It's not my fault you're upset because your dad's here and you're worried he's going to yell at you after the game." Stuart said. "And Kimberly's not my girlfriend."

"Because you're too chicken shit to talk to her," Race snapped. Stuart glanced back at the cheerleaders with such a look of longing that it was pathetic, and Maverick wanted to yell at him for letting a woman get in the way of an important football game. But just as he opened his mouth, he closed it again.

He couldn't get after Stuart when he'd spent the last two games glancing back at the bleachers with the same look of longing. Even now, he couldn't help looking at the middle of the third row where Autumn sat with her family. She wore a bright red scarf that helped him easily pick her out of the crowd. A scarf that she'd used the night before to tie his hands to the headboard of his bed.

He blinked away the erotic image and returned his attention to Stuart. He could tell the kid to stop looking at his cheerleader crush and focus on the game, but Maverick had just proven that was easier said then done. Not that Maverick had a crush on Autumn. He just liked her . . . a lot.

In the past two weeks they'd spent every day

together. He stopped by the bakery in the mornings after his run to see her. After football practice, they either ate dinner with Spring and Waylon or with Ms. Marble. They'd even had dinner with Summer and Ryker. Which had been awkward, but not nearly as awkward as he'd thought. And at night, Autumn would come to his room.

They didn't hurry through the sex like they had in Houston. Instead, they took everything slow. He spent hours exploring Autumn's body with his hands and lips. And she did the same to him, until he couldn't take the torture any longer and needed to be deep inside her. After they made love, they'd lie together in the dark and talk. They'd talk about everything. Autumn's excitement over getting the job as the town's new librarian. Dirk becoming the new mayor. How cute Raff and Savannah's new son was. Or the funny things Stuart and Race did.

But the two boys weren't being so funny now. And Maverick needed to figure out how to get his star players to focus on the game. The first step was to take care of their problems.

"I agree with Race," he said. "You won't know if Kimberly likes you unless you talk to her." He shrugged. "Of course, if you win this game, there's always the chance that she'll approach you."

"What do you mean?" Stuart asked.

"It's been my experience that woman use the excuse of celebrating a win to give guys they like hugs."

Stuart's eyes widened, and he swallowed hard. "No shit, Coach?"

"No shit. But we're not going to win if you don't pull your head out and start protecting your quarterback." He turned to Race. "And Stuart isn't the only one who needs to pull his head out. I get that you're nervous about your dad being here and reaming you out after the game. My junior year in high school, my dad reamed me out right in front of the entire team and the coaches for losing a game. I was so embarrassed that I never wanted to pick up a football again. But I did. That was when I figured out that I wasn't playing for my dad. Or the coaches." He glanced at Stuart. "Or the girls. I was playing for myself. I was playing because I love this game. Because it's the greatest game in the world."

Stuart and Race glanced at each other and grinned. "Hell yeah, it is," they said in unison.

The ref blew the whistle to resume the game, and Maverick slapped their shoulder pads. "Now let's win this game and go home."

That's exactly what they did. The Stuart and Race who played in the second half weren't anything like the Stuart and Race who played in the first. When they started playing well, the entire team started playing better. They ended up winning by one point. But it was all they needed to head to the state championship in Arlington the following week.

As soon the whistle sounded for the end of the game, the entire town of Bliss converged on the field. Maverick was mobbed by well-wishers and a television reporter who wanted to get some footage for the Austin ten o'clock news. Although the blond reporter didn't want to talk about the game as much as Maverick giving up the NFL to coach small town football.

"I haven't given up playing professional football,"

he said. "I'm still training hard and looking for the right fit. In the meantime, I was given the opportunity to coach this great group of boys and I took it."

"Well, it certainly looks like your team won the lottery when they got a professional quarterback as their coach," the reporter said.

Maverick shook his head. "I'm the one who's the winner. These boys have taught me more in the last couple months than I could ever teach them." It was the truth. His team had reminded him of all the reasons he loved the game. Something he had forgotten after Robby's death.

Before the reporter could ask another question, Stuart and Race ran up and dumped an entire cooler of ice water over his head. The reporter and cameraman jumped out of the way, and Maverick took the opportunity to end the interview and celebrate with his team.

While he was slapping shoulder pads and butts, a cheerleader with freckles and pretty blue eyes came running up and threw her arms around Stuart. The stunned look on Stuart's face was priceless. Maverick gave him the thumbs-up sign, and Stuart grinned broadly and hugged the cheerleader back. Numerous girls ran up to hug Race as well, but he seemed distracted. When Race's dad finally showed up, Maverick headed him off before he could reach his son.

"Mr. Dunkin, could I have a word with you?"

"If you want to talk to me about my son's pathetic first half, there's no need. I saw what he was doing wrong and I intend to set him straight."

Maverick knew it wasn't his place to interfere

with his player's personal lives, but he couldn't stop himself. "I don't want you talking to Race."

"Excuse me?"

"Can't you see what you're doing to your own son? One word of criticism from a father can tear down a hundred words of praise from anyone else. I can't stop you from ridiculing Race for the rest of his life, but I can stop you from ruining his victory tonight."

"What the hell are you talking about? I don't ridicule my son. I give him advice like a good father should. And if I want to give him advice tonight, I damn well will."

Waylon stepped next to Maverick. "Leave it alone, Dan."

"Or what, sheriff? You'll arrest me? That's bullshit and you know it."

"You're right," Waylon said. "I can't arrest you for wanting to belittle your son, but I can arrest you for the speeding ticket you got last month and have yet to pay."

Dan Dunkin stared at Waylon for a long moment, before he turned and strode away. When he was gone, Waylon shook his head. "What an asshole." He glanced at Maverick and smiled. "Good game, Coach."

"Ditto, Coach." They did a half man-hug and slapped each other on the back before they drew apart.

"The entire town's heading over to the Watering Hole to celebrate," Waylon said. "You're coming, right?"

A flash of red caught Maverick's eye, and he turned to see Autumn standing there. The stiff wind blew her dark hair across her face, but he could still see her soft smile and the pride in her eyes. Pride that made him feel ten feet tall. A lump formed in his throat as the emotion he'd felt at the church had his heart racing like he'd just run a marathon.

"I think I might have other plans," he said before he walked over to Autumn.

"Congratulations, Coach," she said.

"That's all I get? No hug for the winner?"

She pushed her hair out of her face and held it behind her neck. "I think the winning coach deserves more than just a hug." She placed her mitten-covered hand on his chest and leaned up to whisper in his ear. "I'll be waiting at your apartment."

Maverick tried to hurry the celebration along, but it took over an hour for the field to clear. He broke numerous traffic violations in his hurry to get back to his apartment. When he opened the door, he found the room filled with lit candles. He stepped inside, expecting to see Autumn lying on the bed naked. When she wasn't, he glanced around in confusion.

"Autumn?"

The bathroom opened, and she stepped out in the sexiest lingerie he'd ever seen in his life. A black corset cinched her waist so tightly he figured he could span it with his hands. A matching scrap of lace peeked from between her thighs, and her bare breasts spilled over the top of the corset like dollops of pink cherry-topped whipped cream. Instead of thigh-high stockings and heels, she wore thigh-high black shiny boots with stiletto heels. In her hand, she held a riding crop that she casually tapped against one boot.

"Are you ready for your next lesson, my naughty pony?"

He smiled. "I've always been ready."

An hour later, Maverick was snuggled beneath the down comforter with a satisfied smile on his face and Autumn cuddled against his chest. "I think you left welts on your pony's ass, Miss Horse Trainer. It's still stinging."

She lifted her head, her eyes filled with concern. "But you told me that it didn't hurt."

He tried to keep a sober look on his face. "It hurt bad. And I think you need to rub your abused pony down with liniment oil."

The concern left her eyes, and she swatted his chest. "Maverick Matthew Murdoch, you had me thinking that I'd really hurt you."

He grinned and hugged her tighter. "I'll be your undisciplined pony anytime, sweetheart."

She snuggled against him, wrapping her arm around his waist. "You aren't undisciplined. You take instruction very well for an arrogant coach who is going to the state championship." She paused. "Have you told your players yet that you won't be back next season?"

"No. I thought I'd wait until after state to tell them. Or maybe until after the holidays."

She lifted her head. "You're staying until after the holidays? But I thought you were leaving as soon as the football season was over."

"I was, but I've been thinking that maybe I'll stay a little longer. I've been traveling around from one football tryout to another. It will be nice to have a base to come home to."

The candlelight reflected in her eyes and made her expression hard to read. And suddenly he wondered if he had everything all wrong. If Autumn didn't like him quite as much as he liked her. He was surprised at how hurt he felt.

"Do you have a problem with that?" he asked. She took too long to answer, and he started to backpedal. "Look, if I read this entire thing wrong, just tell—"

She placed a finger on his lips and cut him off. "I don't have a problem with it." She leaned in and kissed him. "I think I can put up with you for a couple more months. Can you put up with me?"

"It will be hard, but I'll do my best. And speaking of hard." He rolled her onto her back and smiled down at her. "I think it's your turn to be my pretty pony."

The following morning, he woke to his phone ringing. He eased away from Autumn so as not to wake her and quickly got out of bed to answer it. He assumed it would be Waylon wanting to go over some game film before the state championship, but a number he didn't recognize popped up on his phone screen. He tapped the accept button.

"Hello?"

"Is this Maverick Murdoch?" A male voice asked.

"It is."

"Good morning, Maverick. This is Stan Weaver from the Miami Dolphins." That woke Maverick up. He became even more awake as the man continued. "As you probably know, our first-string quarterback was injured in last week's game. Our second string will be taking his place while he's out, but we could use another good arm as backup. We thought you might fill the spot nicely."

Maverick was too stunned to speak. He started pacing and running a hand through his hair. He should be excited. He should be jumping for joy. Instead, he had a weird tightening in his stomach like the floor was falling out from under him and he had nothing to grab onto.

"You there, Maverick?" Stan asked.

"Yes, sir, I'm here. It's just that I wasn't expecting this. I tried out in the summer as a walk-on, but you didn't seem interested then. I was just wondering what changed."

"We were interested, but we were worried that you didn't have the right mental motivation."

"And what makes you think I do now?"

"We saw the interview you did last night. It's all over the internet. And you can't take a bunch of high school boys all the way to state if you don't have your act together. So what do you say? You want to be a Miami Dolphin?"

This was his dream. It was happening. And he'd be the stupidest fool in the world if he didn't grab it. Because if he didn't grab it now, it might not ever come again.

Still, it was an effort to get the words out. "Yes, sir. I'd love to be a Miami Dolphin."

"Great. Can you be in Miami on Monday to sign the contracts?"

"This Monday? But my team is going—" He stopped. He couldn't take his team to state. Not if he accepted a job with the Dolphins. His stomach clenched even tighter. "Yes, sir, I'll be there."

After he hung up, he just stood there with the phone in his hand, trying to conjure up some kind of excitement. But all he felt was like he wanted to throw up. The feeling intensified when Autumn spoke.

"You got your dream."

He turned to find her sitting up in bed, her eyes filled with hurt. They made him hurt too. "I'm sorry," was all he could get out. It wasn't enough, but it was exactly how he felt. He was sorry. Sorry that his big opportunity had come now and not later when he'd had more time with her. He needed more time with her.

He waited for her reaction. If she were like his mother, she would start screaming. His mother screamed whenever she felt hurt. And he almost welcomed her anger instead of those deep twilight blue eyes of pain. But Autumn didn't scream. Without a word, she got out of bed and started to get dressed.

"What are you doing?" he asked.

"I'm leaving."

"You don't have to go now. I'm not leaving until Monday."

She stopped and looked at him. Tears shimmered in her eyes, and he felt slayed. "It's okay, Maverick. I knew you weren't going to stay forever. I knew I only had you for a short time. But I'm not good at goodbyes."

Talk about a dagger through the heart. He walked over and pulled her close, burying his face in her neck. She smelled of a sweetness that he'd come to crave. "I'll come back. I promise I'll come back. All you have to do is wait for me. Just wait for me."

She pressed against him for one heart-stopping moment before she drew back and smiled softly. "That's the one thing I can't do."

CHAPTER TWENTY-THREE

WALKING AWAY FROM MAVERICK WAS one of the hardest things Autumn had ever done in her life. Bad boy or hero. Arrogant jock or wounded soul. It made no difference to her heart. She loved all of him. She understood that now. She also understood why her mama had taken her daddy back every single time. Because when you love someone, it's hard to let go. But she knew that if she didn't let go, she'd spend the rest of her life like her mother: waiting for a man who rarely showed up.

As heartbreaking as it was to look in Maverick's hurt-filled eyes and say goodbye, it was better to end it now and save any further heartbreak. He would get over her with some beautiful model or celebrity. And she would get over him. She had to.

When she arrived back at Waylon's and Spring's house, it wasn't difficult to put on a brave front. Autumn had spent her entire life hiding her true feelings from her family.

Granny Bon had arrived from Waco, and the entire Hadley family met at the bakery for breakfast. The adults chatted over coffee, donuts, and muffins while Dirk and Gracie's three girls toddled around causing havoc. To keep her from thinking about Maverick, Autumn took over the job of watching her nieces. She scooped up Lucinda before she could place her donut-sticky hands on the glass of the display case, stopped Luana from eating a muffin crumb off the floor, and tried to block Luella from getting into the kitchen.

But when Autumn was busy keeping Lucinda from toppling over a chair, Luella got past the counter. Thankfully, Christie was there and picked her up before she got to the kitchen. Luella didn't usually warm to people quickly. But she seemed to warm right up to Christie. She gave her a toothy grin before she started playing with one of Christie's dangly earrings.

"You obviously have a knack with children." Autumn said.

"I love children. I wish I'd had more." Christie studied her. "Are you all right? You look a little sad this morning."

She pinned on a smile. "I'm fine. Where is Carrie Anne?"

"Ms. Miller is babysitting her, and Carrie Anne is not too happy about it. Cord offered to watch her today so she could see the new horse he just bought, but I refused. It was very nice of him, but I learned from experience that rodeo cowboys don't make the best babysitters—especially when horses are around."

Autumn didn't agree. "Cord might've been irresponsible in his youth, but he isn't like that now. He would never let anything happen to Carrie Anne."

Christie smoothed one of Luella's curls off her forehead. "I'm just not willing to take that chance."

Autumn figured her daughter wasn't the only thing Christie wasn't willing to take a chance on. And Autumn couldn't blame her when she wasn't willing to take a chance on love either. It seemed that the two women were a lot alike.

Luana started to fuss because she wasn't getting the same attention as her two sisters. Before Autumn could pick her up, Granny Bon appeared and lifted her great-granddaughter into her arms.

"Feeling a little left out, are you?" Granny tickled Luana's belly until the baby giggled, then Granny held out a hand to Christie. "We haven't been introduced. I'm Bonnie Blue Davidson, but everyone just calls me Granny Bon."

"Christie Buchanan." Christie shook Granny Bon's hand. "Nice to meet you."

Granny Bon studied her for a long moment. "Have we met before? You look familiar."

Christie immediately shook her head. "No. We haven't met. I'd better go check those cookies in the oven." She handed Luella off to Autumn, then headed to the kitchen.

Granny watched her go with such intensity that Autumn thought for sure she was going to have some questions about Christie, but instead she turned to Autumn. "Let's get the triplets back to their mama and daddy so you and I can have us a little chat."

Autumn was instantly wary. Her grandmother rarely had little chats with anyone. She was always too busy puttering around to sit down to talk . . . unless she was giving you a lecture. "A little chat?"

Granny didn't answer the question. Instead, she called Dirk over and handed the babies off to him before leading Autumn out the door.

It was a chilly November day. The wind was sharp and cold as they headed down Main Street. Granny Bon seemed to be immune to the weather. She didn't shiver like Autumn or show any signs of being cold. She just kept her stride steady and her gaze straight ahead. When they were almost to Waylon and Spring's, she finally spoke.

"So would you like to tell me why my granddaughter, who just got out of the kitchen and into a library, doesn't look happy?"

Obviously, Autumn wasn't hiding her feelings as well as she thought. Still, she didn't want to worry her grandmother with her problems, so she tried to bluff her way through. "I'm happy, Granny. I just didn't get a lot of sleep last night"

Granny Bon glanced over at her and lifted an eyebrow. "Sneaking out and meeting your boyfriend can sure play havoc with your sleep."

Her mouth dropped open for a second before she closed it and frowned. "Okay, who told you? Spring or Summer?"

"Neither. I'm not stupid, Autumn Layne. I knew your sister was lying as soon as she told me you'd gone for an early morning walk. If you had gone for a walk, there is no way Sherlock would've let you out the door without him. Plus Spring has never been able to lie to save her soul. Guilt was written all over her face. Maybelline had mentioned that Maverick Murdoch was staying over her garage. And since you used to have a mad crush on him, I put two and two together."

"How did you know I had a crush on Maverick?"

"Whenever you three came home for the weekend and I asked Summer about her quarterback beau, she couldn't tell me one thing about him. You, on the other hand, seemed to know what he was majoring in, all his football stats, and what his favorite flavor of ice cream was."

"He doesn't eat ice cream."

Granny Bon shot her a knowing look as they walked up Waylon and Spring's front path. "Exactly. You know that. Summer never did."

"Well, it doesn't matter now." She swallowed down the lump in her throat. "Maverick is leaving."

"Ahh, then that explains the sad face."

"Okay, I'm a little unhappy. But it's not a big deal. I'll get over it."

Granny Bon studied her. "Yes. I know you will. You've always been my stoic girl, the one who can get through whatever life throws you with a stiff upper lip. Which can be an advantage, but also a major flaw." She paused as she took the spare key out from under the garden gnome on the porch and unlocked the front door.

Once inside, Granny Bon patted Sherlock on the head, greeted Watson, and then walked into the kitchen where she filled up a tea kettle and put it on the stove. While the kettle was heating, she turned to Autumn.

"Tell me about what happened with Maverick."

"There's nothing to tell. He showed up in Bliss looking for Summer"—she refused to tell her grandmother about Houston—"and we . . . started dating."

Her grandmother sent her a knowing look. "And you fell in love."

Autumn wanted to say it was just sex, but like Spring, she struggled with bald-faced lying to her grandmother. "I fell in love, but it doesn't matter. He's leaving. He has an opportunity to play professional football with the Dolphins and I could never ask him to give that up. I know how much football means to him. But he shouldn't ask me to wait for him either. I can't do that, Granny. I just can't."

"He asked you to wait for him?"

"Yes. But I saw what that did to Mama and I refuse to live my life like her. I want a man who's there for me like Ryker and Waylon are there for Summer and Spring. Like Dirk is there for Gracie and their daughters. I don't want a man who shows up occasionally and the rest of the time is gallivanting all over the countryside. I don't want that for me and I certainly don't want that for my children. I know what it does to kids."

"Ahh, I see." The teakettle whistled, and Granny took two cups down from the cupboard and went about making tea. Instead of setting the cups on the table, she put them on a tray and carried them into the living room, leaving Autumn to follow.

It was chilly in the house. When Autumn saw that the embers were still hot from the fire Waylon had going earlier, she took a few pieces of wood from the basket on the hearth and tossed them on the coals. Once they caught, she turned to see Granny sitting on the couch sipping her tea and watching the flames as they licked over the wood.

Autumn sat down in the opposite chair and picked up her cup of tea. Watson hopped on her lap, and Sherlock flopped down at her feet. Within minutes, both animals were snoozing. Their deep, even breathing was soothing. As was the fire and the tea. But there was a hole inside of Autumn that couldn't be soothed. That she was afraid would never be soothed. And she was desperately afraid that her grandmother knew it too. This was confirmed when Granny Bon finally spoke.

"Did you know that you were my rock after your mother died? While I knew I could count on Summer to watch out for her younger siblings, she was a little too impulsive and hot-headed to leave in complete charge. There was no telling what plan she would come up with while I was at work. Fortunately, I had you to control her impulsiveness and keep things running smoothly. You were the calm, cool, and collected one. The one who didn't let her emotions rule her logical thinking. With both you and Summer there, I knew I didn't have to worry. But I made a mistake. I put too much responsibility on you and your sister. I made you take each of your jobs a little too seriously. And as adults, you've both suffered for it. Until she met Ryker, Summer couldn't give up control and learn to trust a man. And you can't seem to let go of your emotions and trust yourself."

"What do you mean?"

"I mean that you're too logical, Autumn Layne. And love isn't logical. It's the most illogical emotion there is. Illogical, irrational, and totally senseless. There's no rhyme or reason why people fall in love with the people they fall in love with. Those online dating sites try to act like they have it all figured out, but they don't have a clue. They're just randomly pairing up people until two people finally click. It sounds like you and Maverick clicked. It sounds like you clicked with him from the first time you saw him. And love like that doesn't come around every day. So why wouldn't you wait for him? Why wouldn't you throw caution to the wind and see what happens?"

Autumn stared at her. "Because of Mama. Because Mama waited for Daddy and look how that turned out!"

"How did it turn out? Your mama ended up with four amazing kids that she adored until the day she died. And you know who else she loved until the day she died? Your daddy."

"And look how much pain that love caused her."

Granny Bon shook her head. "If you think that love doesn't have its moments of pain, then that's just plumb crazy. But I'll agree that your mama was a glutton for punishment with your daddy. He made one promise right after another and never did keep a one. And I never want any of my grandchildren to go through what my daughter did. But what makes you think that this Maverick won't be there for you? Just because he has a job where he has to travel, doesn't mean he can't be there for you—maybe not in person, but there are other ways to be there for someone. Your grandfather worked road construction when we were first married. He'd be gone for weeks at a time and we couldn't afford long distance phone calls. So we wrote letters. About every other day, I got a letter from him and he'd get one from me. We were apart, but I don't think we ever felt closer. We didn't have to be in the same house or even the same town. Our love transcended space and time." She patted her heart. "And I still feel his love, even though he's been gone all these years."

Autumn finally voiced her biggest fear. "But I don't know if Maverick loves me like Grandpa loved you."

Granny Bon lowered her tea cup. "You told him you loved him and he didn't tell you the same?"

Her cheeks heated. "I didn't exactly tell him that I loved him."

"Ahh, then I'd say you have a lot of talking to do. And people can't talk if one of them is running away—and I don't mean Maverick."

Granny Bon had a good point. Autumn should've told Maverick how she felt instead of just leaving, and it only took her a moment to figure out why she hadn't.

"But what happens if he does love me, Granny?" When her grandmother looked confused, she explained. "All my life I've been doing what other people expect of me. Even if it's only what I think other people expect. For the first time, I've started thinking about myself and what I want. I love living in Bliss. I love the town and the people. And I love living close to my family. And I'm going to love working in a library filled with books. But if Maverick does love me and things get serious, he'll want me to move to Miami. Which would make sense. But as much as I love him, I'm tired of following other people's dreams. I did that with Summer and Spring. Now, I want to follow my own dreams. I know it's selfish and horrible of me. And I feel guilty even putting it into words."

Granny Bon smiled. "You are about as far from

selfish as you can get, Autumn Layne. All your life you've put others first. I'd say it's about time you put yourself first. But who says you can't have your cake and eat it too? Who says you can't have your dreams and Maverick too?"

"It's the NFL, Granny Bon. This is what Maverick has been working for his entire life. Just like I don't want to give up my dreams, I can't expect him to give up his."

"Why does it have to be one dream or the other? Why can't you give a little and he gives a little."

"So you think I should wait for him?"

"I think you should ask yourself one question. Can I be happy without him?"

Autumn already had the answer. She'd always had the answer.

CHAPTER TWENTY-FOUR

AFTER AUTUMN LEFT, MAVERICK HOLED up in his apartment and brooded. What did she want from him? She'd acted like she couldn't ask him to give up his dream, but that was exactly what she expected him to do. But instead of yelling like his mother had with his father, Autumn had used her big innocent blue eyes and silence to make him feel guilty when he had nothing to feel guilty about. She'd known that he was leaving from the get-go. He never planned on living in Bliss. He'd been forced to live here. And it wasn't like he hadn't given her an option to be with him. He'd asked her to wait for him, and she'd acted like he'd asked her to dive into the mouth of a volcano.

How hard was it to wait?

The more he thought about her rejection, the angrier he got. Finally, he couldn't take the four walls of his room anymore and decided to go for a run. He ran as if he were being chased by demons. And maybe he was. A demon of a woman who wouldn't let go of his mind . . . or his heart. With every step, his mind went over and over all the moments they'd spent together while his heart felt as if it was being squeezed tighter and tighter. The ache grew even worse as he neared the bakery. For a moment, he wondered if he was going to be one of those athletes who goes for a run and ends up dying from a heart attack.

He slowed his pace, then stopped completely when he saw that the lights were still on. The scent of baked goods was strong in the air. Suddenly, he realized that he hadn't eaten and was starving. But not for something healthy. He wanted a donut. Maybe a dozen. And he refused to let Autumn keep him from getting them.

He opened the door of the bakery, formulating what he would say when he saw her. Maybe he wouldn't say anything. Maybe he'd totally snub her. Or maybe he'd ask her what the hell was her problem. He didn't get to do either. It wasn't Autumn behind the counter. It was Carrie Anne Buchanan. She was sitting on a high stool and pretending to tap the keys on the cash register. When she glanced up and saw him, her smile lit up.

"Hey, Coach!"

He forced a smile. "Hey, Carrie Anne. Did you get a new job?"

She giggled. "Nope. I'm just hanging out while my mama cleans up in the back. The bakery is closed. Didn't you see the sign on the door? I turned it myself."

"And I told you not to turn it until I locked the door." Christie came out from the back, holding a set of keys. "Hi, Maverick. Are you looking for Autumn?"

"No," he answered a little too quickly. "I just

came in for a donut. I didn't realize you were closing."

Christie looked thoroughly confused. "A donut? I thought you didn't eat sugar."

"I don't. I mean I don't usually, but sometimes I do."

"Can I give him one of the day-old donuts that Summer said I could take home, Mama?" Carrie Anne asked.

"Sure," Christie said. "They're in a bag in the back." Carrie Anne hopped off the stool and raced to the back. When she was gone, Christie studied him. "Are you okay? You don't look so good."

"Great." He ran a hand through his mussed hair. "I'm just great."

Christie didn't look like she believed him. "You're just great and Autumn is just fine. But both of you look like you just lost your best friend."

He latched onto that like a dog to a bone. "Autumn looks unhappy?"

"As unhappy as you do."

He couldn't help but take his anger out on Christie. "Well, she doesn't have to be unhappy. Yes, I'm leaving. I was always leaving. But I'll be back. All she had to do was wait for me."

Christie sent him a sympathetic look. "Which is exactly what she can't do."

"That's what she said, but I don't get it. It's not like I'm going to be gone forever. Even if the Dolphins make the playoffs, I'll only be gone a couple months. What's a couple months?"

"It's a lifetime if you're waiting for someone to come back." Christie smiled sadly. "I'm going to assume that Autumn didn't tell you about her father."

"She mentioned that he left when she was little. But what does that have to do with me leaving?"

Christie sighed. "A lot, I'm afraid. Daddies teach their daughters what to expect from men. I chose a man who wasn't there for me, or Carrie Anne, because my dad was never there for my mother or me. Autumn's father showed up occasionally, but never stayed. She spent her childhood waiting for her daddy. So I think you can see why she's through with waiting and hoping that a man will come back."

Maverick released his breath and rubbed a hand over his face. Well, that explained things, but it didn't change anything. "So what do I do? I have to be in Miami on Monday, and I doubt anything I say is going to make her believe that I'll be back."

"You're leaving, Coach?"

He turned to see Carrie Anne standing in the doorway holding a donut. The confusion and hurt on her face were easy to read. He wished he could say something that would take away the look. But there was nothing to say but the truth. "I got picked up by the Miami Dolphins. I'm going to be their back-up quarterback."

Carrie Anne's eyes filled with tears. Damned if he didn't feel like crying himself. "But what about state? You can't leave before the state game."

He cleared his throat and forced a smile. "Coach Waylon will be here, and he's a much better coach than I am."

Carrie Anne stared at him for a second before she threw the donut at him. For a kid, she had a pretty good aim. The donut hit him right in the stomach before she whirled and ran back into the kitchen.

Christie picked up the donut from the floor and tossed it in the trash. "I'm sorry. She has a bit of a temper like her mother."

"She has a right to be mad," he said. "It's crappy of me to leave the Bobcats right before state. As crappy as it is of me to leave Autumn when she has trust issues. But I don't know what else to do." He looked at Christie as if willing her to understand. "I have to go."

"Of course you do." For some reason, he didn't think she was agreeing with him. He felt like she was appeasing him and had put him in the same category as all the other deadbeats in her life. She moved toward the front door. "I need to lock up and get Carrie Anne to bed." She held open the door for him. "Autumn will be fine. She's a strong woman. Even if you don't come back, she'll survive and move on."

That was exactly what Maverick was afraid of. He was afraid that once he left, Autumn would move on. Probably with Cord Evans. And if not with him, then with someone else. Autumn was sweet and beautiful and kind. She would make the perfect wife. If Ms. Marble had her way, Autumn would be married by Christmas.

As he left the bakery, he couldn't help thinking about Autumn exchanging vows with another man. It wasn't just the vows. It was all the things that went with them. Her laughter. Her kisses. Her hot sex games. But mostly her love. Maverick couldn't stand the thought of her giving her love to another man. Not when he wanted it. He knew it was selfish. Especially when he was probably too screwed up to ever love her back. But he didn't care. He wanted Autumn's love. He needed it.

It started to rain. Not a light rain, but a heavy downpour that plastered his hair to his head and soaked his sweats and running shoes. The lights of the bakery turned off, and he stood there in the dark and the rain feeling as confused and lost as he'd felt after Robby died. That's when he heard his name.

"Maverick!"

He glanced up to see Autumn running towards him. She was drenched from head to toe, and there was a panicked look on her face that made him instantly concerned. She ran right into him and burrowed against his chest, her arms wrapping around him and holding tight. Suddenly, he wasn't lost anymore. Suddenly, he was found. Enfolded in Autumn's arms, he realized that he wasn't too screwed up to love again.

"I'd thought you'd left already." Her voice broke, and he realized she was crying. "I thought it was too late to tell you."

He drew back. "Tell me what? What happened?"

She took his face in her hands and spoke above the pounding rain. "I love you, Maverick. I've always loved you."

It was raining cats and dogs, but Maverick felt as if the sun had just broken through the clouds and consumed him in light. His heart no longer felt tight. It felt like it could float right out of his chest. He took her face in his hands and kissed her. It was frantic with need and wet with rain, but it was the best kiss he'd ever had in his life. And when he drew back, all he could do was laugh from sheer joy. The words he didn't know if he could ever say spilled out.

"I love you." He tipped back his head and shouted to the weeping sky. "I love Autumn Layne Hadley!" When he looked back at her, her eyes were wide with disbelief.

"You do?"

He smiled. "I do. And once I get you out of this rain, I'm going show you just how much." But before he could, Race and Stuart came running down the street. They were as soaked as he and Autumn were. Trailing behind them was an equally soaked Carrie Anne.

Stuart's big shoes hit a puddle and splashed them as he ran up. "Carrie Anne said you're leaving. Is it true?"

Before Maverick could answer, Race spoke. While Stuart had sounded hurt, Race just sounded angry and belligerent. "What do you expect, dumbass? Of course he's leaving. Who wouldn't choose an NFL team over a bunch of stupid high school kids?"

Carrie Anne pushed her way between them, looking like a little drowned mouse. A devastated little drowned rat. "Say he's wrong, Coach. Tell him that you aren't leaving." She wiped at her cheeks, and Maverick knew it wasn't just rain she was wiping away. "Say it, Coach." Her voice broke. "Please."

Just like that, Maverick saw what he hadn't been able to see before. Or maybe what he hadn't wanted to see. He hadn't wanted to get attached to anyone after Robby. He hadn't wanted to feel the devastating pain of loss ever again. So he'd stayed away from people and concentrated on football. He'd trained hard and took to running all by himself in an effort to outrun the pain.

Then he came to Bliss.

Here, he couldn't outrun Stuart or Race or Carrie Anne. Or Waylon. Or Ms. Marble. Or Autumn. They had stuck right with him, believing in him when if he hadn't believed in himself. Looking at these four rain-drenched faces, he realized that he was glad that they hadn't given up on him. And he realized he couldn't give up on them either.

He smiled at Carrie Anne. "I'm not leaving." He looked at Stuart and Race. "I'm staying here and helping a bunch of high school . . . men take the state title."

As soon as the words were out, he felt as if a huge weight had been lifted off his shoulders. Like everything was suddenly right in his world. It even stopped raining as Carrie Anne ran to him and hugged his legs tight. Even Stuart gave him a hug. Race only stared at him as if he couldn't quite believe it.

"You're crazy. Only an idiot would give up a chance at the NFL to coach a high school team."

Maverick shrugged. "Then I guess I'm an idiot. And while I'm doing crazy things." He looked at Autumn. "Marry me."

She stared at him. "Are you drunk?"

"Maybe he fell and bumped his head," Stuart said. "My cousin had a concussion once and he acted really loopy. Of course, he never proposed to a woman in the middle of a rainstorm."

Maverick laughed. "I don't have a concussion and I'm not drunk—okay, maybe I'm drunk." He smiled at Autumn. "On love. So answer the question, Autumn Hadley."

She flung her arms around him and kissed him. When she drew back, there was love in her eyes . . . and stubborn determination. "Yes, I'll marry you, Maverick Matthew Murdoch. But only if you leave."

"Excuse me?"

"I want you to leave. It will be hard to let you go, but it's something you need to do. It's something I need to do too. If I never let you go, I'll never learn that you're the kind of man to come back."

"I'll always come back to you."

"Then I want you to follow your dreams."

All his life, he'd thought that his dream was to become a pro football player. But now he realized that his dreams were much smaller. He wanted to help the Bobcats win a state title. He wanted to give Stuart, Race, and Carrie Anne a man to look up to. And he wanted to give Autumn the kind of man she could trust.

He looked around at all the faces he'd come to love and smiled. "I think all my dreams have come true."

CHAPTER TWENTY-FIVE

IT WAS A SIMPLE WEDDING. Just family and a few close friends filled the front two rows of the little white chapel. There were no lavish decorations. No swags of tulle or sprays of flowers adorned the pews or the altar. The lit candles that flickered from every corner were decoration enough.

The groom wore a designer suit and Stetson and the bride wore her grandmother's wedding gown and handmade Cord Evans cowboy boots. The groom had one best man who was also his assistant coach and the bride had two maids of honor who were also her sisters. It was a short ceremony. Vows were exchanged to love, honor, and cherish while the guests looked on with joy in their hearts. When the pastor finally pronounced them man and wife, the groom kissed the bride with such enthusiasm that it elicited whistles from the two teenagers in attendance.

While Maverick pulled back from the kiss and shot a warning look over at Stuart and Race, Autumn only laughed. Both boys had won her over in the last week by working so hard to help her and her sisters pull together the quick wedding. She now understood that their razzing of each other was the way they showed their affection. They were inseparable, more like brothers than friends. Today, they were dressed almost identically in wrinkled dress shirts, ill-fitting dress pants, and matching letterman jackets that boasted state championship patches. Carrie Anne sat between them wearing a frilly dress beneath a much smaller letterman jacket. A jacket she had received from Maverick for handing out water and towels to the team at the state game.

"You shouldn't egg Stuart and Race on," Maverick said as he escorted her down the aisle and out of the church. "They've gotten a little too big for their britches since taking state last weekend."

"Cockiness is just part of being a stud football player. And you certainly were a stud on Sunday."

He laughed. "I was in for less than five minutes before they blew the whistle to end the game."

"And in that time, you passed for twenty-seven yards. The sportscasters on Fox were extremely impressed."

He opened the door of the chapel for her. "I think you're prejudiced, Mrs. Murdoch."

"I think you're right, Mr. Murdoch." She leaned up and gave him a kiss on the way out the door. "Now get me to the reception and feed me. I'm starving."

Just like her sisters', Autumn's wedding reception was held in Dirk's barn. Because it was so cold outside, they kept the doors closed and had rented space heaters. A long banquet table was set up in the middle and laden with a feast that was fitting for the day. The turkeys had been roasted to perfection by Granny Bon and Ms. Marble and Carly had made all the trimmings. The cake was a five-tier work of art that had been decorated by Summer. Although the wedding guests were a little puzzled by the two pretty ponies sitting on the top of the cake, Maverick and Autumn weren't confused at all.

"Your sister has a wicked sense of humor," Maverick said as he lifted his fork with the last bite of cake and offered it to Autumn.

Autumn took the bite and closed her eyes at the delicate flavor of moist white cake and whipped buttercream frosting. "But Summer can bake." She opened her eyes. "Do you mind sharing our anniversary with Thanksgiving?"

He brushed a kiss over her mouth, licking off a dab of frosting. "Why would I mind when you agreeing to marry me will always be the thing I'm most thankful for?" He glanced down the long table at the Arringtons who were mixed in with the Hadleys. "But I've got to tell you that the size of your family gatherings are a little intimidating. I didn't realize you had so many cousins."

At one time, she'd been intimidated by her new cousins. Now they were just family. She looked at the two other people who had become part of her family. Maverick's mother and father sat a little farther down the table from them. They were an attractive couple—if not a little too tanned from the Phoenix sun. They had been pleasant enough to her, but there was an underlying sadness whenever they dealt with Maverick. Maybe he reminded them of Robby. Or maybe they were just sad that they didn't have a better relationship with their son. Autumn hoped that would change in the future.

"I'm glad your parents could make it," she said.

He nodded. "They haven't argued once since they got here. Maybe they've changed. Or maybe Ms. Marble gave them a stern lecture about arguing. I saw her talking to them at the rehearsal dinner."

She laughed. "I wouldn't put it past her. But all married couples argue occasionally. We already had our first fight."

He scowled. "Because you're too stubborn for your own good."

"It's not stubborn to refuse to let the man I love give up his dream. And you have to admit that things have turned out pretty perfect. The Dolphins let you come back for the state high school game and now your wedding. I'm really starting to like the Dolphins coaching staff—although the Dallas Cowboys will always be my team."

His eyebrows popped up. "Your husband plays for the Dolphins and the Cowboys are your team?"

"Sorry, you married a woman who has a mind of her own." She kissed him. "But I promise to root for you in the game on Monday night. I have no loyalty to the Steelers."

"You better root for me. You'll be sitting in my box seats—along with your siblings."

Summer walked up with Spring. "I just hope my new brother-in-law doesn't embarrass the family too badly. Although I don't know how you're going to do well in the game when you couldn't even keep up with me on our run this morning."

Maverick grinned. "I was holding back because

of your condition. But after you have the baby, I'll be happy to show you a real NFL workout."

Summer shrugged. "We'll see. Right now Spring and I need to borrow my sister."

"We'll bring her right back, Mav," Spring said.

Maverick held up his hands. "I've been informed by Waylon and Ryker to never interfere in sister time."

Autumn laughed as her sisters pulled her away from the table to the stalls at the back of the barn. A few of Dirk and Gracie's horses stuck their heads out as the women stopped in front of the stalls.

Spring smiled brightly. "Well, we did it. We all three found our happily-ever-afters. Even Summer."

Summer scowled. "What's that supposed to mean?"

Before there could be an argument, Autumn cut in. "We did do it. And I want to thank you both for accepting my relationship with Maverick so quickly and welcoming him into the family." She looked at Summer. "Especially you, Summer."

Summer's scowl softened. "It wasn't that hard. Maverick and I were too much alike to be anything more than friends. We knew that even when we were dating." She smirked. "So basically, you married your sister. And I married you. Ryker is just as level-headed, shy, and bookwormy as you are."

"And I married a combination of you and Summer," Spring said. "Waylon is as controlling as Summer and as level-headed as Audie." She frowned. "I guess no one wanted to marry me."

Autumn put an arm around her sister. "Because

there's not a man alive with your charisma and charm."

"Except maybe Ryker's dad," Summer said. "That man could charm a snake out of its skin. But unfortunately, we don't have another sister to pawn off on him." She hooked her arms around her sisters. "It's just us three old married ladies."

Tears filled Autumn's eyes as she hugged her sisters close. "I love you. I love y'all so much. And I'm going to miss you."

"Good God," Summer said. "Once the season's over, you're going to be right back here in Bliss with that stud of a football player of yours. Then you'll be decorating your new house that Spring and I are going to find for you and working as our new librarian. So there's no need for waterworks."

Spring sniffed. "When are you going to learn the difference between sad tears and happy tears? These are happy tears. We're crying because all our dreams have come true. We're going to be living together in a town we love with the men we adore." She placed her hand on her stomach. "And raising our adorable children side by side."

Autumn's eyes widened. "You're pregnant?"

Spring nodded her head and laughed. "I just couldn't let Summer outdo me. And wouldn't it be wonderful if Audie got pregnant too, then all our kids would be close to the same age and be best friends just like we are."

Autumn smiled at the thought of a sweet little baby boy who'd they name Robby or a precious little girl who they'd name Dotty after her mom. But there was no hurry. They had time.

Granny Bon walked up. She wore the wide-brimmed felt hat that Ms. Marble had given her for her birthday a few days earlier and a soft smile that said she too was happy that all her grandchildren were married and content. "What are you three planning? When you're huddled together like this, it usually means you're up to no good."

"We're just having a little sister time," Spring said.

"Well, enough of that. Right now, Autumn and Maverick need to get to Austin and get some sleep so they can catch their plane bright and early tomorrow."

"I hate to break this to you, Granny," Summer said. "But people don't usually sleep on their honeymoons."

Granny Bon lifted an eyebrow. "Watch your p's and q's, Summer Lynn. I still have my wooden spoon." She gave Summer a playful swat on the bottom.

A few minutes later, Maverick and Autumn had thanked all their guests for coming and were on their way to Maverick's truck. He had opted to keep his beat up old truck instead of buying a new one in the Dolphins' colors. Someone had placed a big sign in the back window that read, "Blissfully Married." Truer words had never been written.

Before they reached the truck, Ms. Marble came hustling up with Autumn's wedding bouquet. "I think there's something you forgot to do." She handed the bouquet to Autumn, and then directed all the single women to get in a group in front of Autumn. There was only Granny Bon and Christie. As much as Autumn had started thinking about her grandmother finding a male companion, the one she wanted to catch the bouquet was Christie.

Not only did Christie need to learn to love again, but Carrie Anne needed a father she could count on.

Autumn looked to see where her friend was standing before she turned her back and tossed the bouquet. She turned around to see the pretty autumn-colored flowers heading straight for her friend. Unfortunately, Christie didn't lift a finger to catch it. But her daughter did. Carrie Anne made a diving jump that any NBA player would be proud of and plucked it out of the air before it could end up on the ground. Obviously, she'd changed her mind about getting married.

"I got it!" she crowed with delight. As everyone laughed, Carrie Anne took a dramatic sniff of the flowers. "And I know exactly who I want."

Both Stuart and Race looked at each other and spoke at the same time. "Not me."

Maverick laughed as he opened the door of his truck for Autumn. "It would serve those boys right if they ended up with wives as sassy as Carrie Anne." He waited until he got in the truck before he continued. "Of course, I got myself a sassy wife and couldn't be happier."

"I'm not sassy." Autumn swatted him.

"I don't know what you'd call it. You've certainly been speaking your mind lately." He started the truck, and they waved as they pulled away from their family and friends.

"You were the one who taught me that there's nothing wrong with letting people know what you want."

He took her hand and brought it to his lips as he glanced over at her. "And what do you want, Mrs.

Murdoch?"

She didn't even have to think about the question. "You. For the rest of my life."

With her hand in his, she settled back in the seat as they headed down the road to bliss.

Here's a sneak peek of the next book in the
BRIDES OF BLISS TEXAS
series.

CHRISTMAS TEXAS BRIDE
Will be out November 2018!

"I'M NEVER HAVIN' S-E-X."

Cord Evans almost choked to death on his own spit. After he finished coughing, he glanced over at the little blond-headed girl who perched on his brand new fence. Carrie Anne Buchanan's face was serious and her hazel eyes were intense. Since the last thing he wanted to do was get into the can of worms she'd just opened, he kept his mouth shut and went back to spreading the load of coarse sand in his new corral. He hoped she would get the hint and move onto a more appropriate subject. But he was learning that six-year-old little girls rarely did want you hoped they would.

"Do you know what S-E-X is?" she asked.

Cord knew. In his heyday, he'd been quite the ladies' man. Every town he'd traveled to had been filled with women wanting to take a ride with a real-life rodeo cowboy. And he'd always been happy to oblige. He'd been in bed with so many women that he couldn't remember their names or their faces. Or maybe he couldn't remember because he'd always been drunk off his ass. When he'd finally given up the bottle and realized what a shit-fest he'd made of his life, sex was the last thing he worried about.

He continued to smooth out the sand and tried to change the subject. "How was school today, Half Pint?"

"Okay. We got to draw a picture and talk about what we did on Thanksgiving break and I drew a mag-nificent picture of a wedding and told everyone about Coach Murdoch and Autumn getting married and about how I got to drink Sprite from a champagne glass when we made some toast and how I catched the bouquet and now I gotta get married." She paused for a quick breath. "And my friend Mia asked who I was gonna marry, but I didn't tell her 'cause my grandma—God Bless her soul—said that sometimes girls need to have their secrets. But I did tell Mia that it wasn't gonna be a deadbeat like my daddy. 'Cause we Buchanan women are through with deadbeats."

He cringed. According to what he could piece together, Carrie's father had been a rodeo bum like Cord. And like Cord, he'd chosen horses and bulls over wives and cute kids. It was a bad choice, one Cord regretted and wished he could fix. Unfortunately, as much as he might want to, he couldn't go back. His first wife had divorced him long ago and was now happily remarried. And his only son was grown, married, and starting his own family. Cord could only hope that he'd be part of that family. Which was exactly why he'd moved here to Bliss, Texas.

"I'm sorry about your daddy, Carrie Anne. Sometimes daddies are just lost and think that running from their responsibilities is the way to be found. But running just makes you tired and even more lost. Hopefully, your daddy will figure that out like I did."

Carrie Anne scrunched her face in thought. "Mama says that once a deadbeat always a deadbeat." Which probably explained why Carrie Anne's mother didn't care for Cord. She was always polite, but he'd caught her more than once looking at him like he was a cockroach she'd like to crush under her boot heel. Thankfully, her daughter didn't feel the same way. She flashed a bright smile. "But after meeting you, I think my mama's wrong."

He winked at her. "Thank you for the vote of confidence, ma'am." He went back to raking. "So what else did you do in school?"

"We had a snack and went to recess where Jonas Murphy chased me on the playground and told me that he'd marry me. That's when he told me about S-E-X. He said that husbands and wives do it at night in the dark when all their kids are sleeping. He found out about it because he woke up one time and heard his mama moaning like she was in pain. And when he woke up his big brother, his brother said, 'They're just havin' S-E-X, stupid. Go back to sleep.' And I figure if something makes a woman moan out in pain that it can't be fun, so that's why I ain't doin' it never with my husband." She paused and when he glanced over, she gave him another bright smile. "And I just wanted you to know."

Cord continued raking. On one hand, he was relieved that she didn't know the particulars of sex, but on the other, he was annoyed at Jonas and his big brother for tarnishing her innocence even as much as they had. Carrie Anne was a sweet little thing who Cord had gotten quite attached to since her mother had started working for him. She followed him around like a little lost lamb, and damned if he didn't feel protective of her.

"Jonas Murphy, huh?" he said. "And he's in your class at school?"

"He's six like me, but he's not in Mrs. Trammel's class. He's in Miss Jules. I wish I had Miss Jules 'cause she's nice. Mrs. Trammel is a meanie. She talked with mama and told her that I need to get better at phone-tics because I don't sound out words when I'm readin'. I just make them up. And I don't make them up. I look at the pictures and tell a story, and that's exactly what reading is. But now mama feels all bad 'cause she drugged me all over the countryside this summer and didn't teach me enough phone-tics."

He had to bite back his laughter. "Your mama shouldn't feel bad. I'm sure you'll figure out phonics soon enough. It's pretty easy. Every letter has a sound. Once you remember each letter's sound, you can sound out a word. C-A-T spells cat." He said the word slowly, enunciating each sound. "Do you hear the three different sounds that come together to form the word?"

"CCC-aaa-ttt," she mimicked.

As he continued to rake, he gave her a few more examples of three-letter words and sounded them out for her. After she finished sounding out the word bat, there was a long pause. "So what does S-E-X spell?"

Cord mentally cussed himself for walking right into that trap. Thankfully, before he could figure a way to get out of it, her mama showed up.

Christie Buchanan was a good-looking woman. She had pretty hazel eyes that were more green than her daughter's and wheat-colored hair that she kept in a braid that hung all the way down to her butt. She was petite and couldn't weigh much more than a hundred pound sack of feed. But he'd come to realize that inside the small package was the heart of a tiger. And he had to confess that he was a little scared of her. Which was complete nonsense seeing how she was closer to his son's age than his.

"What are you two up to?" She asked as she rested her arms on the fence next to Carrie Anne.

Before he could say a word, Carrie Anne jumped in. "Me and Cord was just talkin' about S-E-X."

He cringed. Oh boy. This wasn't going to be good.

Christie's eyes flashed fire, and he watched her hands grip the fence railing as if she was about to vault over it and rip him to shreds. Before she could, he held up a hand.

"Now, Christie, it's not what it seems." He looked at Carrie Anne. "Why don't you run into the barn and give Maple a treat? When I was talking with her this morning, she told me how much she was looking forward to seeing you after school."

Carrie Anne sprang down from the fence, her tattered tennis shoes sinking into the thick sand. "See, Mama, I told you that horses can talk. They talk to Cord all the time. And he said when I become better at listening, they'll talk to me too." She looked at Cord as if he were the best thing since Cracker Jacks.

It had been a long time since he'd gotten that kind of adoration from a kid, and damned if it didn't make him feel ten feet tall. He reached out and ruffled her hair. "Horses do like listeners, but they don't mind talkers either. Just keep your voice low and soothing. And stay away from Raise a Ruckus. He's not ready for polite company just yet."

"Will do, Cord." She raced out of the corral.

When she was gone, Christie gave him that same look she always gave him. A look that knocked him down from ten feet to about two . . . inches. "Well, explain."

He leaned on the rake handle. "I was not talking about sex with Carrie Anne. In fact, I was trying my darnedest to avoid talking about it. But Carrie Anne isn't the type of little girl who lets you avoid anything. She's as headstrong as her mama."

"I'm not headstrong." Christie's brow crinkled. "If she didn't learn the word from you, where did she learn it?"

"From a little boy at her school."

Christie's eyes widened. "Oh my God."

Cord held up a hand. "Now before you go postal. He didn't give her any details other than it's something a husband and wife do at night in the dark."

He figured he could leave out the moaning part. This conversation was uncomfortable enough as is. "His older brother was the one who spelled the word out for him. I figure he's the one who needs a good talking to."

"Talking? He needs his ears boxed. And I plan to go up to the school first thing tomorrow morning and make sure the principal does something about it."

He leaned the rake against the fence. "Now I don't know if I'd do that. I think that might be pretty embarrassing for the parents to be called in front of the principal. I think it would be better if you talked with Jonas Murphy's mother yourself. I'm sure she'll handle it from there."

He thought his solution was a pretty damned good one, but Christie didn't agree. "Thank you for the advice. But Carrie Anne is my child and I'll deal with the situation as I see fit."

He wasn't surprised by the prickly response. He was learning that Christie Buchanan was one prickly woman. She reminded him of the abused filly he'd helped train when he was working at a ranch outside of Amarillo. The horse hadn't trusted any human to get too close. If you did, you got bit, kicked, or bucked off on your ass. It had taken Cord months of soothing talk and gentle handling to get the horse's trust. But it had been worth it. Best damned horse he'd ever known.

He handled Christie the same way he'd handled the horse. He kept his distance and his voice low and calm. "Of course she's your daughter. I was just trying to help."

"I don't need any help raising Carrie Anne. I can

do it just fine on my own. I appreciate all you've done for me in the last couple months. I appreciate the job you gave me and I appreciate the loan to fix my car. But your kindness doesn't give you any rights to my daughter."

"Neither the job or the loan was a kindness," he said. "It was purely selfishness. I desperately needed someone to help me with my website and social networking and I didn't want to have to go pick my assistant up if I needed her to come out here and take pictures of an old rodeo cowboy's—" he held up his hands and did quotation marks—"'ranch life.'" He lowered his hands. "So I didn't do you a favor. You did me one. But you're right. I don't have any business butting my nose into things that don't concern me. Especially where Carrie Anne is concerned. As everyone knows, I'm the worst father this side of the Pecos."

Her shoulders visibly relaxed and most of the fire left her eyes. "Believe me, you aren't the worst. And you and Ryker seem to have a good relationship."

"Twenty years too late."

"Better late than never."

Cord wished that was true, but knew that it wasn't. His son still hadn't completely forgiven him for all the lost years. And Cord hadn't forgiven himself. Late at night, when he was lying on his blow-up mattress in the big ol' empty ranch house he'd built, he thought about all those years he'd missed. All the time he and Ryker could've shared as father and son. He wasn't a crying man, but he'd shed more than a few tears for those lost years. And what broke his heart even more was that he knew his son had too.

"I don't think Ryker would agree," he said. "I think he would've preferred a daddy who was there for him when he was kid. A dad to play catch with and to talk to about important things like S-E-X."

A smile broke out on Christie's face. The only word that came to mind was *Dazzling*. Christie had the kind of smile that lit up the world. It was a shame she didn't use it more off.

"S-E-X." She shook her head. "Good Lord. What's that child going to come up with next?" She paused and looked at Cord with those big hazel eyes. "I'm sorry for assuming the worst. I should've known better."

"Don't ever apologize for watching out for your daughter. Carrie Anne is lucky to have a mama like you."

"I don't know about that. Sometimes I feel like all I do is get after her. In case you haven't noticed, she's been quite a handful lately. I realize that her acting out has to do with starting a new school in a new town, but it doesn't make it any easier to deal with. And now that Mrs. Miller has gone to spend the holidays with her kids and grandkids, I have to bring Carrie Anne to the bakery with me. I'm sure Summer isn't happy about having a six-year-old around."

When Christie wasn't helping him with social networking, she worked at The Blissful Bakery in town. He thought she worked way too much, but he wasn't about to tell her that.

"Summer would tell you if she had a problem with you bringing Carrie Anne to the bakery. My daughter-in-law isn't the type to beat around the bush. But if you want Carrie Anne could always hang out here. Besides the occasionally uncomfortable conversation topic, she doesn't cause me any problems."

She shook her head. "Thank you, but you've done enough for us. I'm sure I'll figure something out." She took her hands off the fence and pulled a cellphone out of her back pocket. "For now, I need to get a couple pictures of you working on your corral for today's posts."

"You want to post a picture of me raking dirt?"

"Yes. The picture I took of you shoveling horse manure got over five thousand likes on Instagram and even more on Facebook." When he looked shocked, she laughed. "I know. I don't get it either, but for some reason people like to see you getting dirty. Or maybe they just like to see that famous folks work just as hard as they do. Of course, you being shirtless in the last picture probably helped. Women love a hot cowboy with a nice, hard bod—" She cut off, and her cheeks flushed pink.

He felt a little flushed himself. Christie thought he was a hot cowboy with a nice body? Before he could even digest that piece of information, she quickly hurried through the gate of the corral. "Well, we better get that picture. Just go back to raking and act like I'm not—" The high heels of her city boots sank into the deep sand, and she stumbled. Her cellphone flew out of her hands and hit the sand, but before she could, Cord reached out and caught her.

It had been a long time since he'd held a woman. Too long. The libido he'd put into hibernation woke up like a hunger bear ready to feast. And what it wanted to feast on was the woman in his arms. She smelled like a mixture of ripe strawberries and fresh baked bread right out of the oven. Which didn't help his hunger. Nor did the soft breasts that pressed into his chest or the trim waist his hands could almost span. And when she lifted her head, he got lost in twin pastures of brilliant green and earthy browns that brought up thoughts of springtime and picnics . . . and rolling naked with a woman in fresh-cut grass.

"You were right, Cord!" Carrie Anne's voice broke through his misbehaving thoughts. "Maple missed me." He quickly released Christie and stepped back just as Carrie Anne came tearing into the corral.

"And Raise a Ruckus missed me too," she crowed as she stopped between him and Christie. "When I went by his stall, he stuck out his head and grinned at me. Just like this." She bared her teeth. When neither Cord or her mother said anything, she looked between them. "What's wrong? Why are you both all red in the face? Are you still talking about S-E-X?"

They hadn't been talking about it.

But now Cord sure as hell was thinking about it.

DEAR READER,
Thank you so much for reading *Autumn Texas Bride*. I hope you enjoyed Maverick and Autumn's love story. If you did, please help other readers find this book by telling a friend or writing a review. Your support is greatly appreciated.

Love,

Katie

Be sure to check out all the books in Katie Lane's
The Brides of Bliss Texas
series!

Spring Texas Bride
Summer Texas Bride
Autumn Texas Bride
Coming soon…
Christmas Texas Bride (November 2018)

Other series by Katie Lane

Tender Heart Texas:

Falling for Tender Heart
Falling Head Over Boots
Falling for a Texas Hellion
Falling for a Cowboy's Smile
Falling for a Christmas Cowboy

Deep in the Heart of Texas:

Going Cowboy Crazy
Make Mine a Bad Boy
Catch Me a Cowboy
Trouble in Texas
Flirting with Texas
A Match Made in Texas
The Last Cowboy in Texas
My Big Fat Texas Wedding (novella)

Overnight Billionaires:

A Billionaire Between the Sheets
A Billionaire After Dark
Waking up with a Billionaire

Hunk for the Holidays:

Hunk for the Holidays
Ring in the Holidays
Unwrapped

Anthologies:

Small Town Christmas (Jill Shalvis, Hope Ramsay, Katie Lane)
All I Want for Christmas is a Cowboy (Jennifer Ryan, Emma Cane, Katie Lane)

About the Author

Katie Lane is a USA Today Bestselling author of the *Deep in the Heart of Texas*, *Hunk for the Holidays*, *Overnight Billionaires*, *Tender Heart Texas*, and *The Brides of Bliss Texas* series. She lives in Albuquerque, New Mexico, with her cute cairn terrier Roo and her even cuter husband Jimmy.

For more on her writing life or just to chat, check out Katie here:

Facebook www.facebook.com/katielaneauthor
Instagram www.instagram.com/katielanebooks

And for information on upcoming releases and great giveaways, be sure to sign up for her mailing list at www.katielanebooks.com!